TIMEDRIFTER

THE
VEIL
OF
SMOKE

LAUREN LYNCH

You turn people back to dust, saying,
"Return to dust, you mortals."
A thousand years in your sight are like a day
that has just gone by, or like a watch in the night.
  - Psalm 90:3-4

The Veil of Smoke
Copyright © 2014 by Lauren Lynch

All rights reserved under International and Pan-American Copyright Conventions. No part of this text may be reproduced, stored in or introduced into any information storage and retrieval system, or transmitted in any form or by any means electronic, mechanical, or otherwise in any form or by any means, whether electronic or mechanical, now known or hereinafter invented, without prior written permission.

This novel is a work of fiction. Names, characters, places and incidents are either products of the author's imagination or used fictitiously.

ISBN: 978-1503272057

Published by Psyche Press.
Printed in the United States of America.

Cover and interior design:
Lauren Lynch Design & Writing
www.laurenlynch.com

Requests for information should be sent to:
info@laurenlynch.com

Excerpts were used from *The Aeneid*, written by Virgil in 19 B.C. and translated by John Dryden in 1697.

All scripture quotations, unless otherwise indicated, are paraphrased from The Holy Bible, New International Version®, NIV®. Copyright © 1973, 1978, 1984, 2011 by Biblica, Inc. ™ Used by permission of Zondervan. All rights reserved worldwide. www.zondervan.com The "NIV" and "New International Version" are trademarks registered in the United States Patent and Trademark Office by Biblica, Inc. ™

For Patrick, with love

AUTHOR'S NOTE

The character of Julia Felix is based on an actual historical figure in Pompeii, created after researching her home, the location and features of her estate, the advertisement (used verbatim in the book) for leasing part of her compound, her social status as the wealthy daughter of an imperial freedman, and the cultural impact on women in first century Rome. Julia had the privilege of being a woman of independence in an era when women had few rights or opportunities.

The characters of Lucius Istacidius Zosimus and Gaius Julius Polybius are also historical characters from Pompeii. Zosimus is believed to have owned the villa and winery northwest of the city know today as the Villa of Mysteries. Julius Polybius owned a home in town just a few blocks west of the estate of Julia Felix.

The descriptions of the buildings are based on what existed from records at the time of excavation and taking in to account the fact that most buildings in Pompeii were hundreds of years old and being repaired from the devastating effects of the massive earthquake of 62 A.D. We tend to forget when reconstructing Pompeii in our mind's eye, that much of the city was already very old and still in disrepair when Mount Vesuvius erupted in 79 A.D.

A glossary of Latin terms used in this book may be found at the end. I tried to use only what was necessary for accurate descriptive and just enough to bring out the historical flavor of Pompeii.

The Veil of Smoke is the second book in the TimeDrifter series. Read *The Place of Voices* first to get a fuller understanding of the characters and their journeys.

PROLOGUE
Rancho Los Amigos Medical Center
California, 1961

Brendan grasped at consciousness. Dragging his eyelids open like a pair of heavy blinds, he blinked at the light beyond them. Pulling his surroundings into focus proved equally challenging. Murky light filtered through dismal green fabric suspended from tracks on the ceiling, creating a threadbare illusion of privacy from his left to the foot of his bed. To his right, a radiant white figure came into partial focus.

Sleep's magnetic embrace lured him, but he struggled against it. He had a visitor. Brendan wanted little more than to rub the fogginess from his eyes, but his leaden hands wouldn't cooperate. The figure next to his bed glowed with angelic warmth. This place was no heaven though. He was too worn out. Heaven, he believed, would deliver him from the prison of his polio-ridden body.

Here, behind the drab green partition, his wasted form still trapped him. After several surgeries he'd heard many medical terms he didn't understand—and a few that he had … infection … possible amputation.

Brendan wanted to squeeze a fist over his eyes, but he couldn't summon the strength to lift a finger. Everything was wrong. Everything was worse. He would never possess the body of a typical nineteen-year-old, but he'd hoped to get a little closer at least. Now, that might never happen.

The woman in white leaned close and whispered in his ear.

"Brendan?"

Her voice penetrated the fuzzy edges of lingering sleepiness, yet he couldn't quite escape the desire to close his eyes.

He tried to move his legs, but a wave of pain engulfed his body, sharpening his unwilling senses. He heard a moan — probably his own, but his body and mind seemed to have disconnected to some degree, and he was currently incapable of bridging the gaps. He wasn't even sure he wanted to any longer.

"I am going to give you something for the pain. It will help you sleep." A cool hand swept over his brow. Oh, the happy promise of those words.

Big brown eyes held his with an intensity he couldn't match. A silvery brown curl escaped her starched white nurse's cap. She bit her lip and twirled the stray lock onto her forefinger, concern etched in the lines of her face. Warmth drifted up his arm and spread throughout his body. He sunk back into the deep pleasures of blissful oblivion.

The woman's gentle voice inspired unquestioning trust. "Come with me…" Anna's whispers tugged him deeper into the warm comforts of sleep, and this time, he didn't fight it.

1

Hooves clattered against stone, jarring Brendan's mind awake. He wrenched his eyelids open, immediately discerning two things: the rustic enclosed carriage he'd found himself in traveled a very bumpy road, and his waking brain was now sharper than it had been in weeks. Vague images from interrupted dreams drifted to the far reaches of his consciousness as his senses snapped to attention.

A dusty film permeated the air, robbing his eyes and mouth of their moisture. His joints ached as if he'd slept in one awkward position for far too long. He stretched, and a robed arm extended from his body draped in layers of scratchy white wool—not the faded hospital gowns he'd grown accustomed to, but something equally coarse and oversized. He tugged at the heavy folds of fabric covering his chest.

Alarm jolted his mind as he realized the hand, although it obeyed his bidding, did not appear to be his own. The manly fist sported a bulky iron signet ring on the index finger. Brendan's gaze drifted down his body. His chest had widened with well-defined muscle. He lifted a hand to his cheek. Stubble.

Strange. Brendan found he didn't care where—or even who—he was as long as he was no longer trapped in a feeble body and confined to a hospital bed. Given any chance to escape his frustrating circumstances, he'd gladly embrace it—real or not. This body was strong and healthy—a glorious improvement on what he'd endured over the past several years. If his mind had resorted to mental diversions to cope, so be it.

Next to him, a veiled woman kept vigil over the passing scenery outside her window. He leaned forward quietly, so as not to disturb her, and drew back the curtain on his side of the carriage.

Hilly fields rolled toward a large cone of a mountain he couldn't identify. Rows of neatly trellised grape vines trailed into the distance, interrupted only by an occasional cluster of cypress trees. The carriage rattled past a group of robed travelers already filthy from foot travel, now grimier by far from the cloud of dust their wheels churned up.

"Did I wake you?" The woman next to him interrupted his thoughts, her voice barely containing amusement. Brendan turned to face her, his eyes roving her concealed features without gleaning much information. She lifted her veil and leaned closer. "You look much better now. Just look at that vigorous color. Do you feel well?"

When he didn't answer immediately, she bit her lip. Her long, delicate fingers fluttered to her hair. They latched onto one of the wavy brown tresses escaping her elaborate hair arrangement and wound their way into a corkscrew curl as if soothed by the mindless action.

"We rode through the night," she said, turning back to gaze out the window. "We must be nearly there by now."

She pulled a small bronze mirror from a purse at her waist and examined her face. As she patted the skin at the corners of her eyes, he waited for her to echo his complaints about the dust. "Amazing," she said shaking her head.

While he might have chalked her self-assessment up to ego, her pronouncement seemed less smug than amused. Something in her manner tugged at his memory, yet he was certain he'd never forget a face so breathtaking.

THE VEIL OF SMOKE

He turned back to the vast miles of vineyards outside the window and tried to gather his thoughts. He'd last drifted off to sleep in a dismal hospital room. He'd been lonely—far enough from his hometown that his father and brothers had only been able to visit on occasion. Between visits, he'd drifted in and out of consciousness. Now this. It was tempting, so tempting to believe again—to hope. His threadbare mind grasped at happiness, re-fabricating his greatest adventure, the dream that had held his imagination for years ... and yet ...

The scene outside the carriage remained as foreign to him as the mode of transportation was primitive. Brendan struggled to come up with a rational explanation, but favored silent observation until he could figure out his situation. A walled city appeared on the horizon. Buildings spilled out across the hillside surrounding it, as if it had burst at the seams.

"You really aren't going to question me about it?" The corners of the woman's mouth twitched and her eyes hinted at a smile. Apprehension tugged at him, but he didn't want to give her the satisfaction of knowing she had the upper hand. He would keep silent and alert until he had a better grasp on his situation.

"Very well. I'll explain it all when we get there," she promised the back of his head when he refused to respond. This hallucination was particularly convincing, but he'd ride it out and maybe even enjoy the scenery in the process.

An important detail seemed to elude him, dangling just beyond the grasp of his recollection. His traveling companion's voice rang with a familiar lilt he couldn't quite place—and those nervous fingers of hers. His memory sparked, wrenching his stomach. No, it couldn't be. Not after nearly four years of trying to convince his bewildered mind their shared adventure had been nothing more than a dream. If it was Anna, then she had aged exceptionally well in the decades it took for her to catch up with him in time. This woman couldn't be more than twenty-five at the most, and significantly less awkward than the young girl he remembered.

The carriage clattered to a stop at a narrow gate in the city's high outer wall. The road continued beyond it, flanked on either side by high-curbed walkways.

"This is as far as I can take you." The driver hopped down from his seat. "Carriages cannot enter the city at this hour. You might arrange for a lectica, but it is just a short walk to the estate of Julia Felix. Just past the vineyard, you will find the entrance to her thermopolium and beyond that her baths and the main entrance to her residence. If walking is acceptable, you may send a servant back to collect your things. I will water the horses and wait here."

A man seated on a bench outside the gate strode over. "The well is bone dry today, you must go farther down the road, past the necropolis, where they will bring you water from a cistern."

Their driver threw his hands toward the sky. "Ah — of course, welcome to Pompeii."

Brendan latched onto his traveling companion's elbow. She turned to him, eyebrows raised in an unspoken question.

"Anna?"

"You should call me Annthea here, Brendanus." Her graceful lips curved into a triumphant smile. She was a little too proud of her kidnapping coup.

Her eyes held his for a moment before winking. "I hoped you might figure it out if I gave you enough time. I'll explain it all as soon as we have a moment alone," she whispered before turning back to take the driver's extended hand. She gathered her gown neatly around her ankles and made an elegant exit from the carriage. Not much in her appearance to hint at the tomboy he'd once known, but something of the old spitfire Anna remained.

Brendan fumbled with his own awkward garment before stepping out. The fabric hung in heavy folds from his shoulders. A leather strap from his sandal caught in the narrow doorway as he maneuvered out of the carriage and he made a clumsy landing on the cobbled walk.

"He just woke," Anna said to the carriage driver with a shrug.

The driver grunted his indifference.

"We'll manage on foot," she added, taking Brendan's elbow and steering him toward the pedestrian gate. "I'll send a porter."

"Pompeii? Anna, what on earth were you thinking bringing us here? I studied this in school once. It doesn't end well."

"Keep your voice down," Anna whispered, looping her arm through his. "We do not want to draw attention to ourselves as outsiders."

Outsiders. They'd defied the laws of time before. Still—trying to blend in here would not only make them obvious outsiders, it would put their lives at risk. Then again, he had little left to lose.

2

Chicago, 1985

Marcus stepped into a pair of ragged jeans he'd grabbed from the floor near his bed, followed by a faded black T-shirt and Doc Martens. He squirted a handful of mousse into his palm and ran it through his dark hair, tugging it into a more intentional mess. Before pulling on his leather jacket, he made a Billy Idol face in the mirror and mouthed a silent rebel yell. If he could slip out the door before his mother cornered him, he would count it a good morning.

Marcus edged past the kitchen doorway and crept down the hall, avoiding the squeaky spots. Ambitious pot banging signaled the beginnings of a large breakfast. Just as his fingers hit the front door knob, his mother called out.

"Marcus, I'm making pancakes."

Just a few seconds too slow. "I'll grab something on the way to school," he lied.

His mother stepped into the hallway before he could escape. "On Saturday?" she demanded, one dark eyebrow disappearing into her thick bangs.

"Son of a..." he muttered under his breath.

"I beg your pardon?" His mother's eyes narrowed, arms clamped across her chest. She somehow managed to make her five-foot-one frame appear threatening.

He brushed past her, shrugging off his jacket as he flopped face down onto his bed.

"Did you talk to Mr. Salvatore about a summer job?" she asked

11

from his doorway. "You only have a few weeks of school left."

Marcus jammed a pillow over his head, muffling his reply. "The band will get some gigs and I'll need to get some sleep during the day."

"What ... the band?" His mother groaned as she tugged at pillow, but he held tight. "Marcus, we've discussed this. We don't have your father to take care of us anymore. We must find a way to survive on our own. You need to get your grades up and start applying to colleges. It was what your father wanted for you—what we both wanted."

As much as the reminder of his old man stung, he couldn't get hung up on what might have been. He hated the way she referred to Pop as "his father," like she hadn't lost a husband. She seemed to place all her hopes on his shoulders these days—and that was way too heavy to deal with right now. All her dreams for the future seemed to involve his life, not her own. Even if he did go to college, his father would never see it—not any more. What was the point?

"Pop and his American dream." He might still be alive if he'd stayed in Italy. Marcus was a first generation citizen of the United States. His parents had always resented the fact that he wasn't more connected to his Italian roots. It was ironic since their dreams for a better life had brought them to Chicago in the first place. They wanted the best of both worlds. Had they really thought that was possible?

"What did you just say?" His mother yanked at the pillow and he loosened his grip on it, knowing it would send her back a step or two.

Marcus sat up and sniffed the air. "I think your pancakes are burning."

She dropped his pillow and gave a loud groan of frustration.

"Don't go back to sleep, Marcus. Don't waste the day. I don't have to be into work until ten. We can talk over breakfast." She darted back to the kitchen.

"Just a couple more hours, Ma." Marcus grabbed the pillow, shoving it back over his head. "I'll go talk to Mr. Salvatore later."

His mother would never accept his music as a way to make a living, and he had no interest in college. With a little more sleep, he could practice late into the night at his friend Jeremy's loft where the killer acoustics made them sound even more hardcore. Jeremy's parents never hassled him about the band. Of course they weren't around much to complain. Maybe he should just start crashing there.

He closed his eyes. It would be great to have his own life — away from his mother and her plans to stamp out each of his life choices with a cookie cutter. Maybe she'd allow him a few minutes of peace before the pancakes were ready.

∞

Marcus's heart skipped a beat as he opened his eyes. A haze of smoke surrounded him.

"Ma?" Had the stupid pancakes started a fire? No answer. He tried to lunge out of bed, but his legs held fast as if pinned to the ground. Hammering pulled his attention to the right, but it was too smoky to make anything out. A dog barked nearby. He pounded on his thighs — must have slept on them weird.

The smoke shifted and a man appeared in front of him. At first, he seemed to reach out to offer help, but Marcus soon realized the man made shooing motions with his hands. He scowled, bellowing in some foreign language. At first, Marcus mistook him for a fireman. Wishful thinking. He appeared to be some crazy immigrant neighbor wrapped in a sheet.

Marcus had grown up in Chicago's Little Italy neighborhood. He knew Italian dialects, but he couldn't place this guy's accent. Fresh off the boat, the old dude probably wouldn't know what to do in a high-rise fire.

The yammering man stood over him now, hands on hips, sheet flapping in the breeze with disgust etched on his face. He wanted to stand up and give the man a shove—tell him to back off, but searching for an escape route would be a better use of time. He had to get to his mother first.

Blue sky loomed above the smoke. Had the roof caved in? He twisted his torso, checking out his surroundings as best he could with legs still tangled in sheets. A crumbling masonry wall loomed behind him. A wooden cart loaded with debris had rumbled away, revealing the area Marcus appeared to have slept in. Dust had clouded his view, not smoke. The foul-tempered man continued to swear at him in an indecipherable tongue. Marcus got the message despite the language barrier. The man wanted him gone. Somehow, he had ended up outside—and on a construction site no less.

The archaic demolition site bustled. Carts hauled away piles of debris. Two bare-chested men with sledgehammers pounded away at the remains of a plastered brick wall. Pulverized plaster and brick showered down around them, kicking up another cloud of dust.

A younger guy loading debris into a ramshackle cart approached the grouchy foreman. He gestured to Marcus, himself and the cart. Wariness settled over Marcus along with the layers of grit. He shook his wilted hairstyle from his eyes to keep an eye on the two. The pandering debris hauler shuffled over to Marcus, threw him over his shoulder as he might have any other piece of rubble and dumped him onto a cart.

Marcus's legs flailed as he landed in a painful heap. He yelled in outrage at his would-be rescuer — shocked as much by the sight of his withered limbs as from the pain shooting through his hips as he slammed onto the jagged mound of refuse. His twisted legs refused to cooperate. A pair of primitive wooden crutches landed next to him. Nausea swept through his gut. Where was he and how long had he been here? For that matter — who was he? He studied his arms, which appeared in every way to be his own — down to the dirt encrusted tribal tattoo on the back of his hand — but the legs were definitely not ones he recognized. Sleep deprivation might cause nightmares, but this bad dream was as lucid as they got.

A dog bounded up behind them and leaped to his side, hunkering down as the cart groaned to a start. The grimy cart attendant gave him a disgruntled snarl, hands on hips, and asked a question Marcus had no way of translating. He read both pity and exasperation in the young man's eyes. The frustrated worker frowned as he pointed to the tattoo on Marcus's hand, muttering something about stigmata.

"Where am I?" Marcus asked, hoping the guy might recognize English and respond in kind. The laborer only shook his head with a groan and threw his hands toward the sky. He wiped his face with a rag as he followed along next to the cart, prodding the old mule with the handle of a whip instead of lashing it into submission. Compassionate.

The cart creaked through an arched doorway and into a large, open space lined by columns stacked two layers high. Sunlight crept over the top of the structure they had just left. It had to be dawn and the area — some sort of marketplace from the looks of it — would soon bustle to life. Merchants set up stalls on both sides of the courtyard. Some raised portable awnings to shelter them from the rising sun.

Before he had a chance to wonder where they might be headed, the cart ground to a halt across the courtyard. The man gestured for him to scoot forward, which he did as best he could with limited use of his legs. The dog hopped down and barked his encouragement. The man heaved Marcus over his shoulder again and set him down in a grassy corner where a column had toppled, creating a small niche of shadowed privacy amid the chaos of construction and commerce. He propped Marcus against a block a crumbling stone then stepped back and frowned. He leaned forward again, took the rag from his shoulder and spread it over Marcus's legs as if hiding them might improve his situation. He tucked the edges under the twisted limbs as a mother might tuck in a boy at bedtime. Maybe the man was trying to make him comfortable. He tilted his head and gave him a shrug as if to say, it's the best I can do. Spinning on his heel, the man strode back to the cart, nudging the mule forward.

"Wait," Marcus called after the man. "My crutches—" The man was already ambling away, oblivious to his panic. What was he thinking anyway? They weren't his crutches. Were they?

Marcus squeezed his eyes shut. He took in a deep breath through his nose and exhaled slowly through his mouth. "Just a dream, just a dream, just a dream—"

He visualized the comfortable bed at home he'd burrowed into to escape his mom's relentless demands. The tension between them must be messing with his head. That was all. Maybe this was some sort of nervous breakdown.

He opened his eyes as the scent of fresh bread wafted past. It was obvious wishful thinking hadn't made the marketplace disappear. If anything, the traffic had increased. "No, no, no—no!" He wanted to shut his eyes again and hide his head under his pillow, but the growing clamor of unintelligible chatter remained whether his eyes were open or not.

The dog tilted its head and stared at him with soulful eyes.

"Thanks for sticking with me." Marcus gave the dog a half-hearted pat on the head.

The dog acknowledged his belated gratitude with a hearty snort.

"I've been having this disagreement with my mother," Marcus added aloud, feeling foolish, but grateful for the companionship. "We used to be so close, but lately—"

The dog pawed at Marcus's forearm as if to get his attention. As he turned, it pressed its nose against his. Before Marcus could shove the cheeky mutt away, the dog exhaled a purple vapor. Marcus held his breath as the sparkling purple cloud shrouded his face. No matter how much he swung his head from side to side, the vapor clung to him like a mask. The dog stepped back and snorted again. Marcus shook his head, trying to rid himself of the strange dog's breath clinging to him. Eventually, he could hold his breath no longer. Desperate for air, he drew the purple vapor deep into his lungs. A tickling sensation prompted him to cough. He had half expected purple vapor to accumulate again when he exhaled, but it remained inside him.

Without thinking, he shook his head—as if it might clear his overloaded mind. Something was different. He scanned the growing crowd of shoppers gathering in the plaza.

"They're speaking English now." Marcus had to remind himself to close his mouth as he eavesdropped on several conversations in the vicinity. He turned to the dog. Nothing made sense.

"No, nothing about them has changed, but you are now capable of universal communication." The dog sat back on its haunches.

Marcus rubbed his forehead. "I'll be able to speak their language?" No. While he now comprehended conversations he once found foreign, he still heard himself in English.

"Wait a minute—" Marcus's eyes locked onto the dogs'. "What?"

"Yes," the dog replied in flawless English. "You can understand me, as well."

"I don't get it." Marcus shook his head.

"You have made that abundantly clear." The dog appeared to frown at him in return. "Have you heard of the Tower of Babel? It's something like that, in reverse."

Marcus bit his lip. He had no snappy comeback for a smart-mouthed dog.

The dog crouched, as if ready to bound away. "Come with me if you want to live."

"Wait!" Marcus yelled. "I can't follow you just like that. The workman took my crutches." Marcus wasn't sure they would be much use even if the man had left them behind. They weren't much more than two worn sticks with a crook at the top. The dog ran off.

"Wait—" Marcus rolled to his side and pulled himself up on his arms. He managed to get a couple feet before tumbling over. "Wait," he whimpered into the ground, blinking back tears of frustration. He rolled onto his back. "Help!" he yelled to anyone who might listen.

A small girl, not much older than a toddler, peeked around the toppled column. She held a wedge of bread in one tiny fist. She tipped her head toward her shoulder and gave him a shy smile.

"I need help." Marcus wiped his eyes with the back of a filthy hand.

She pressed her lips together as if debating her options, then handed him her hunk of bread. For a brief moment, Marcus considered handing it back. Desperation won over and he shoved it into the belt of fabric at his waist instead. A woman grasped the toddler's hand and tugged her back away from Marcus with a scowl of annoyance on her face.

"Stay with me, Iris," she scolded, lifting the girl into her arms to speed their escape. The girl watched him over her mother's shoulder as they retreated and waved.

"Thank you, Iris," Marcus called after the tiny girl with the closest thing to a smile he could muster. He held his hand up in a weary wave before collapsing onto his back. A cone-shaped mountain rose above the triangular crest of the marble building towering over him. There were no mountains in Chicago. He was far from home.

3

Sandals were new to Brendan. Accustomed to booted polio braces, the soft leather footwear he now found himself in was as curious as the strength in his legs. They caught on the curb as he stepped onto the high sidewalk, causing him to stumble into a clay jug leaning against a doorstep. He dove forward to right it before it fell. Who designed clay jars with rounded bottoms? They should never be stood on end. On the upside, whatever he lacked in dexterity, he seemed to make up for in quick reflexes. Moving had never been so easy. The momentum still caught him by surprise.

An unfamiliar fierceness shone in Anna's eyes. "Are you trying to draw attention to us? We are here to observe — to help someone. It will be difficult to do that if everyone is watching us instead." Anna's eyes softened as she leaned closer to him. "Brendan, this is as much for you as it is for me."

What was that supposed to mean? He should have taken advantage of the time in the carriage to question her instead of stewing. Now he would have to wait for details.

Anna and Brendan walked two blocks in awkward silence. The confident woman next to him wasn't the wild-haired, anxious Anna he had known when they first met. She carried herself with a sophistication that, in comparison, cast him in the role of a bumbling oaf. His admiration grew as she strode up the worn walkway with the poise of a foreign dignitary. No one would question her presence here.

A handsome man rounded the corner from a side street, an appreciative smile twitching at his lips as he appraised Anna from head to toe. He nodded, wishing Anna a good morning and turned as she passed to steal another glimpse. The man's Latin greeting dawned on Brendan's mind as if uttered in English. Of course. Years ago, Ben had given Tzutz Nik the ability to communicate with them in the same way. Brendan had a new appreciation for Nik's stunned reaction to the effect.

Before he could voice his thoughts, they arrived at a dramatic columned entrance. Painted in narrow red lettering on the exterior wall of the luxurious estate, a notice read: To let, in the estate of Julia Felix, daughter of Spurius: elegant baths fit for the finest, shops with living quarters above, and apartments on the upper floor. From August 1 next to August 1 of the sixth year. The lease will expire at the end of five years.

"Five years?" Brendan couldn't be sure what the present date was in Pompeii, but the dry well hadn't been a good sign. He racked his brain for the details he had learned the year before when studying Pompeii and the Roman Empire in history class.

"Sad, isn't it?" Anna's brows bunched as she examined the façade of the Felix estate.

Brendan smirked. "You mean, how eager Pompeians are to use their walls as billboards?"

Anna rolled her eyes, but her lips hinted at amusement. "The hopefulness—all the dreams that will never be."

"How long do we have before things start heating up around here? I won't be going anywhere fast in this thing." Brendan tugged at the cumbersome layers of heavy fabric draped over him. "—so it'd be great to have a little notice."

Before Anna could answer, an elegant woman clothed in extravagant silks appeared at the front entrance, a servant close at her heels.

"I am Julia Felix, owner of this establishment," she announced. "Would you, by any chance, be Brendanus and Annthea? I apologize. The letter Theophilus brought with him when he arranged your accommodations only mentioned your praenomina."

Anna paused in dumbfounded silence before confirming their identity, but offered no additional information.

Lady Julia seemed unconcerned by her omission. "Normally, I would not extend hospitality to strangers from foreign lands. As an independent woman, gaining respect is difficult enough without drawing negative attention, but you came with the highest recommendation. Your charming friend made all the arrangements for you in advance." A young boy appeared at Julia's side, opening a parasol to shade her from the intense morning sun. "I was expecting you yesterday. Please forgive me for continuing with my business this morning. I was just heading to the Forum."

"You are renting out much of your estate." Brendan peered into the open doorway as their hostess stepped into the sunny street.

"Oh—yes. That was the point of my investment. Pompeii is a popular vacation destination. Many Romans keep modest villas here in Pompeii, but they are usually not adequate for entertaining on a grand scale. This estate will serve that need. I hope to soon have a long-term arrangement with a committed investor—someone who will appreciate the choice location. The grounds are well equipped for hosting lavish parties and the extensive gardens at the rear of the estate feature gates that open right in front of the amphitheater. I will personally escort you on a tour of the property when we return."

"You are an astute businesswoman," Anna gushed. Brendan doubted the girl he'd once known would have been impressed by such things, but the older version appeared sincerely impressed.

"I am sure you understand—few women have the opportunity to conduct business with the freedom that I do. I intend to use my circumstances to the fullest advantage."

"Wise, indeed." Anna joined Julia on the sidewalk.

"I know you've only just arrived, but would you care to walk with me to the Forum?"

"We'd love to," Anna said without hesitation. Had she allowed Brendan to speak first, he might have declined, but Anna was already immersed in her mission. "We haven't seen the city yet. Our carriage is waiting at the Porta Urbulana with our bags."

"Think nothing of it. Isidore will send a porter to retrieve them." Julia whispered to her dark haired companion, who disappeared through a side door.

"I recently opened my new bathhouse and would like to petition Isis for success in this new venture. I will offer a sacrifice at the temple this morning."

When Isidore returned, they headed west on the main street. Julia and Anna strode arm in arm on the narrow sidewalk, the boy with the parasol dashing to keep up with their pace. So much for catching up.

Brendan stepped into the street—empty of cart traffic during daylight hours. Julia's servant lagged a few steps behind him. The salty Mediterranean air also carried the scent of baking bread. Brendan's mouth was watering by the time they reached a wooden counter piled high with large round loaves.

Food shops with counters open to the street offered steaming food from large clay pots recessed into marble mosaic countertops. Brendan's stomach grumbled a reminder that he hadn't eaten solid food for far too long.

"Have you had your property long?" Anna shaded her eyes as Julia paused to consider her question. Brendan peered into a bubbling pot on a counter open to the street. Inhaling its savory steam, he couldn't identify the contents. It had to be better than hospital food.

"My father purchased the western half of the property long ago, I acquired the rest after he died. Every improvement I make to the property is designed to honor him." Julia continued down the street before Brendan had a chance to hint at his hunger.

Anna hustled after her. "Were the plans for the estate his or your own?"

"My father wanted property for his medicinal gardens. He used the store at the front to sell his remedies. The bathhouse was my own vision. My father died a freedman, but he came to Rome a slave of the empire, forced into public service. He was considered a lucky one, of course. As servi publici can own land, he made investments here in Pompeii, and I have developed the land with great care for my future."

Anna didn't comment for once, perhaps as lost in the curious details of the street as he was. Julia continued, oblivious to Anna's uncharacteristic silence.

"Spurius, my father, was rewarded for his loyal service and freed in his old age. He was a man of the highest caliber. After finding me abandoned in a gutter, he adopted me. Most would have made me a slave—if they had bothered to pick me up at all—but he made me his heir. I will honor his memory by making our estate the finest in Pompeii and leveraging it into—I am sorry. Pardon my oratory. I am passionate to the point of obsession when it comes to my father's dreams for me."

"Your father picked you up out of the gutter?" Anna asked, voicing Brendan's concern. Filth encrusted the edges of Pompeii's well-worn roads. Refuse once flushed downhill by rain now wilted under the relentless summer sun. The stench quelled Brendan's

25

hunger for the moment.

Brendan studied their host's profile, jockeying for position with the parasol-hoisting child. Julia wore her Roman nose well—softened by prominent cheekbones and the graceful lines of her neck. Her fair skin confessed a life of privilege, while her brazen auburn hair shimmered as if made for the sunlight. Saffron yellow gown billowing behind her, she kept an admirable pace as they strode uphill. Julia didn't appear to be the kind of woman that slowed down for much.

"It happens all too often when a woman doesn't possess the means to care for a child. She casts it aside like common refuse—" Julia's jaw clenched. "—especially when that baby is a girl. It may not be the custom where you come from, but in the Roman tradition, a baby is always placed at the father's feet shortly after birth. It is his choice whether or not to take the child into his arms and accept responsibility for it."

"Your father chose you." Anna placed a comforting hand on Julia's arm and their companion seemed to regain her composure.

"In his many years as a slave, my father was not able to have a wife or children. He believed that fortune laid me in his path at the very moment he was contemplating the need for an heir. He believed I was a gift from the gods. A gift." She swallowed hard, as if overcome by her adoptive father's generosity. "It was a joke of fortune—to be cast into a gutter by my mother only to be raised by an old man—but Spurius did choose to have me in his life. He taught me to survive in a man's world and I am better for it."

"I am certain you are," Anna said, stopping herself as she reached for one of her stray curls. Brendan hadn't observed her giving in to her nervous habit as much here in Pompeii. She had matured in the years it took to catch up with him in time.

"How strange," Julia said, placing a hand to her lips, "that

I should be so unguarded with my sordid past." She reddened, raising her palla over her head like a veil, as if it might help her keep her thoughts to herself. "You have witnessed a rare moment. When it comes to business, however, I never leave myself exposed."

Brendan imagined she wasn't exaggerating that sentiment. She wouldn't have accomplished as much as she had by showing vulnerability. Distracted by hunger, his eyes longingly roved trays of olives, bread, cheese and onions on a nearby counter, but his billowing outfit didn't appear to have a pocketful of coins.

Julia must have followed his gaze as she turned. She released a burst of nervous laughter and seemed grateful for the chance to change the subject. "Forgive my rudeness. I should have offered you something to eat before we left. She stopped and reached into a basket Isidore carried, offering them each pears. I always take a few things from my garden when I go to the temple. I'm sure Isis won't resent a few less pears. I was planning on buying some incense at the market anyway."

She waved them on in the direction of the marketplace. "This will give me a chance to show you a bit of what I love about Pompeii."

The Forum bustled with activity. Merchants set up impromptu displays beneath the double layers of columns, a few of which had toppled to the ground in pieces. Julia headed toward a gleaming marble building, its oversized doorway flanked by statuary niches. At every opportunity, the empire flaunted deity and royalty. Graven images of Pompeii's gods cast indifferent glances as they passed. Perhaps the statues' blank stares inspired the growing notion that nothing went unnoticed. Brendan tried to ignore the overactive nerves prickling the hairs at the back of his neck. They headed north across the large Forum courtyard, each step drawing them closer to the ominous mountain.

The crumbling temple of Jupiter dominated the architecture in spite of its obvious decay. Hemmed in on either side by two large archways, it lay like a captive at the foot Vesuvius.

"Amazing isn't it?" Lady Julia followed Brendan's gaze to the temple. "It was built by the Samnites hundreds of years ago, then transformed into the Capitolium once the Romans took Pompeii. Even in its unfortunate state of disrepair, it's stunning."

"I hadn't expected it to be in ruins." Brendan realized too late how stupid his unchecked thoughts would sound from Julia's perspective.

"Well, that happened in the big earthquake, of course—and several smaller ones in the years since then. The city is still recovering, but I'm sure once we've rebuilt, Pompeii will be grander than ever. Until then, it just lends to her mystique, don't you think?"

Brendan and Anna could only nod before Julia continued.

"I'm sure the new emperor will see fit to restore the temple soon since Jupiter is supposed to be the protector of Rome. A generous benefactor has already restored the Temple of Isis, as you will soon see. There are many devoted followers of Isis in Pompeii."

Vesuvius loomed on the horizon, a silent threat. Brendan leaned close to whisper in Anna's ear. "Look how massive that mountain is—and way too close for my comfort."

Anna frowned in response, but her fingers betrayed her uneasiness as they fumbled at her shoulder for a stray curl.

"We're not staying here long, are we? Vesuvius is smoking—building up steam as we loiter here in its pathway."

Anna cleared her throat and scurried closer to their fast-paced hostess. "Were you in Campania at the time of the earthquake, Julia?"

"Yes. I was here in Pompeii and hardly more than a girl then. Tremors plagued us for days, leaving us with an overwhelming amount of reconstruction to deal with afterwards. For days beforehand, we prepared feasts in honor of Pompeii's guardian spirits, oblivious to the chaos they would soon unleash. Toppled lamps caused fires. Nearly every building in the city was damaged in one way or another. It's enough to make a girl lose faith in the guardians."

"Several days? How did you manage to sleep at night?"

"It taught me to accept life as it comes. We can only make the best of what Fortune brings us and make every effort to ease the gods' wrath."

Anna shook her head. "You never considered leaving?"

"Many did, although I cannot imagine why. Does a place exist where you can avoid disaster?" Lady Julia's laugh echoed in the arched doorways to the marketplace. "No, the earthquake only served to make us stronger. None but the cowards abandoned our city. Only those of us who were truly committed remained."

"Or should have been committed," Brendan mumbled under his breath. Anna elbowed him in the ribs.

"Pompeii is now a city of great opportunities. I was able to buy the property adjoining the small estate my father had acquired—and at a much reduced price." A wry smile twitched at Julia's lips. "I even convinced the magistrates to give up the street dividing them so I could combine the two properties and open a bathhouse. With the limited functionality of Pompeii's public baths, it wasn't difficult to convince them my proposal would benefit the town."

Julia leaned closer and lowered her voice. "You have arrived at a most fortuitous time. These little tremors are nothing compared to what we withstood seventeen years ago, yet the fair-weather residents are already retreating back to Rome. You could lease for now—" Julia winked. "—and buy investment properties as the opportunities arise. In no time, you could be in my position." She raised her eyebrows as if the proposition was irresistible.

Brendan's jaw dropped. Anna popped a date into his mouth and paid the vendor with a coin from her purse. The cheerful man handed Brendan several more. From where Anna had positioned herself between Brendan and Julia, only he could see her threatening glare. Brendan offered them both an innocent smile.

Lady Julia and Anna continued toward the back of the market, their conversation lost on Brendan as he lagged behind. He couldn't resist turning to check Vesuvius again, but the pointed peak maintained its illusion of innocence. As Brendan's eyes scanned the bustling marketplace, one person caught his eye. A bedraggled teen languished against a toppled column, his withered legs not quite hidden by the dog at his side. Bridging the distance between them, the boy's eyes locked onto his and seemed to plead.

"Already, I am taking this new strength in my legs for granted," Brendan muttered aloud. "That should be me—" He took a single step in the direction of the crippled boy and his dog.

"Brendanus!" Anna dashed back to his side. "You don't know your way around the city. You should stay with us."

"The crippled boy—that must be polio. I can't just leave him there when I have been so fortunate—"

"You must." Anna looped her arm through his and tugged. "I know this must be difficult for you, but there is nothing you can do for him here. We can't allow anything to distract us from our task. We don't have the time or the power to change much here."

Brendan took a deep breath. "You're right, I guess—but what are we here for if we can't make any sort of difference? I need to know what I'm doing here."

"I know. I'm sorry. This isn't playing out quite the way I had hoped so far. I'll explain what little I know as soon as we can find

THE VEIL OF SMOKE

a moment alone. We're supposed to be helping a relative of mine."

"Who?"

"That's the thing. I don't know. I can only guess Julia is our mission. Why else would Ben have sent us to her?"

"So it's just doom and gloom for these people and there is nothing we can do to help them?" Brendan's eyes returned to the crippled boy who seemed to be as much out of place as he felt. Brendan's stomach tightened. Being a helpless observer was going to be torture.

"Their bodies are of little consequence in the eternal scheme of things. We can't hope to change anything but their hearts." She placed a slender finger on Brendan's chin and pulled his gaze toward her own. "In the end — that's what really matters." Brendan turned back to the boy, and the mountain beyond, once Anna stepped away. This trip would take every shred of his self-control.

When Brendan and Anna caught up to Lady Julia, she was examining a length of coral colored linen. The merchant offered several more for her inspection, but she rejected them with a casual flick of her wrist.

A dozen food stalls opened onto porticos on each side of the entrance, offering amphorae of wine, olive oil, grain, and baskets of fruit. Sheep bleated in a cramped pen at a back corner of the market. In the opposite corner, butchers displayed cuts of meat on marble counters, cooled only by the limited shade. Brendan could only assume the sheep were destined to be sacrifices since the freshness of meat did not appear to be a concern.

In the center of the market, fishmongers hawked their wares among a dozen waist-high pillars arranged in a circle. As with many structures in Pompeii, they appeared as if they had at one time served a more elegant purpose. At the moment, they served as stands for gutting and cleaning fish. A simple wooden structure shaded the seafood displays. As if to draw attention to the fish filets for sale, their former scales glittered in a drainage trough behind them.

"Sold for 625 denarii!" An auctioneer bellowed as they passed a crowded stall near the back corner.

Julia craned her slender neck to peer through the crowd, who also appeared fascinated by the sale. "Did you hear that? 625 denarii for a male slave. At that price, at least, he has worth and should be well-treated."

"And yet, you look disturbed by it," Anna observed.

Julia shrugged. "Slavery is a misfortune we must accept. My father was captured as a young man. Greeks are well respected for their refinement and education. The emperor valued my father's medical expertise. He served the imperial family for many years. In the end, he received a generous reward for his years of service."

"I am sorry." Anna faltered, twisting a lock of hair on her finger. Julia might not know her well enough to read her, but Brendan could recognize the signs of stress and discomfort in Anna's expression and mannerisms.

Julia shrugged. "Don't be sorry for me. Had it not been for his years as a slave, I would not be alive today. He found and adopted me after he received his freedom, so I have full Roman citizenship. My father placed all his hopes for the future in me. He had no son. Fate is a tyrant, but Fortune has been good to me. I am going to make the most of it."

"Do you own slaves?" Brendan stepped close enough for Anna to grab onto his elbow and give a warning squeeze.

"I do have slaves myself, but I allow them to operate their own businesses. In return for a portion of their profits, they enjoy a life of virtual freedom. Some day, they will earn enough to buy their freedom, but for now, I must survive off the income from my properties and the work of my clients and servants. The earthquakes have forced me to make many repairs, but they have provided unique opportunities as well. I might never have had the fortune to open a bath facility on this side of the city had it not been for the earthquake damage to the public baths—and so the Wheel of Fortune makes its endless tumble bringing prosperity from disaster."

"You credit Fortune with your success?" Brendan met Julia's cool gaze.

"It sounds as if you've put a lot of work into your estate," Anna interjected. "You might take credit where it is due."

Julia tilted her head. "They say Fortune is blind to our works, but I do believe in hard work, my friends. I believe in it from sunrise to sunset. Speaking of which, we need to head to the temple for its blessing."

Tucked into the shadow of the theater, the temple of Isis defied its shabby surroundings. The refurbished Iseum stood out as a paragon among Pompeii's older structures. Most were not yet resurrected from the rampant decay of the great earthquake almost two decades ago.

Murals depicting exotic Egyptian scenes adorned the rich red and black portico walls. The inner temple building towered over them, approaching the height of the theater next door.

Priests of Isis, robed in white linen, gathered at the top of the podium, their shaved heads moving in reverent unison. One lifted a sistrum, calling the worshipers to a respectful silence. The soft rhythmic jangle of the bronze rattle mesmerized the crowd. Another joined in with ethereal strains from a flute. Choirs lining the temple steps waved small palm fronds as they broke into a wailing chorus. Brendan edged back toward the outer portico to escape the heady waves of incense drifting from the altar.

A snippet of the liturgy seized Brendan's attention. A priest hailed Isis as "she who knows the orphan." Perhaps that was part of Egyptian goddess' appeal for Julia. Could it be irony that they'd each lost parents?

"Queen of Heaven," the acolytes chanted.

Across the courtyard, a narrowed set of eyes scrutinized him as he backed through the murmuring worshipers. A statuesque blond man loomed above the crowd, his gaze intent upon Brendan instead of the ritual before them. Hatred permeated the man's glare. Brendan darted behind a pillar, chiding himself for his gutless knee-jerk reaction. He clenched his teeth, willing himself to confront the man's piercing gaze with equal intensity.

Brendan stepped beyond the pillar, forced his unwilling eyes to search the crowd. He slowed his breathing, feigning interest in a portrait bust engraved with the name Norbanus — an actor of all things. It would appear that there was nothing new about idolizing actors. No surprise, he supposed. They were in the theater district. Beyond it, a Lucius Caecilius Phoebus touted his donated statuette of Isis with an inscription on the pedestal.

Brendan gave the crowd of worshipers a casual glance. His breath seized in his throat. Hateful eyes again riveted on his own as the man edged closer. Brendan ducked low and switched directions, heading for Anna.

"What are you doing now?" Anna whispered. Her brows creased in warning.

Brendan put a finger to his lips and tugged at her elbow. "I think we need to leave."

Anna rolled her eyes at him, but leaned toward Julia. "Excuse us, Lady Julia, we'll be waiting for you outside."

"We don't want to alienate our hostess," she hissed as soon as they were out of earshot.

Brendan raised his hands in surrender. "Hey, I'm sorry. Some stalker was giving me the evil eye in there. Would anyone recognize us here?"

As soon as the words left his mouth, he knew. He'd seen that malevolent glare before—in the ancient ruins of Mutul. "Fire is Born."

"What on earth are you talking about? We are here on a mission, and we are running out of time, Brendan. Please—focus on what we need to do."

"You don't understand. There is great evil here, just like we faced in Mutul. After you went home, I encountered the real source of all our troubles there." It had all been real. In the years since he'd returned from Mutul, he'd been deceived yet again—lulled into believing he'd imagined it all—that Fire Is Born had never really existed.

Anna frowned, but reached for his hand. "What is it?"

"An evil presence." Brendan's heart raced at the memory of it and a prickle crept over his flesh. "I don't have time to explain it all now, but Fire is Born is not someone I want to cross paths with again. After you left Mutul, I had a run-in with the creep. I overheard him ranting about how he'd led the Mayans to their destruction. You could tell he got his kicks ruining people. Makes sense that he would show up in Pompeii now. This is exactly his kind of scene. I'd recognize that merciless stare no matter what disguise he fabricated. I just didn't expect anyone to recognize me, looking like this."

"Why didn't you mention this before?" Anna's eyes grew distant as if piecing things together in her mind.

Brendan didn't bother responding. There had been little opportunity to discuss the details of their time in Mutul before they returned home, much less since they arrived here together.

"The snake—" Anna whispered. The haunted glaze her eyes held as a girl returned.

"What snake?" Brendan squeezed her hand. "We really need to talk."

"Not important right now. Please continue."

Brendan clapped a hand to his forehead. "I can't believe I didn't think of this sooner. Right before he stepped into the fire portal, Fire is Born said something about being just in time for the Festival of Volcanus." Brendan shuddered. "I didn't think much of it at the time. It never occurred to me I'd cross paths with him again."

Anna gaped at him. "What is it, Brendan? You should see the look on your face."

"He's here. That had to be him watching me across the courtyard." Brendan grabbed Anna's arm as realization washed over him like ice water through his veins. "We've got to get out of here." His eyes darted down the street. His body yearned to follow the same impulse. Only his concern for Anna's welfare kept him rooted where he stood.

"Wait." Anna's face wore a new strength and calmness that became her. "We can't just run off. We were sent here for a purpose, and we might not understand it all yet, but it's important for us to finish the task."

Anna couldn't comprehend the enormity of what she was up against. Brendan took a deep breath and emptied his lungs with force. The urge to flee was overwhelming, but an equally determined look on Anna's face prevented him from taking another step.

"It has taken me a long time," Anna said, with a fierceness etched into every line of her face. "But I have finally learned to face my fears. We escaped him before, right?"

"You don't understand. He doesn't just tempt you. He deceives you. He is a master of manipulation. He makes you believe you've got nothing to lose and everything in the world to gain. In the end, you have no one to blame but yourself. I fell for it once. I can't go through that again."

"Then don't. Stand up to him. Someone here needs us." Despite her petite size, she assumed a battle stance that might have given a gladiator pause. As comical as it appeared on a petite woman, she projected an air of authority Brendan had to respect. "Has Ben taught you nothing?"

Anna couldn't know how close her words cut to the painful truth. "You forget. Our last experience was many years ago for you, but only a few for me. I haven't had time to grow as strong as you have."

Anna's face softened. "I'm sorry. You're right. I'm not being fair, but trust me on this — running will only make it more difficult. Resist. Have faith. I'll help you with everything I've got. What did he look like?"

Brendan's fingers shook as he combed them through his hair. "When he disappeared into the fire portal at Mutul, he was tall, blond, muscular. I think you would call him handsome."

"Handsome?" Anna's eyes narrowed.

"Scared now?"

Anna shook her head, but the line of her mouth betrayed a hint of doubt.

"He was wearing a red robe."

"And he looked the same here?"

"I could only see the top of his head — but, yeah, I think so."

"All right," Anna said, taking a deep breath. "We're going back in there. It's a public place. He's not going to make any moves here in front of a crowd. We'll watch him — try to get a feel for what he's after."

"What he's after? He's an evil, soul-sucking monster."

"Maybe he's trying to get a feel for what we're after."

She had a point. That bolstered his confidence somewhat. If Fire is Born possessed unlimited power, he wouldn't skulk around the temple spying on him. "All right," he said, offering her a half-hearted smile. "Ladies first."

Anna spun on her heel and marched back into the temple. He had to admit she had spunk. If anyone could go head to head with their nemesis, it would be his small friend and her enormous faith.

They stepped back into the temple courtyard. Anna's eyebrows lifted in an unspoken question. Where was this alleged threat? He scanned the worshipers gathered at the bottom of the temple stairs but saw no sign of the conspicuous red robe and blond hair. The choir's keening wail rose to a feverish pitch. They swayed as if in a trance. The priest raised a bronze pitcher, the sculpted image of a snake coiling at the rim.

"Queen of Heaven," the priest roared. The acoustics in the Iseum were impressive. The priest descended the stairs, joining the crowd of revelers. "We invoke you."

Brendan hovered at the outskirts of the gathering, searching the faces of the onlookers. Before, the unmistakable glare had nailed him. Now, no one stood out from the crowd.

"Waters of the Nile," the priest thundered, pouring the contents of the pitcher into a basin on the altar near the base of the stairs. "Cleanse us."

Brendan caught Anna's eyes. He shrugged and shook his head. All eyes focused on the priest. No one appeared to take notice as he crept around the perimeter of the activity. He rounded the temple where arched doorways opened onto a narrow room lined with murals of Egyptian scenery. In one fresco, snakes guarded a basket—always snakes with this goddess. Two tables laden with offerings for a ritual feast stood ready at the center, but the room was otherwise empty.

Completing his circuit of the small temple grounds, Brendan returned to Anna's side. Her eyes followed Lady Julia, presenting her sacrifice to the priest at the altar.

The priest placed her bundles on the altar and poured fluid from a bronze cruet over them. "Inconsumable oil—balsam of life." A young girl brought a small torch. "Immortal flame of Nature, author of life."

"*Una quai es omnia, Dea Isis*— Being one, Thou art all, Goddess Isis."

He shook his head. "Nothing," he mouthed with another shrug. Anna raised her eyebrows and gave him a slow nod.

Julia joined them with a smile. "I have given so Isis may give. I can only pray she'll reward my efforts," she whispered, ushering them toward the door.

No sign of Fire is Born. Brendan shivered, even as they stepped into the blistering Pompeii sun.

LAUREN LYNCH

4

Brendan ducked out of the glaring Pompeii sun and into the cool oasis of Lady Julia's main atrium. Isodore's artful anticipation of his mistress's needs bordered on sorcery. Before Brendan's eyes could adjust to the dimness of the atrium, Julia's faithful servant produced three pairs of slippers. He summoned a girl to remove their street shoes before disappearing through a curtained doorway.

Julia urged them to sit as a willowy olive-skinned girl arrived with a basin of cool water and washed the dust from their feet. While disturbed by the intimacy of the slave's gentle attentions to his filthy feet, he had to admit it was refreshing. The girl hunched over his feet, guarding what dignity remained by hiding her face.

He placed a hand on her shoulder as she gathered her things, forcing her to make eye contact. "Thank you." He learned forward as she helped him into soft leather slippers.

She gave a quick nod. A crease appeared between her brows before she lowered her eyes and scurried away.

Julia was back to business at once. "If you can wait here for a moment, I will give you a tour of the property myself. I just need to get the kitchen staff started on dinner. I hope you don't mind, but I've invited a few more guests tonight—nothing too formal. I hope to give you an unforgettable taste of our colorful Pompeian social life—to leave you wanting more."

Lady Julia glided toward the large doorway leading to a

courtyard garden, but spun back to face them before she left. "Isidore will see to your needs. You might enjoy examining the frescoes in here while you wait. I'll only be a moment."

Brendan turned to the frescoed walls, Isidore hovering close at his elbow. "I've taken your personal items to a cubicula upstairs. I will take your toga there as well." Isidore's lips betrayed an amused smile as he unwound the cumbersome layers of wool. Brendan stretched in delighted relief once he wore only the tunic beneath it. The stoic servant made a hasty exit with their outer garments, leaving them alone to explore the spacious atrium.

"I don't know how they manage to keep such a busy pace in this heat." Anna stifled a yawn. She cast a cautious glance toward the doorways before leaning closer. "Do you get the feeling that Lady Julia is trying to sell us on her rental properties?"

"Definitely," he whispered back. "Who is this friend Theophilus arranging our accommodations? And what did he imply on our behalf?"

"Ben works in mysterious ways. Lady Julia seems intent on offering us lavish hospitality during our stay here. I have to believe he planned for us to meet the person we're supposed to help at this location. Just follow my lead and go along with whatever Julia suggests. We need to be ready for whatever opportunity might unfold."

Brendan couldn't help shaking his head at their situation. "How long do you think we can remain guests before she expects us to lease the place?"

Anna clamped her lips together, suppressing a laugh, but her eyes still sparkled with amusement. "I don't know, but we'll need to stall in every way possible. We need to play the role of discriminating business people. At least it will give us an excuse to be thorough in our exploration of Pompeii."

"Do you really think that will satisfy Lady Julia?"

Anna threw her arms wide. "What choice do we have? She seems to accept us as we are without question so far. It appears the stage is already set for us. We'll need to make the right choices in playing our assigned roles."

Brendan bit his lip. "I have the feeling we don't have much time anyway. Do you know when Vesuvius erupts? I only remember one bit of irony: it erupts the day after a festival for Volcanus — their god of fire."

Anna shrugged. "I believe it happened in late August of 79 A.D."

"How can we find out without being too obvious?"

"Hopefully they'll discuss politics at dinner tonight. Maybe that will give us a clue. Emperor Vespasian died in 79 A.D. and Titus' rule began only two months before Pompeii was destroyed. Even that wouldn't give us an exact date though."

Brendan's chest tightened under the layers of restrictive wool. "We can't just guess. We'll need to get out of here well in advance. They didn't have much warning did they?"

"Not that they would have understood. I remember when Vesuvius erupted in 1944. It was nothing compared to what will soon happen here, but it devastated the area even then."

"You've been to Pompeii before?"

"Last year — well, in 1957 — as a tourist. Among the many ironic twists life seems to throw my way, it was after I left Italy to live in the United States. I was only in Campania for a short stay."

"Just one more reason why time travel isn't supposed to be part of a normal life. It bends the mind at painful angles."

"And, yet — if we had never experienced it, we would have missed out on our friendship altogether." A radiant smile curled across Anna's lips. Her face, framed by its mane of untamed curls, portrayed an innocence and joy that warmed his heart and soothed his ragged nerves.

It was a mental snapshot of Anna he believed would remain etched in his mind—and he already had a few locked away in his memory vaults. Brendan returned her smile. The journey would always be worth it. Living with the after effects of polio had taught him to savor simple pleasures as they came.

"Isn't it delightful?" Lady Julia's over-cheerful voice called from behind them. Brendan's heart skipped a beat. It was as if Julia had read his thoughts and commented on them. He hoped the splashing fountain had masked their whispered conversation as much as it had concealed her return.

Julia joined them in front of the wide fresco depicting various public activities. "The Forum in its prime," she said, her finger tracing the ankle-length gown of a girl standing before a seated magistrate. "It's a daily reminder of what Pompeii can once again become. I, myself, find it inspiring."

"I imagine if someone found this hundreds of years from now, it would offer a fascinating illustration of what everyday life here was like." Anna scowled at him from behind Julia's back.

Julia snorted at the thought. "I suppose it might. I considered having it restored to its original brightness after the earthquake. Time has faded the finer details—but I decided not to destroy its charming rustic qualities."

Anna folded her arms across her chest and nodded as she stepped back and surveyed its full length from a greater distance. "I agree. Old things should be treasured and appreciated—just as they are." She winked at Brendan.

"The men's bathing session has just ended for the afternoon. The staff is already cleaning the facilities, but we can take a quick peek now if you like. The furnace room is just through these doors. I'm sure you noticed the street entrance as you arrived, so

I'll take you around the back way. Lady Julia led them through one of the large doorways at the back of the atrium opening onto a wide portico with courtyard gardens beyond.

Brendan stopped and stepped back a few paces, fascinated by the covered walkway's columns. While appearing grand in scale from the atrium entrance, passing them in the portico revealed their shallow depth. He moved back and forth, amused by the cunning effect.

"We'll dine here tonight in the summer triclinium." Lady Julia indicated an alcove to their right. The front of the room opened onto the dramatic gardens behind them. The back three walls featured built-in stone couches covered in cushions where they could recline during their evening meal.

Brendan turned back to the garden view, again admiring the optical illusion of the columns. From the dining area perspective, they wouldn't obstruct the scenery. "The columns are quite clever. They appear large from one angle, yet from here you hardly notice them."

"Aren't they though?" Julia seemed pleased that he'd noticed. "Every detail of this room was orchestrated for dramatic effect. I commissioned the frescoes in this room myself—scenes from the Nile to honor Isis."

Strange how you could end up in ancient Italy, lounging beside freshly painted scenes of Egyptian riverbanks. They would dine among naive images of crocodiles and pygmies while blundering their way through Roman social customs.

Water trickled down a stepped fountain built into the back wall, disappearing into a panel hidden behind the couches. "The fountain is brilliant." Anna stepped closer and tilted her head. "The sound of water brings the mural to life."

"I am rather pleased with that feature." Julia gave an emphatic nod before turning on her heel to lead them back toward the baths.

"You may explore the gardens more tonight, if you like," Julia suggested as she strode past the lush landscaping. "Beyond the ornamental gardens, I have fruit trees and vegetable gardens large enough to supply not only the household but the tavern as well. The fish pond and flower gardens, however, are my true pride and joy."

"It's amazing what you've managed on your own." Anna's eyes were wide with admiration.

"Well, you can see why I would want to lease part of the complex out. I enjoy the purchase and development of property more than the day-to-day management of it. There is only so much one woman can do on her own."

Julia hailed a servant trimming an arbor vine. "Are the grapes sweet enough yet?" He waved her forward and placed one between her lips. A smile spread over Julia's face as she chewed. "You two have perfect timing. You will sample my grapes at dinner tonight."

Anna's eyes met Brendan's at the mention of their timing.

"This place is massive," Anna whispered to Brendan before dashing after Julia. Neither woman was ever still for long.

"The public baths are barely operable these days," Julia yelled over her shoulder as she hastened them past a series of pergola draped in lush vines. "So my new bath complex should be quite popular."

She paused mid-stride and lowered her voice. "I charge enough to make sure the clientele are strictly upscale. Many stop by the tavern on their way out or order refreshments at the service window as they wait, which adds to the profits."

A narrow hallway opened into a changing room with a cold plunge pool and led beyond into the tepidarium for warm baths with a small steam bath room. They peeked into the caldarium

THE VEIL OF SMOKE

as they passed, but the floor was still too hot to step on in their lightweight house slippers. That explained the wooden soled sandals he'd noticed in the first room. They retraced their path back to the changing room, this time detouring through the waiting room. Peacocks and griffins decorated the bench-lined walls.

Julia looped her arm through Anna's. "If you care to use the baths before we open to the public tomorrow morning, I would be happy to have you join me."

She ushered them through a side door in the waiting room to a private expanse of lawn bordered by a sizable outdoor pool. Brendan loitered near the sparkling water, longing to end the tour where they stood.

Julia offered him a perceptive grin, pointing to an outbuilding with an arched roof. "There are latrines and another changing area at the back wall there. You are welcome to use the pool during your stay, of course. If you wait until the bathhouse closes, you'll have it all to yourself."

Julia directed them back through a door at the front corner of the property. "Located so close to the amphitheater, our tavern is overflowing after every event. As you can see, there is indoor and outdoor seating—both couches and benches." She pointed to the dining establishment they had passed in the morning when they first arrived.

"You truly did not exaggerate when you advertised the property as luxurious," Anna said.

Julia rewarded her with an appreciative smile. "You are kind. If I am rewarded with success, I will be as generous a benefactor as Eumachia once was. Nothing would please me more than to honor my father's memory in that way."

She signaled to a server at the street-side counter and instructed him to offer them whatever they would like to eat or drink. "I apologize for taking so much of your time today. I'm sure you're exhausted. Please take time to refresh yourselves before our dinner guests arrive. Use the pool or explore the gardens. My staff is at your disposal. When you are ready, Isidore will show you to your rooms upstairs and help you prepare for dinner. There is one guest in particular I think you'll find fascinating—at least I found him irresistible."

Before they could offer more than a brief word of thanks, she was gone. Anna collapsed onto a masonry bench. "She is one dedicated businesswoman."

"More than you can imagine." The server reappeared at Anna's side with heaping plates of bread, figs and olives.

"Does she ever slow down?" Brendan asked, rubbing his feet through the thin-soled slippers.

"Only when she sleeps—and we're not even sure she does that." The man shook his head, spinning on his heel to return to waiting customers.

"Julia is so self-reliant and committed to this dream of hers—to this place." Anna groaned. "If she's the one we're meant to help, it's going to be quite the challenge. Can you imagine dragging her away from this even for a day?"

5

Every muscle in Marcus's twisted limbs screamed in pain. There was little he could do to escape the relentless sun, but for once, he was grateful for its soothing warmth. Freedom of movement was something he'd always taken for granted, but after little more than a day trapped in an uncooperative body, he was ready to admit defeat.

Marcus closed his eyes and leaned back against the stone pillar. If sleep had brought him here, there was a chance it might also provide a path home. He willed his mind to take him somewhere—anywhere but this frustrating reality. He relaxed and allowed his mind to drift, visualizing his own soft covers instead of the coarse and filthy rag now covering his legs.

A thump at his side tugged him back to awareness. He opened his eyes, his left hand sliding over an object on the ground next to him—one of the rickety crutches. He smiled in spite of his dark mood.

"You came back," Marcus said, ruffling the fur on the top of the dog's head. "I thought you'd abandoned me."

The dog tilted his head and seemed to ponder that. "Do you often assume the worst?"

Marcus yanked his hand back. "Dogs are usually a lot more easy going."

"I wasn't always a dog. I am, however, here to serve."

"I don't think I'll be able to do much with just one crutch."

Marcus examined the crotchety stick. It was little more than a forked branch trimmed to serve as a crude support. As worn as it was, it appeared to have received many years of use. Marcus couldn't imagine how he'd manage to lift himself and walk with it—even if he still had both.

"I managed to catch up with the cart and grab one of them, but I had no way to carry two, and now the cart is long gone." If a dog could look perturbed, this one had succeeded in it.

Marcus folded his arms across his chest. "You sure are grouchy for a dog."

"I apologize." The dog licked his cheek. "Is that better?"

Marcus wiped his cheek with the back of his hand, but couldn't suppress a smile. "I think we can limit it to words. What should I call you?"

The dog thrust his chin forward and straightened his spine. "You could call me Maximus."

Meaning greatest? Marcus bit back a laugh. "Humble. I like it. I always wanted a dog as a little kid. My mother never would let me get one. She said dogs didn't belong in the city."

"In many ways, she made a valid point." Maximus stretched his body out against Marcus's withered legs.

"How about I call you Max for short?"

The dog groaned and rolled his eyes.

"Thanks, Max." Marcus scratched him behind the ears. Dust rose from the dog's bedraggled fur.

Max used his hind leg to scratch at the back of his neck with the skill of a contortionist. Marcus also found himself grating the coarse fabric of his tunic across his ribs. "Unbelievable." He clenched his teeth against the urge to scratch. "I think we have fleas."

A bald man in a white sleeveless robe shuffled past, sidestepping to avoid any threat of physical contact. Thrust before him, he gripped a parcel in the tips of his fingers as if the contents might soil his pristine garments. The pungent tang of fish lingered in his wake. "There's an odd duck," Marcus said with a snort.

"A priest." Max rose up on his front paws and sniffed the air.

"He doesn't look like any priest I've ever seen."

"In this town, if they're not bowing to the emperor, they're worshiping gods of their own making. Statues of lifeless gods are crammed into every niche and crevice here. Their empty stares raise my hackles." Max plunked back to the ground. "Of course, most seek fulfillment at the altar of their own desires. That is one human consistency I've observed regardless of place or time."

"And where are we exactly? Why am I here?"

The dog pushed himself up to a sitting position again. "That is an excellent question to ask yourself. Has something been weighing on you lately? Where have your circumstances been leading you? What is going on in your life?"

"My life? I'm trying to take charge of it. I should have a right to do what I want with my future, but my mother seems to think otherwise lately."

"In what way?"

"She wants me to get a job this summer sweeping floors or washing dishes or something so I can put that money towards a college education."

"And you think that means she doesn't care about your future?"

"She cares too much! It's not her future. It's my life." Marcus's heart was pounding in his ears. He caught himself glaring at the memory of it and tried to shake the anger loose. "I should be able to live it as I see fit. I was born with a gift for music. My mom told me I would make music with whatever I could find from the time I could pick an object up."

"You mention that you were born with a gift—your own words. Was that your own doing?"

"Well—no." Marcus rubbed at the tension bunching in the back of his neck.

"Could your gift for music not flourish in college?"

"Well, yes, it could—but not everyone needs to go—"

"Is your mother abusive?" The dog pushed his snout a little too close for comfort, eyes boring into his own.

"Of course not." He and his mother had always been close. It was only recently that she crowded him at every turn with her oppressive expectations. Marcus had to fight the urge to give the dog a shove. Why did everyone have to get in his face lately?

"Well, she must be unkind in some way to provoke this sort of reaction from you," the dog suggested.

"No—no!" His voice piped to a girlish octave. He clamped his mouth shut. The dog wasn't giving him a chance to explain.

"Why do you feel that your life is your own? Did you create yourself or your gifts?" Max flopped to the ground. "If my life was my own, I wouldn't be squandering it here in a dusty corner of Pompeii with you."

"Wait—dusty corner of what?"

"Pompeii," Maximus said with a slight growl. "In 79 A.D., no less."

"What do you mean? What happens in 79 A.D.?" The tension in his neck intensified.

"They teach these things in history classes, you know." Max tilted his head and waited for his words to soak in. "If we want to live much longer, we need to leave this place—so the sooner you can figure out why you're here, the better."

Marcus stared at his lifeless legs. His stomach growled. He had never been less equipped to survive on his own. He couldn't do much more than grovel in the dust, clothed in filthy rags and unable to walk. Even if he could, he didn't have a clue where he would go.

Max put his furry chin on Marcus's leg and released a deep sigh. "You need to ask for help."

"That's not my style." Marcus realized how stupid the words sounded the moment they left his mouth.

"You must humble yourself, or we will both perish here."

"Why are you doing this to me?"

Max groaned. "No one is doing anything to you."

"Then why am I here? What happens if I die here?" Marcus squeezed his hands into fists.

"I find it's best to be prepared at all times. We never know when our earthly lives may end, no matter what the location."

Marcus rubbed his forehead. He hadn't parted with his mother on the best of notes. She was all he had left.

Max lifted his head. "Ben chose you."

"Ben? Who on earth—" Purposeful movement in the open expanse of the courtyard drew his attention. Amid the meandering traffic of socializing market shoppers a head bobbed toward them. The man's height alone made him stand out in a crowd. The sea of faces parted, revealing the only man to make eye contact with Marcus all day—at least since the incident with the construction foreman. The man had a loping gait and the kind of rugged face women would call handsome. Something in his lopsided smile put Marcus at ease.

"Is that Ben?"

"Certainly not, but I have a feeling he knows Ben."

Marcus scrambled to gather any remaining dignity he might posses as the man strode toward him at a determined pace, flicking his dark hair out of his eyes.

Once the man drew near, he seemed to hesitate. Perhaps he suspected the fleas they both harbored. "Hello. May I sit?" He pointed to a toppled chunk of marble.

Marcus gave him a sheepish shrug over the formalities. It wasn't like he had a front door to knock on. "Sure, pull up a boulder." He could only hope the guy wasn't a local authority, here to dump him someplace worse.

The man took a deep breath. "My name is Brendanus. I couldn't help noticing you sitting here with your dog."

"I am Marcus, and this is my dog, Max."

"Are you here alone?" Brendan asked.

Would giving an honest answer put him in danger? "Yes," Marcus finally admitted. As tempting as it was to beg for help, but didn't want to scare the man off. He wouldn't know what to ask for anyway.

"Do you have family in the area?" The man seemed sincere enough. His kind eyes had a way of putting Marcus at ease, but the questions still made him nervous. He couldn't offer blind trust. He was in no position to defend himself here, but he also didn't have many options. He was going to have to take some risks and hope to survive it all.

The man's eyes softened. "I'm sorry. I didn't mean to pry. Are you hungry? A friend of mine grows pears. She gave me two."

He tossed one to Marcus and took a bite of his own. "Wow—they're great too." He wiped juice off his face with the back of his hand.

Marcus's stomach betrayed him with a deep growl. No point in trying to keep up appearances. He chomped into the pear and closed his eyes to savor the juices on his parched tongue. Fruit had never tasted so good.

The man picked up Marcus's lone crutch. "Is this how you get around? If you don't mind me saying so, it's a bit beat up — and it must be hard to get around with only one. Maybe I could help you out with that."

Marcus didn't know what to say. He had nowhere to go here. He just wanted to go home. "There were two." Marcus shrugged.

"You'd never know it now, but I've suffered from a handicap myself," the man confided. "I know how hard it is to sit on the sidelines while an oblivious world speeds by. I understand your predicament better than you'd imagine."

"I wasn't always crippled." Marcus's throat tightened. He hung his head to hide the unshed tears burning his at eyelids. How had he sunk so low in just one day of groveling in the dirt? "I — I —"

Max scratched at his arm twice as if prodding him to say more. What did he want him to say anyway? It was obvious Max wanted him to ask for help, but growing up on the streets of Chicago, he'd learned to hide any vulnerability. Showing weakness never worked in your favor.

"Brendanus!" Two beautiful women strode up behind him.

Marcus shifted in the dirt, throwing the tattered rag over his withered legs. It was stupid really. Like he could hide any part of his current affliction. He was still filthy and covered in fleas, but he'd do whatever he could to avoid one more look of pity or disgust.

"We must be on our way. Julia needs to visit the temple and there are the dinner guests tonight. We still need to walk across town and bathe before we — oh, hello. I didn't realize you had a friend here." The shorter woman offered Marcus a radiant smile. He had to give her credit for that. She hadn't so much as flinched at the sight of him.

The other woman looked as if she had a mouthful of something sour she didn't want to swallow. She took a step back, but managed a strained smile.

"Go on ahead, I'll catch up in a minute." Brendanus waved the two women on.

The tall one set off immediately. The nice one tugged at Brendanus's arm before chasing after her friend. "Remember to stay on task, my friend."

Brendanus clapped Marcus on the shoulder. "Sorry to rush off. Look—if you don't mind, I'll look into a better mode of transportation for you. I'll come back when I can. Do you live around here?"

"I'll be here," Marcus said with a shrug.

The man scratched Max's head. "Take good care of him, buddy."

As soon as Brendanus was out of earshot, Max gave him a nudge. "Why didn't you ask him for help?"

"Well, what was I supposed to say? I can't just blurt out that I don't belong here," Marcus snapped.

Max sighed. "I don't know, but you'd better come up with some idea before he comes back—if he comes back at all. I can sense the trouble brewing in that mountain. It tests my perseverance. Every fiber of this body yearns to flee."

6

Anna paced the floor of the small bedroom Isidore escorted her to. Ben had charged them with helping a lost family member in need, but left them to discern the details on their own. When she attempted to press him for details, Ben assured her she'd know what to do when the time was right. Nothing about this place in time seemed right though.

Meanwhile, north of Pompeii, the volcanic monstrosity roused from its slumber. Thousands lived within the city walls. Time was short and so much about this mission was yet to be revealed.

Ben's mysterious nature bewildered Anna, but she trusted him. He could easily handle whatever this task was without her assistance, yet he chose to involve her—as if the process of discovery held more importance than the undertaking itself. It was Ben's way and she had grown to accept it. Indulging in worry or fear would be pointless. When she needed assurance, she could call on him. He was always as near as she wished him to be.

Worn wooden steps to the upper rooms creaked as soft footsteps approached the drapery at her doorway. "Lady Annthea, may we come in?"

Anna pulled the heavy curtain aside, revealing the demure olive-skinned girl who had bathed her feet earlier. Again, she carried a basin of scented water. A younger girl followed in her wake. "I apologize for our early arrival. Lady Julia instructed us to assist you before coming to her."

Although Anna yearned for a few moments of solitude, she welcomed them into her room to complete their assigned tasks. One washed her face and arms with a damp cloth while the second fanned her with a peacock feather flabellum. Anna closed her eyes and did her best to relax, inhaling the heady scent of cinnamon and balsam as the girl rinsed her neck. Gentle fan strokes cooled her damp skin. She had to admit, it was an invigorating break from the incessant heat.

The girls draped a sheer indigo blue stola over her simple gray tunic, securing the lightweight fabric at her shoulders with two golden ivy leaf brooches. Ben had arranged for them to stay in a place where they would have help dressing—a luxury Anna was grateful for. She could never have figured out what to do with the baffling layers of draped fabric on her own.

"The air here is scorching," Anna said, certain perspiration would bead on her upper lip again the moment Julia's attendants left. "Much hotter than where I'm from."

"It will cool off a little when the sun goes down," the younger girl promised. "This summer has been hotter than usual. Take advantage of the pool when you have a chance."

Anna cleared her throat and decided to risk making a fool of herself with someone other than Julia. "The new emperor … what is his name?"

"Titus?" The girl suppressed a giggle, eyes rolling toward her workmate.

So it was Titus. Time was short. But how short? Ben was with them, whatever he was doing had their best interest at heart. They'd have to trust him and work fast.

Trunks of clothing had shown up with them on the carriage ride to Pompeii, making their arrival appear more natural than it actually was. Lady Julia's servants had already unpacked the contents into a wardrobe in her room. If the amount of clothing provided was any indication, their stay in Pompeii would last several days at least.

Once they had dressed her, the girls worked together to subdue Anna's stubborn curls with an elaborate hairstyle. She summoned the last of her patience as the girls tugged at her hair. One weaved in a variety of ribbons and ornaments as the other pinned it all into place. Their deft fingers worked in unison with few words exchanged. At last, they stepped back and handed her a polished silver mirror, waiting for her approval.

She turned her head to admire their work. "It's beautiful, thank you." Once more, they had accomplished a feat she could never have managed on her own, not that she often attempted to dress in such a lavish manner.

The women dipped their heads in humble acceptance of her praise, the youngest offering her a shy smile. They gathered their supplies and left Anna alone with her thoughts. She returned to the mirror, fascinated as much by its unusual qualities as by the elegant transformation of her reflection.

"What am I to do, Ben?" she asked aloud. "We have little time and much to accomplish."

"You will gain confidence in your abilities to listen and discern by moving past these uncertainties. Draw near to me, dear Anna. I am here with you." She could almost see Ben's eyes reflected in her own as she held the mirror to her face. She couldn't be certain whether his words were audible or a sensation of her mind — but she believed them without question. "Watch for opportunities. Heed your inner prompting. The path unfolds before you even now."

"I will do my best."

"I can ask for nothing more, Anna."

"Is Julia my ancestor? At times I imagine I recognize something of my mother in her eyes or laugh, but perhaps I am only grasping at what I long for."

She blinked at her silent reflection. "Ben?"

"I am here."

"Must we allow these people to die?"

"I don't want them to perish any more than you do, but they must make their own choices. If I forced my will upon them—protected them from every danger—they would only resent their lack of freedom."

It called to mind a sentiment her uncle had often expressed: no good deed goes unpunished. "Is there nothing we can do to help?"

"We can love them."

∞

Anna followed narrow wooden stairs to the dim hallway below. Although the sun still blazed outside, bronze oil lamps suspended from the ceilings lit the cramped and windowless interior halls. She marveled at the oddities of Pompeian architecture. Pieced together over the centuries, the city melded the ancient with the new in an eclectic mosaic of styles. The Etruscan foundations of Julia's estate displayed Egyptian influence while it offered Roman luxury. As Rome pushed its boundaries outward, the cultural mix intensified.

The hallway opened into an extravagant reception area. Lamps lit the shadowy back corners of this room as sunlight streamed in from the columned garden beyond.

Flirtatious giggling drifted across the courtyard. A copper-haired girl in a gauzy blue dress tiptoed on the ledge of the fishpond. She struck a playful pose, brazen as a goddess in her youthful beauty. Golden highlights danced in her hair as sunlight glimmered on the pond's surface.

The girl reached for someone hidden by the garden's large topiary bushes, attempting to lure them across the narrow bridge. It was Brendan she finally tugged with her to the edge, pulling with such gusto, he had to grab onto her to keep them both from plummeting into the water. She latched onto his neck with another burst of laughter.

Anna sighed. This was the taste of Pompeian social life Lady Julia had promised to show them? She had to admit, Brendan seemed charmed. Anna had yet to explain what few details she knew of their mission, but she'd hoped he might take a more purposeful approach.

Concealed by the unlit room she stood in, Anna lingered in the shadows as the girl twined her arm around Brendan's. They disappeared from view among the vines of the pergola.

The irony hadn't escaped her. The playful girl she was dismissing as flighty and immature was centuries older than her—more than a millennium in fact. When Anna had left her own time for Pompeii, she was aging and unmarried. Here in Pompeii, she'd returned to a more youthful body. Time was a matter of perspective—beauty was fleeting and appearances deceiving. The body containing her spirit had always been a temporary vessel, but she had never been more aware of that concept than she was in this moment.

The copper-haired girl embraced life—as she should. Her body might be destined to perish in a few days, but she was living fully in the present. Anna clenched her jaw tighter with each mischievous giggle, but she knew she had no right to be resentful. She had encouraged Brendan to explore the garden—pushed him, in fact, to interact with the other guests. He was simply doing her bidding. Anna took a deep breath and stepped into the sunshine.

7

As a coppery sun blazed a trail toward the western horizon, Pompeii's streets grew still. Isidore urged napping or bathing during the stifling afternoon hours, but Brendan couldn't seem to unwind in Vesuvius's looming shadow. He'd decided, instead, to wander the estate's vast gardens. When Julia's attendants arrived to help Anna dress for dinner, Brendan figured he'd have plenty of time to explore on his own while he waited.

Impeccable topiary shrubs bordered the pathway to a narrow fishpond extending the length of Julia's formal garden. Trellised vines framed a brick wall separating the courtyard garden from extensive vegetable and herb gardens beyond. Those outside the property's staid walls, could never imagine the beauty of the oasis within. A peacock was the only other creature in sight and the garden remained peaceful aside from the occasional squawk it let out.

Brendan leaned over the pond's brick ledge to get a closer look at the fish lurking in its depths. A mirror image of his face wavered on the surface of the water, squinting back at him in the fierce sunlight.

Having no one else to talk to, he interrogated his own reflection. "What are you doing here? Since when does Anna accept any help? What possible help can you offer?"

Brendan bit his lip, but reflected image of his face seemed to offer him a wide grin.

"Don't worry. I am always with you."

Brendan scanned the garden. Confident he was alone, he drew closer to his smiling reflection. "Ben?" he whispered, kneeling down and bracing himself at the edge of the pool.

"Yes," his reflection answered.

"How?" He felt foolish as he spoke aloud to his own watery image. The act was both disturbing and comforting.

"I promised to be with you always. I am here. Inside you." His eyes blinked back at him, deep and mournful. "Why didn't you seek me sooner? You've denied me since your return to the world."

"When I returned home, I was confused—slipping in and out of consciousness. At first, I believed, but eventually I convinced myself I'd only imagined my time with you. You were right there and I couldn't see it."

"If only you'd spoken to me. I would have shown you the way." Ben's voice was gentle, even as it pierced him.

"First I betrayed you, then I denied your existence. Why do you bother with me?" Ben had suffered a horrible death as a result of Brendan's poor choices and had given his own life to save theirs. "You forgave me—and now you still want to be a friend to me. I just don't understand."

"It was a sacrifice I chose to make. I forgave you long ago. You know that in your heart. When will you forgive yourself?"

Tears pooled in Brendan's eyes. He clenched his teeth.

"You are forgiven," his reflection repeated. Seeing his own face produce the words still didn't help him accept it as true. "Don't dwell on the past. You have more important things to focus on."

Brendan nodded, not quite convinced—and yet he could sense Ben's love overpowering his doubts. "There is evil here too, Ben."

"Yes."

"And we are running out of time." Brendan's head jerked toward the mountain again. His fingers tightened against the pool ledge.

"You are an eternal creature—beyond the limitations of time—limited only by your lack of faith. If only you would trust and believe. You would have access to unlimited power. Mine."

Was anything worthwhile ever that simple? He'd never found it easy to trust. Some part of him clung to the idea that he needed to rely only on himself. "Why am I here? I don't know how to help Anna. How are we going to accomplish anything when we don't know what to do?"

"There are times when you need to do, but there are also times when you just need to be. Be still. For now—here in the garden—just be with me. When the time comes to do something, you will have an overwhelming urge to act. You'll know what to do. Follow your inner prompting."

"Why am I here, Ben? How can I help Anna? She's much stronger and wiser than I am."

"Is she? Or is she a better listener?" The reflected eyes held his. "What has been revealed to you?"

"I'm not sure I understand. I don't think anything has been revealed to me."

"Nothing here has made an impression on you yet?"

"That evil creature called 'Fire Is Born' is here. He manipulated me. I fell for it once. I can't let that happen again."

"Focus on what you can change. Nothing here inspired you to act—to give of yourself in any way?"

"The crippled boy at the Forum. He's been on my mind all day, much to Anna's frustration. She has reminded me several times to focus on the mission."

"And what do you think the mission is?"

"According to Anna, she was sent to help a family member in need. I guess I am here to help, but—"

"Again, I ask: who has made an impression on you?"

"The boy? Am I supposed to help him? Because I'm not sure what I can do—"

"When prompted to a selfless act, heed that inner calling. What I have done for you—you can do for others. What you do for them, you do for me. You are called to act, but you are not alone. Remember—I am in you."

A stone plopped into the pond, hitting his reflection square in the forehead. It scattered in a myriad of rippled fragments. An amused giggle followed.

"It's amazing, isn't it?" A coy voice enticed him from his thoughts.

A girl had tiptoed to his side by balancing on the raised ledge of the pond. He noticed her delicate slippers first. Crafted from gilded leather, tiny pearls embellished the toes. She wore a simple, sleeveless gown of the palest blue and it swirled like sea spray as she jumped down to kneel beside him. Her mounded chestnut curls revealed a graceful neck.

"It's the finest garden I've ever seen," he admitted, trying to hide his frustration at the interruption. At least his tormentor was dazzling.

"I was referring to your reflection," she laughed. "You seemed quite absorbed by it."

Brendan's cheeks burned. He stumbled to his feet, brushing dirt from his tunic.

"I am Livia. My father is an old friend of Julia's. We have come for the Volcanalia Festival." She extended her hand. The festival. Exactly what Fire is Born had mentioned before leaving Mutul.

"I am Brendanus." Unsure what the acceptable custom might be here, he took her hand and gave an awkward bow before releasing it.

Livia rewarded him with a coy smile. "You're not from around here are you?"

"Is it that obvious?" Brendan ducked his head to hide his flaming cheeks. This brash redhead, young as she was, possessed unnerving skills for making him squirm. He peered over her shoulder, plotting an escape route.

Livia shrugged one shoulder. "Well, that just makes you all the more interesting, doesn't it? Would you care to stroll the garden with me?"

"I was waiting on my traveling companion, but—"

"I'm sure he won't mind." She gave him a confident smirk, her hands encircling his bicep.

Brendan didn't correct her. Anna had encouraged him to explore the elaborate gardens. Livia peered at him through her lashes. A shiver of pleasure coursed through his arm when a stray lock of her coppery curls brushed his shoulder. Who could resist?

"Follow me," she said with a wicked giggle.

She leaped cat-like onto the ledge of the fishpond. Three small decorative bridges spanned the narrow width of the pond at regular intervals. From where they stood at the center, it would be a lengthy jog for him to span the outer edges of the pool to meet her on the other side. Either option seemed a bit foolish.

Livia paused on the narrow bridge, her sea nymph blue gown swirling around her with the evening sun glowing through her curls. Every bit as bewitching as a mythical siren, she projected just enough playful innocence to lure him.

"Come on," she urged, reaching for his hand. She tripped, tantalizingly close to the edge as she backed across the narrow bridge. "Follow me."

"I'm not sure these bridges were meant to support a man's weight."

"Don't be ridiculous." Livia traipsed across the small bridge and jumped to the other side. "There is nothing to it."

Casting a brief glance over his shoulder, Brendan stepped up to follow. He made it to the other side in two large steps.

Livia clasped his arm and tugged him under a pergola extending the full length of the pond. Bronze lamps twinkled among the draping vines, creating a dramatic hallway of foliage. "It's quite private in here, isn't it?" A mischievous smile spread across her lips.

"How did Lady Julia manage to find an estate this large in the city?" Brendan wondered aloud.

"She didn't find it." Livia leaned toward him as if sharing a secret, then whispered: "She created it. Lady Julia convinced the city council to give up one of their precious roads, allowing her to connect the two properties. She can be persuasive. This part of the garden, right here, used to be a street to the amphitheater. Isn't she clever?"

"She's certainly ambitious."

"She sacrificed a bit of property to widen the street to her east," his chatty companion continued, "but it was of no consequence. She had her gorgeous gardens. Julia is an enterprising woman. It is one of the many things I admire about her."

"This place is pretty amazing," Brendan agreed, only half listening. He glanced back toward the reception area. How long could it take for two serving girls to dress one woman?

"Tell me — are you going to lease Lady Julia's entertainment complex?" Livia raised her eyebrows and glanced at him from the corner of her eyes.

Brendan tugged at his tunic, beginning to feel a bit clammy. "We are exploring possibilities in the area." Brendan scanned the courtyard for any sign of Anna.

"Well you couldn't find a more intriguing place." Livia

entwined her arm through his. "My father and I visit Pompeii several times a year." A sly smile spread across her face. "It never fails to excite me."

They walked the length of the pergola and reached an arched garden shrine to Isis at the end. The bottom half of the structure was painted to blend in with the bushes flanking it. Only the images of two snakes stood out from the leafy artwork. Anubis attended a likeness of Isis on a throne. Within the arched sacrarium, a bronze brazier stood on tripod legs formed in the shape of satyrs.

"Snakes again," Brendan said with a shudder. "What are they supposed to symbolize?"

Livia's eyes narrowed as if gauging his sincerity. "Rebirth, healing … here they are protectors of prosperity."

"Where I come from, they're usually considered evil or cunning, but I suppose they are symbols of healing too."

Livia shrugged. "Snakes have their place."

"Brendanus?" Anna's voice drifted from the far side of the garden.

Livia released Brendan's arm. "I think I'll freshen up before dinner. Father and I are staying in Lady Julia's personal quarters just through there. She pointed beyond the shrine to a series of large windows with a view of the vegetable and herb garden beyond. "I'll see you again soon." She gave his arm a squeeze and darted through the vines around the corner, disappearing through a doorway beyond.

Brendan stepped out of the pergola and waved to catch Anna's eye. If he hadn't heard her call his name first, he might not have recognized her. Brilliant blue fabric draped her slender figure in all the right places. It suited her. Anna sat on the pond's marble edging and waited for him to cross the garden.

He gave a low whistle as he sat beside her. "You're beginning to look native." He craned his neck to peek at the back of her head. Her wild, dark curls had been tamed into something impossibly intricate. "Nice do. No wonder it took so long."

Anna rolled her eyes and turned an amusing shade of pink as she touched the elaborate hair-do. "Julia's servants dressed me and fixed my hair. It's a bit much, isn't it?" She groaned. "I just hope they help me back out of all this."

Brendan had to chuckle at his tomboy friend, all grown up and dressed like a lady. Somehow, in this dusty city, her beauty became more dazzling. The long, flowing gowns suited her. He nudged her with his shoulder "You look great—like you belong here. I get the feeling I'm not fitting in quite as well."

Anna's lips twitched. "You're rather handsome in a toga. I just haven't noticed many men wearing them here."

Brendan tugged at the steamy folds of wool. "I can imagine why in this heat. It's just not practical. Have you figured out the mission here yet?"

"Ben assured me that I would know," Anna said with a frown, "but I still can't say for sure. It must be Julia, don't you think?"

Brendan had his doubts, but decided to keep that to himself for the moment. "I guess we'll have to see what unfolds."

"Why else would Ben arrange for us to stay with her? It just makes sense." A wayward curl escaped her fussy hairstyle. She twirled it on her finger, her gaze preoccupied. This was the Anna he remembered. "We should take advantage of every opportunity to met people here. I am confident Ben will orchestrate circumstances so we will be able to do what we came to do."

Without warning, the earth lurched. Brendan stumbled forward as if a rug had been yanked from under his feet. Anna tumbled to the ground, a pond-side statue toppling down next to her. Brendan dropped to his knees at Anna's side as the rumbling swelled. Crashes and screams resonated from the kitchen. Several clay tiles slid from the portico roof and shattered on the ground. Ceiling lanterns swayed on their chains.

Lady Julia stumbled through the portico, swooping in to rescue a tottering statue of Isis from a niche in the wall. "Oh, not again. I have finally completed repairs from the last major earthquake. Gods have mercy." She lugged the marble goddess into the triclinium, wedging it into the seat cushions.

With a fading groan, the ground shuddered to a standstill. They remained frozen in place moments longer, alert for aftershocks that never came. Julia smoothed her gown and tucked a stray hair back into place. She cleared her throat and gave the dusty air a dismissive wave. "Ah … well. Nothing like a few tremors to get us going after our afternoon naps, right? Pompeii is a city of great vivacity. Nothing can take that away from us."

Brendan stood and offered Anna a hand up. He brushed dry, powdery soil from his knees. Anna looked as dazed as he felt—and this was only a taste of what was yet to come.

Julia tilted her head and examined Brendan, a slender finger pressed against her lips as if stifling an amused smile. "Please—make yourself comfortable, Brendanus. You need only wear your tunic in my home. It's so sweltering hot this time of year. You'll suffer heat exhaustion in that thing."

Isidore waved him into a side room. He managed to keep his expression blank as he helped Brendan back out of the heavy woolen robes he had earlier suggested forgoing. Once freed from its constricting weight, Brendan could have bounded back to the courtyard. The weight of what they still needed to accomplish hung on him instead as he rejoined Anna in the garden.

She paced the short pathway to the fishpond. "I wonder who

this mysterious Theophilus is who arranged our accommodations with Lady Julia. Ben is always so mysterious about everything. Surely one day he'll let us in on his plans."

"I'm far more concerned with Fire is Born. The fact that he's here with us isn't a good sign." Brendan tugged Anna toward the pond and sat on the ledge. "Ben spoke to me today."

Anna's head swung toward him. "He did? I heard from him too."

"I saw him in my reflection in the pond."

"He does that. Did he give you any sense of what we should be doing?"

"We were interrupted, but it sounds like I'm supposed to keep an eye out for something selfless to do. I felt like he was telling me to be patient — that we'll know what to do when the time is right."

Anna hugged her waist, and for the first time since they had arrived in Pompeii, he could see hints of the fearful girl he'd known in Mutul. She'd been much more withdrawn then, plagued by the physical and emotional scars she guarded closely. "How are we supposed to be patient in this nerve-racking environment?"

Brendan put an arm around her shoulders and drew her toward him. "I'm sure we'll learn to trust him."

"I still feel like it must be Julia we're meant to help. I just can't imagine how. When I asked Ben what we could do for these people, he said we could love them."

"Love them? Can't we warn them, or something?" Brendan asked, shaking his head. "Can't these people see the signs of impending doom?"

Anna sighed. "Remember what Ben told Nik when we were in Mutul? We can't change events, only hearts. We have the luxury of hindsight, but they don't seem to read danger in any of the warning signs."

"Then why are we here?"

"I sometimes wonder if we're just looking at time through a spyglass," Anna said. "We enter as if in a dream, perhaps a shared dream. I'm not even convinced any of what we're experiencing is real — and if that's true, then we're not here to change anything. Maybe we're here to be changed."

She had a point. They were more likely to change themselves than to change anything here. "This feels about as real as anything I've ever experienced. What are we supposed to learn from this anyway?"

Anna leaned toward him, her eyes intense. "Be observant. Nothing happens by chance. We will be shaped by the currents of time, no matter where we are."

Brendan eyed Vesuvius over Anna's shoulder. A thin trail of smoke hovered near its pointed peak, tinted a brilliant orange by the evening sun hovering unseen at the Mediterranean horizon.

Isidore bustled toward the estate's street front entrance followed by the servant girl and her washbasin. Moments later, Julia sauntered in draped on the arm of a tall, blond man. A pang of queasiness clenched Brendan's stomach as they approached. The man's features were finely sculpted — a chiseled jaw line, a strong Roman nose and a full-lipped smile. He displayed to advantage every flattering physical feature a sculpted Adonis could with an equally cold and lifeless stare. The red synthesis he wore over his pristine white tunic hung flawlessly from his broad shoulders. A tiny monkey sporting a collar and thin bronze chain perched on his shoulder.

"Our guest of honor has arrived," Julia said with a flourish. "Fulgentius Iacomus Basilius is staying with friends in the theatre district. He is sponsoring a wild animal hunt in the arena this week. I happened upon him in the praetorium only yesterday and insisted he join us tonight."

The man gave a slight nod, his gaze sliding over each guest in the reception area without any perceptible reaction. Livia and her father applauded at the mention of a hunt and managed to get a smug smile from the honored guest.

Julia guided him closer. "These are my dear friends, Quintus Livius Camillus and his daughter Livia Camilla, visiting us from their seasonal country home and vineyard. They live in Rome most of the year, but have come for the Vinalia rustica festival."

"Salve!" Camillus raised his arm in greeting.

"And who is your friend, Basilius?" Julia reached up to stroke the monkey's tail.

"Ah — this is Perseus. He refused to be left behind this evening. I hope it wasn't too rude of me to indulge him."

"Not at all," Julia gushed. "I have a feeling he'll be a great source of entertainment."

Brendan choked back bile. That hair, those chilling eyes. It had to be Fire is Born — had to be the same man eyeing him at the temple. He needed to warn Anna. He searched for her eyes across the room, but her attention remained riveted on the new guest.

8

"What an unusual name you have, Basilius," Camillus mused aloud.

Basilius dipped his head in agreement. "Indeed. There is nothing ordinary about me. My name might as well reflect that."

"Well, ordinary hardly makes for stimulating dinner conversation now does it?" Julia's hand hesitated on Basilius's bicep as she guided him toward the dining couches.

Camillus hovered at Basilius's side as Isidore removed his street shoes and replaced them with slippers. "I suppose a man of your profession must travel extensively to acquire exotic animals."

Servant and guest alike buzzed about him like flies to a dung heap. To be honest, Brendan had to confess a morbid curiosity drew him closer.

"Sometimes it seems as if I wander the earth endlessly." A smirk curled at Basilius's lips as he nodded. Brendan bristled at his brashness. Could the others not see him for what he really was?

"So we'll have a hunt in spite of all this heat?"

"A little heat never slowed me down. I will take the advice of Quintus Horatius Flaccus and seize the day—and the moment," Basilius said with a disarming smile.

Livia fluttered closer to him, like a moth to a brilliant flame, and matched him quote for quote. "Happy the man, and happy he alone, He who can call today his own; He who secure within can say, Tomorrow do thy worst, for I have lived today."

"Well said, daughter." Camillus clapped Basilius heartily on the back. He lowered his voice as he leaned closer. "I must confess, the hunts remain one of my guilty pleasures."

Basilius's eyes flashed as his grin stretched even wider to reveal impeccable teeth. "It's a rare man who is mindful of his own depravity, Camillus. I like that about you."

Julia directed Basilius to the couch along the far wall — the seat reserved for guests of honor — and seated Anna beside him. Camillus and his daughter, Livia, settled on the couch to the right. Julia reclined facing Basilius and requested that Brendan take the seat beside her.

"Only five guests tonight, Lady Julia?" Camillus raised a brow, but gave her an approving smile all the same.

"Unconventional, perhaps," Julia said, with a flippant toss of her head. "But I was in the mood for something a bit more intimate tonight."

The last rays of sunlight disappeared below the roof line as they found their seats, leaving the sky with a faint purple glow. Lamps glittered in the garden creating a scenic stage before them. Brendan turned his back on Basilius and tried to compose himself. The sight of his simpering face over Lady Julia's shoulder turned his stomach. Flanked by two beautiful women, Basilius triumphed in his momentary celebrity. Brendan had to admit, he looked enough like a Greek god to turn even his own head. If he allowed his gaze to linger on the man's flawless physique, he battled something close to envy.

With a husky whisper, Basilius lured Anna and Julia into an intimate circle. Only their laughter rose above the sound of the fountain's musical play. They were getting way too cozy in the corner for Brendan's comfort, but there was little he could do at the moment. He turned his attention to Livia. Eyes intent upon Basilius, the poor girl strained to catch tidbits of conversation from the chummy huddle opposite her.

A handsome young servant set a tray of radishes and mushrooms on the small table between them, yet Livia seemed oblivious of his presence. He reappeared moments later with dishes of oysters and filled their glasses with honey-sweet mulsum. As they devoured the first platters of food, attentive servants replaced them with bowls of olives and chunks of smoked cheese.

Livia reached for a mushroom with her spoon. "Usually, I don't have much of an appetite, but Julia always spoils me with my favorite dishes and I can't resist." She closed her eyes as she savored the tiny mushroom. Livia dipped her fingers into the water bowl, wiping them on a napkin that complemented the pale blue fabric of her dress.

The other guests had brought their own napkins. Brendan hoped his lack of social graces wasn't too evident. He'd already cast himself in the role of an eccentric by arriving for dinner in a toga.

"I don't have much of an appetite myself tonight," Brendan said, casting a glimpse in Basilius's direction. A servant replenished his empty glass as he turned his attention back to Livia. Brendan's thoughts drifted to the crippled boy at the Forum. Did he have anything to eat?

"Tomorrow is uncertain," Camillus said with a wink. He slurped an oyster off his spoon with gusto. "It's wise to enjoy your evening to its fullest."

"Sensible words, my friend. I will do my best to embrace them tonight." Camillus's passionate enjoyment of his food brought an amused smirk to Brendan's lips. It saved him from wincing at the prophetic nature of Camillus's philosophy. Brendan hoped their stay in Pompeii would be brief. He could only maintain the guise of ignorance for so long.

Brendan took a bite of a crisp, mild radish. "The best I've tasted," he had to admit, although he rarely ate them.

"It's the soil here in Campania—the richest you'll find. Crops thrive with little effort." Camillus indicated his daughter with a tilt of his head. "Livia tells me you're considering the lease of Julia's fine entertainment compound."

Brendan offered a noncommittal shrug. "Julia has an impressive estate to be sure."

"That she does." Camillus nodded in Julia's direction. "I knew her father well. He would be pleased with her many accomplishments."

"Julia is everything I one day hope to one day be," Livia said, her eyes wide with obvious admiration.

Brendan forced a smile. Ash and pumice would soon engulf Julia's beautiful estate. She'd created an oasis of beauty within the estate's imposing walls—walls that might be able to shut out the chaos of Pompeii, but not the devastation of Vesuvius. As beautiful as the city was, it was the people who weighed on his conscience. Those who couldn't run didn't stand a chance. He had to do something to help Marcus.

The women's laughter rivaled the splashing fountain as they howled at the monkey's impish antics. Brendan gritted his teeth in his efforts to ignore them.

"I have a bit of amusing news." Camillus raised his voice so that all in the room could hear. "A neighbor on the north boundary of my property, Sabinus, was preparing for the festival of Vinalia Rustica tomorrow and sent a few servants to his mountainside vineyards to assess the grapes before the harvest. They came running back early, terrified over rumbling in the hills." Camillus slapped the cushion in front of him, sloshing his drink. "They actually believed that giants roamed the mountainside, threatening to crush us."

Julia shook her head, disgust etched on her face. "We rid the city of cowards every time the ground rumbles."

"We've always had tremors." Livia added, sweeping a stray lock over her shoulder.

"Well here is the odd thing: he ended up making the inspection himself. Although he didn't hear or see the thundering of any giants, he did find the ground had swelled on his eastern slopes. The leaves on the vines nearby were wilted and the grapes had turned to raisins."

"Perhaps Volcanus is among us, preparing for his impending festival." Basilius suggested with a sly grin. "Those who can't take the heat, shouldn't worship a god of fire."

"You may well be right," Camillus raised his glass with a hearty guffaw.

Hours passed as Julia's servants brought tray after tray of finger food. Chicken, mullet, and eel were prepared tableside on a brazier laced with sprigs of fresh herbs. Several courses followed with trays of prawns, boiled quail eggs and yet another tray of raw oysters. In his desire to be polite, and his ignorance of the many courses to follow, Brendan overindulged. He now had a whole new appreciation for the reclining position and loose clothing the Romans favored.

A willowy girl appeared at the garden's edge. The same meek servant who'd washed his feet that morning lifted a flute to her lips, mingling its wistful strains with the fountain's trickling harmony. In defiance of Roman tradition, her dark hair hung in long loose tendrils down her back. The coarse undyed fabric of her simple tunic could not disguise the gracefulness of her waif-like form. She closed her eyes as if to shut out the room around her, perhaps offering her music in worship to a god of her homeland. Lost in the soothing melody, she swayed to the tune.

For a few precious moments Brendan shut his eyes on Pompeii's ill-fated luxuries. His empathy for the beautiful slave girl grew with each note rendered by her delicate fingertips. Her performance went otherwise unnoticed as Basilius's monkey beguiled the dinner guests with his antics. How did such a fragile looking creature survive a life of slavery? Although Julia appeared to be a gentle and caring mistress, it was little consolation for a lifetime of lost freedom.

When he opened his eyes, the girl and her flute had disappeared. Livia eyed him with a stifled smile.

She slid with practiced grace from her couch and took a seat on the narrow bench in front of him. "There are times when the old traditions suit a woman. Reclining with respectable men is enjoyable enough, but I believe I'll enjoy my honey cake all the more seated by your side."

A bite of chicken lodged in Brendan's throat despite its tenderness. Livia flustered him. Worse, she appeared to not only recognize her power to bewitch, but to revel in it. Chestnut curls brushed his cheek as she leaned toward the table in front of them, overpowering his senses with the fragrance of rose petals. He couldn't seem to put two rational thoughts together in her presence.

Fresh trays arrived with luscious fruit from Julia's orchard: pears poached in honey and wine, figs and small honey cakes with raisins and walnuts. Each course offered a simple decadence. Julia had a rare gift for showering her guests in luxury without appearing showy.

As the final platters of food were removed from the table, Julia clapped to get their attention. "We have another treat tonight. Basilius has honored us with a private gladiatorial show.

He arranged for a retarius and secutor to battle here in our own garden." Julia's smile was wide and genuine. Basilius just might win her over with his cunning charms and flashy stunts. Brendan's gag reflexes threatened.

Julia guided her guests to the poolside exercise area where servants arranged garden benches and stools around a makeshift battlefield.

Basilius glided to the forefront, preening in the ring of lamplight, and gave a slight bow. "Our retiarius, must rely on speed as he evades his attacker. A man of the sea, he must depend upon his net and his trident to defend himself."

The gladiator wore nothing but a loincloth with a single plate of armor extending from his shoulder to his wrist on his net arm. He swung the weighted net in his left hand and jabbed at the night sky with a trident held in his right. Although tall and lean, the man's oiled muscles gleamed in the lamplight. Pale scars slashed his sun-bronzed skin. He hunkered down in front of a campy wooden fishing boat prop and whirled his net to garner applause from the small audience.

"Our champion, the secutor, will pursue the unsuspecting seafarer with a vengeance." Basilius ran a finger across the gladiator's muscular chest. The secutor assumed a fighting stance and roared, his angry bluster muffled by a full helmet. The hulking man wielded a sword while hiding behind a generous body shield. Fairness seemed to be less of an issue than dramatic effect.

Basilius stepped back as the secutor lumbered forward, growling at his lanky adversary. The retiarius readied his net, sidestepping a lunge from his attacker and circling wide. The challenger charged again, jabbing at the retiarius, who evaded the sword once again.

The retiarius cast his net and missed, but managed to retrieve it while ducking yet another blow from his rival's sword. The secutor dodged cast after cast of the retiarius's net, landing an occasional whack with the flat of his sword—enough to make his opponent stumble.

Julia cheered with each blow the muscle bound secutor landed. He'd strut close and reward her with a flex of his sword arm after each small victory. Although his armor had at first appeared to give him an advantage, his swaggering steps began to falter as the contest wore on. It had to be sweltering inside the heavy, full breastplate and helmet in the lingering evening heat.

The retiarius closed in, jabbing with his trident. He swung the net wide and yanked his captive toward him. Writhing in his captor's net, the secutor sealed his fate as he tumbled to his back. The retiarius made several mock jabs with his trident before retrieving a dagger from his waist and adding a few more. Primal grunts added an air of authenticity to the simulated battle each time the retiarius pretended to stab his fallen opponent. Straddling the secutor's deathlike form, the retiarius thrust his trident high in triumph.

Julia broke into enthusiastic applause. "Bravo!" She looped her arm through Basilius's. "Thank you for the front row seats, Basilius. Your barbarians have left me breathless." She fanned her flushed face with a bejeweled hand.

Basilius grasped her fingers and held them to his lips. "If I have tantalized you, then my evening has been a success."

Brendan offered a few polite claps as he backed away from the sordid scene. The fig bush behind him rustled, wrenching his attention from the revolting exchange. The bewitching slave musician hovered in the shadows, her dark eyes wide with fear. Of what?

"It's okay." Brendan reached for her. He'd only meant to reassure her, to soothe the tormented lines from her brow. His outstretched hand swept through her billowing hair as she beat a hasty retreat.

Nausea rippled through Brendan's gut. Why had he said that? It was not okay. Things were far from okay in this doomed city. As a slave, she was likely a prisoner of war. Romans were as cavalier about their perverse entertainment as they were with warfare. A survivor of their ruthless appetites would not find their playacting amusing.

The girl disappeared into the leafy pergola bordering the courtyard garden. Even his days spent captive in an iron lung suffering the effects of polio had left him with more hope. He turned back to the group, imagining their raucous laughter from her perspective.

Basilius pushed past Brendan. "I must get these men back to the training compound."

Julia dashed after her guest of honor as he trudged toward the front atrium. "Basilius, the streets are dark at this hour. Let me send Isidore with a torch to accompany you home."

Basilius raised a palm. "Please—Lady Julia, I do not need an escort. Pompeii's streets do not inspire fear in me." He gave a parting stroke to the monkey nestled on her shoulder. "You keep an eye on the enchanting lady for me, Perseus."

He turned to face the other guests. "Good evening, my friends. Your company was most amusing."

"It was our pleasure," Livia cooed, lunging for Basilius's arm.

Her father caught her by the elbow before she could latch on. "We also bid you all a good night," Camillus said with a nod to each of the guests. Lips pressed into a pout, Livia managed a reluctant farewell as her father steered her toward their guest rooms.

Lady Julia and Isidore accompanied Basilius to the front door.

Brendan tugged Anna toward the shadowy perimeter of the formal garden. "If ever there was a wolf in sheep's clothing ... Basilius is pure evil," he hissed. It was all he could do to keep his voice down.

"What? Don't be daft." Anna crossed her arms over her chest, one eyebrow raised. The cocky attitude and Australian accent of her childhood reappeared when her patience grew thin.

He motioned her toward the poolside fountain where he hoped their conversation couldn't be overheard. "Fulgentius Iacomus Basilius is Fire Is Born. They are one and the same."

"No." Anna's eyes narrowed. "You can't be serious. He was witty and charming and handsome. He couldn't possibly—"

"Oh—he could and he is—" Brendan raked his fingers through his hair. "And it gets weirder. Do you know what his name means?" He paused, giving Anna time to draw her own conclusions.

"That's the strange thing about our ability to communicate here. Now that I think of it, I do know what his name means: Shining Supplanter King. Okay, that's a bit strange but I still can't imagine—"

"Well, there was nothing attractive about Fire Is Born in Mutul. I have to admit, it's difficult to make the connection between the cackling old geezer I saw in the jungle and Julia's sophisticated friend here. I'm not sure I would believe it myself if I hadn't seen the transformation with my own eyes."

"The initials FIB—his blatant lies—is he just toying with us? I doubt there's anything we can do to expose him without drawing unwanted attention to our own situation. Is Fulgentius Iacomus Basilius even a name that would be used in the first century Roman Empire? It's been a long time since I studied this period, but I don't think those names were used for a couple centuries at least."

"What—like Brendanus and Annthea are common around here? No one has even asked for a surname. It's like they've been blinded to our oddities. Even my painfully obvious lack of fashion sense doesn't seem to give them pause. I'm sure Basilius could care less about historical accuracy. The name was probably thrown out there for his own amusement."

Anna shook her head. "It's not like we've been so forthcoming ourselves."

"But we're here to help in some way." Brendan bit his lip as he met Anna's gaze. "At least we're supposed to be helping."

Anna rubbed the back of her neck. "Ben once warned me that an evil one roams the earth, masquerading as an angel of light." She shivered despite the oppressive heat lingering past nightfall. Her mouth contorted as if words had soured in her mouth. "I found Basilius ... attractive."

Brendan's hands curled into fists as he groaned in frustration. "That's what he does. Heck—I knew who he was and I couldn't help admiring him. He knows how to work a crowd."

"What is he doing here? What does he want?" Anna crept closer to Brendan, eyes roaming the shadows shifting at the edges of the garden. She looked as if she might jump onto his back at the slightest cricket chirp.

Brendan shrugged. "Maybe what we're doing here is more important than we thought."

"We have no clue what we're doing here. We're flying by the seat of our pants trying to figure out what our purpose here is, but I don't feel like we're getting anywhere—do you?"

"We must be. Why else would he care?"

Anna let out an ear-piercing shriek. Her arms flailed as something dropped from the trees and onto her shoulder. No lamps lit the back part of the garden at this hour. She lunged toward him in the darkness, diving into his arms with a wail.

"You—" Brendan growled as recognition dawned. The monkey.

A large figure stepped from the shadows, blocking the pathway and the lamplight beyond. The monkey leaped from Anna's shoulders to the dark silhouette looming over them.

Anna's hand fluttered to her heart. "Oh—you startled me." She managed a stiff smile.

"There is no need for pretense now. I believe you have something of mine." Basilius crossed his arms over his chest.

"The monkey?" Anna's voice quavered.

"Don't be absurd," Basilius hissed.

"There you are." Julia rounded the corner. An orange glow radiated from the oil lamp she carried. Her cheeks were rosy and her breath came in soft gasps. She laughed as the monkey pounced onto her shoulder.

"And there you are, my pet." Basilius gave a light laugh and stroked both the monkey and Julia's bare shoulder. "He's a spirited little fellow, but there will be no end to the entertainment he provides. Enjoy him." He clipped a thin chain onto the monkey's collar and handed it to lady Julia. "Now behave, Perseus," he said to the monkey.

Julia giggled like a young girl as the monkey gave the ornate comb in her hair a playful tug.

Basilius turned to Anna and Brendan. "I will see you all tomorrow night and we can continue our conversation." He kissed Julia on the cheek. "Good evening." He sauntered toward a small side gate.

Julia stroked the monkey's tail. A dreamy gaze filmed her eyes as they followed Basilius. "He's a charming man, isn't he? He'll celebrate Vinalia Rustica with us tomorrow. We're invited to join a dear family friend at his winery. He lives just outside the city walls."

Brendan watched Basilius retreat into the distance over Julia's shoulder. Before he passed through the side gate, he turned, met

Brendan's gaze and pulled the hem of his red synthesis aside to reveal a torn edge. Brendan's heart skipped a beat. He was wearing the same garment Brendan had ripped a piece from as Fire Is Born disappeared into the fire portal at Mutul.

Was that what he wanted — the piece of his robe? If so, it had to be of value for him to threaten them over. He'd be unsuccessful on that point, at least. Brendan had no idea where the scrap was. In fact, he'd spent a significant amount of time trying to convince himself it had never existed.

Anna and Brendan followed Julia as far as the fishpond. With uncharacteristic giddiness, their hostess excused herself to arrange accommodations for her new pet. Anna sunk to the marble ledge of the pond, looking almost as dazed as Julia. Brendan plunked down beside her, a bit bewildered himself.

"What was that about?" she asked, a crinkle surfacing between her brows.

"When Fire is Born walked into the flames at Mutul, something snapped in my mind. All that anger and frustration exploded inside me. I leaped out of my hiding place and all I could think about was trying to stop him. I managed to grab onto the hem of his robe just as his ankle was about to disappear into the portal. He was gone — just like that — " Brendan snapped his fingers. "But when I opened my hand, there was a scrap of red fabric in it."

Anna grabbed his hand. "A piece of his robe?"

"That piece of fabric went back home with me when I left Mutul. I held onto it as a reminder that it had all been real. I guess I needed to convince myself that I wasn't losing it mentally as well as physically." Brendan's cheeks burned. "At least I thought I did. One day, it was just gone — along with my confidence that any of it had ever happened. After a time, I convinced myself it had all been in my imagination."

Anna's eyes were wide. "Brendan, you know I've been working in the hospital where you are being treated, right? On one of your particularly difficult days, I took your hand in mine, and found that piece of fabric clutched in your palm. I always wondered what the significance was. I knew it had to be important to you."

"It disappeared." Brendan shook his head. "I—"

Anna pressed her lips together, her eyes locked on Brendan's. She seemed to be holding her breath.

"What?" he finally asked to break the uncomfortable silence.

Anna stared at him for a moment longer and them seemed to sigh in defeat. "I didn't want to tell you everything," she said, as if that explained what was going on behind her puckered eyebrows.

Dread clutched at Brendan's throat and he swallowed hard. "What do you mean?"

Anna opened and closed her mouth without a word. What was she hiding? She opened the satchel at her waist and handed him the familiar scrap of red fabric, crumpled by weeks of being clutched in his sweaty palm.

"You have it?" Brendan felt his brows bunch together as he tried to sort out his mixed feelings of relief and annoyance.

Anna's shoulders slumped. "I spent many hours at your bedside," she admitted. "You were unconscious much of the time following your surgery, and when your health took a turn for the worse—well—I wanted something to remember you by."

"Remember me by?" Brendan gripped her elbow. "What do you mean, remember me by? Is it that bad?"

She pressed one of his hands between hers as she met his eyes. "Do you remember waking after your surgery?"

Brendan searched his mind. He had only vague memories following the surgery to improve the use of his legs. "My father and brothers visited. I was so weak and tired."

"Yes." She stooped to look into his downcast eyes.

"I had another surgery afterward, didn't I?"

"Yes. Infection set in, you went into septic shock."

Feverish images flashed through his mind: the hospital staff hovering over him, concern etched on their faces—including the face he now knew had been Anna's.

"But I feel wonderful," he said, stretching his strong legs.

Anna nodded. "And you will here." Her smile was strained. "The virus that caused your polio isn't active yet."

"I hadn't thought of it that way. It isn't alive yet here?"

"Well, that's a whole debate in itself. A virus is never truly alive on its own. It's more like the undead." Their bodies weren't limited by age and circumstance here. Their souls were the only thing unaffected by time.

Another question jolted his mind. "What will happen when we go back to our own time?" His heart thudded as if in answer.

Anna's brows puckered again. "You will return to a body in critical condition."

Brendan's stomach lurched. "So I am given time with the use of my legs, and placed in a doomed city. And if by some chance I survive that, I can go back to a wasted body."

Anna gave an almost imperceptible nod, but her eyes betrayed a deep sadness. "I did everything I could for you, Brendan. Please believe me."

Brendan squeezed her hand. "Of course you did. I'm sure you did. I don't mean to complain. I—well maybe I do—but I have nothing but appreciation for you, Anna. You've always been there for me."

"More than you know." She pressed her lips into a thin line.

"What do you mean?"

Anna bit her lip and sunk to the bench next to him. "I was

a bit obsessive about finding you, and then getting the training I needed to help care for you."

"You came to America to look for me." Brendan paused to consider the many years that had passed for her, while for him it had only been a couple years.

"I'll turn 40 this year—well I will in 1957. I'm a bit on a shelf there—what you might call a spinster." Her fingers fumbled for a stray curl. "It's like I don't belong there. Like I'm misplaced or something. I spent my best years looking for you."

He let her words sink in. "You did that for me?"

"Of course I did. I would do it again too." Anna's eyes were earnest as she turned to face him, yet they hadn't lost their youthful sparkle. He reached for her hand. "Ben was right. He told me that if I chose this adventure with him, it wouldn't be easy, but I would never regret it. I never have. It has changed me for the better. I am not the fearful person you once knew. I trust him completely."

"You've been spending time with Ben?" Brendan couldn't seem to get enough air.

"A lot of time." Anna ducked her head to meet his lowered eyes. "Haven't you?"

Brendan tugged at the grating wool tunic. "I have only seen him once since we were last together—and that was in the fishpond this morning."

"Have you looked for him?" Anna asked. "I sometimes find him in the most unexpected places. His spirit is here among us—in all that is good."

There was a refinement to her now that was beyond him—some sort of acceptance, or peace—something he longed for. Anna had been spending time alone with Ben. She'd changed. In the meantime, he had limped along, falling behind, as always. The girl he'd once thought odd had grown and matured into a exquisite woman who had sacrificed much of her life in an attempt to save his. What price had she paid for her efforts?

"Why am I here, Anna?" This is about you, not me." Bitterness crept into his voice, but he was too tired to pretend his mood hadn't soured.

"Well, women can't just cavort about the first century Roman Empire alone, and—"

"You needed an escort," Brendan interjected.

"I was going to say: I thought you would enjoy coming with me," Anna said, her smile fading. "Truthfully, I wanted you here. I knew you'd understand."

Brendan stood and ran his fingers through his hair. "I'm sorry, Anna," he said, shaking his head as if it might scatter his poisoned thoughts. "I don't know what to say. This hasn't quite sunk in yet, but thank you for thinking of me."

"I have thought of you often over the years, Brendan," Anna confessed. "Don't forget, I am behind you in time. Our bodies are close in age here—youthful, healthy vessels for our journey together, but over the years, I have ... earned more experience."

Brendan shrugged, fingering the folds of his tunic. "I still think of you as a child. It is the only way I've known you."

Anna nodded, eyes downcast. "I understand. I do. This takes some getting used to. I've had years to sort it out."

Brendan examined the scrap of fabric in his hand and attempted to shove his fears aside. For some reason he was yet to pinpoint, it gave him a shred of hope.

9

A peacock roaming Julia's gardens squawked, wrenching Anna from a fitful sleep. She stretched and attempted to rub the stiffness from her joints. The small sleeping couches here might be better than a pallet on the ground, but spoiled as she'd become by modern luxuries, she found hers cramped. Poor Brendan must have slept folded in half. Anna was all the more grateful for the youthfulness of her body here.

Unsure of the protocol for dressing and dining in the morning, Anna opened the wardrobe and found a simple cream-colored stola to throw on over the inner tunic she'd slept in. She'd try Julia's bath facilities if the opportunity arose. Although Anna had spent much of her life in Italy, she had only a limited knowledge of ancient Roman customs.

While she and Brendan were obvious outsiders in Pompeii, their ignorance of social customs never seemed to draw suspicion. Either Ben was protecting them, or the people of Pompeii were gracious in accepting people of diverse backgrounds. So far, they'd been able to observe and interact without offending. She had to believe they were protected from Basilius and his trickery as well.

Anna tiptoed down the creaky wooden stairs, her path lit by a solitary oil lamp hanging from the rafters in the downstairs hall. She crept into the open courtyard, past the pond and into the orchards beyond. She sampled a few grapes as she passed the pergola. They had sweetened to perfection on the vine.

Julia's adoptive father had used his medical training in service to the imperial family. Julia confided he'd taught her much about medicinal herbs. The estate's herbal gardens were extensive. Anna found a few she could identify: dill, rosemary, thyme and basil—but many of the plants were a mystery to her.

Every inch of the grounds was well groomed and lush despite the climbing temperatures. Vesuvius's fertile slopes were as nurturing as they were deadly.

Anna ventured into the orchard near Julia's private quarters at the back of the estate. A high wall enclosed the entire property, carving privacy from the chaotic street traffic beyond. Only the amphitheater's upper section, visible between the treetops, encroached on the garden's seclusion. She shaded her eyes against the stark morning sun as she gazed up at it. A man in a red tunic stood at the top of the stairway leading to the highest seats in the arena. Basilius?

A loud bang pierced through the panic gripping her and she jumped, spinning to face its source. Wooden shutters had been thrown open on a large window nearby, slamming against the stucco walls. A bird burst from a laurel bush outside the gaping window, fluttering away with a chirp of alarm.

Anna cast a furtive glance back at the amphitheater. No one loitered at the top of the stairs now. Frayed nerves would wreak havoc on her mission if she didn't remain calm.

"Annthea!" Julia called, with a vivacity most wouldn't be able to summon at such an early hour. "Wait there. I'll join you."

Anna stole another quick glance at the amphitheater, but its vacancy failed to comfort her. She couldn't seem to shake the notion she was being watched. Julia rounded the corner, waving as she dashed toward her.

"I'm glad I've caught you alone." Julia strode across the garden to her side.

"Brendanus expressed an interest in Camillus's vineyards. He and Livia left for their country home before dawn this morning, but they urged me to extend an invitation on their behalf. Livia made me promise to persuade him to celebrate Vinalia with them. He's welcome to join us, of course, but if he's interested in touring the mountainside and observing a harvest, I imagine he'll want to take them up on their invitation. I'm quite sure Livia would provide enthusiastic hospitality." Julia raised her eyebrows and seemed to study Anna for a reaction.

"I can't speak to his preference, but I'll be sure to mention it to him this morning," Anna promised. Perhaps it would be wise for them to double their efforts by splitting up.

"You will join me at my friend's house for Vinalia, won't you? I would love to have your company—and I don't want to invite rumors by spending an afternoon alone with Basilius. Do say you'll join me. My dear old friend is the most entertaining host and it's only fitting to observe the festivities at one of the finest wineries in the region."

Julia knew how to spin anticipation. Anna found herself nodding without a second thought. "I would love to go. I'll need to confirm our plans with Brendanus, of course, but I'm sure we'll find an arrangement to satisfy all our interests."

The only way Anna could envision succeeding in this puzzling mission was to stay open to all the possibilities—to be the proverbial leaf in the stream as Ben had taught.

"I'll have the staff fire up the balneum furnaces early if you'd like to join me for a private session before the bathhouse opens."

"I would love that." Anna was eager to wash the grime of the previous day's travels from her body.

Julia plucked a fragrant rose from a bush beside her and offered it to Anna. "Allow me a few minutes to give the staff their assignments for the day and I'll meet you in the tepidarium. If you arrive first, help yourself to the bathing sandals in the changing room and start without me."

"I will—thank you," Anna said to the back of Julia's head as she hustled toward the service rooms. The woman's non-stop energy far eclipsed her own.

The sun's rays had yet to breach the courtyard and already sweat trickled down her spine. Although hot water and steam didn't sound appealing at the moment, she'd follow the lead of the natives as much as possible. What could be more intriguing than an authentic Roman bath?

Anna headed back up the dim hallway stairs, nodding at Isidore as she eased past the kneeling servant. As busy as his mistress despite the early hour, he appeared to be replenishing the oil lamps. Anna declined his offers for assistance and made her way to Brendan's doorway.

Unable to knock, she cleared her throat outside the drawn curtain. "Brendanus?"

A faint groan was his first response. "Come in."

Anna whisked the drapery aside and stood at the threshold. She placed a finger on her lips, trying to suppress a giggle. He had dressed in fresh clothing, but had returned to his sleeping couch and curled himself like a contortionist into its confining shape. His bare feet dangled over the edge.

"Oh, no. I wondered how you were managing." She did her best to keep a straight face, but ended up bursting into laughter.

"I didn't get much slept last night. We have got to get moving on this mission though." He unfolded himself from the small couch. "If I can manage to get moving at all." He stood and stretched.

"Julia tells me you requested the use of a cart."

"I want to move Marcus from the Forum to this side of town where I can keep an eye on him."

"Have you shared these plans with him? I'm guessing he chose that area for its traffic."

"I can't imagine why he would."

"Brendan, this isn't the twentieth century where you can just go on the dole. It's the first century where begging is a way of life for those who can't manage work. He needs to be around people. I'm sure he's getting castoffs from the market at the end of the day."

"Anna, it's hard to explain. I just have a gut feeling about him. You never know. He could be your ancestor. He might be your mission."

"Oh, come on. You're letting your emotions get the best of you. I understand why he'd get to you, but we can't interfere." She knew the feeling all too well. Caring for someone from another time came with a price.

Brendan's eyes tugged at her heart. "He has no options — no choices. He doesn't even appear to have family here. We could give him a chance at least. Anna, aside from Ben, you're the best friend I've ever had. I'm your partner in this and I'll do whatever I can to help you, but the kid in the Forum — I feel a connection to him too."

"Don't you think I feel the same grief for every person we meet? Julia has dreams for this place that will never see completion. It's agonizing to watch." Anna rubbed her temples. "I understand how difficult this is, but I think we should try our best not to become ... attached."

"Julia's connection to this place is so strong. She'd never willingly leave it. Ben told me — "

Anna met his eyes, eager to find hope in them. Instead, they revealed only sorrow.

"Livia interrupted, so we didn't have time to discuss much. You know how Ben always seems to answer a question with a question. When I asked him why I was here and how I could help, he asked me if anything had inspired me to give of myself. I immediately thought of Marcus."

"It's Marcus, is it—the crippled boy? If you know his name, I suppose you consider him a friend." Anna bit back a warning. She had no right to judge.

"He seems as out of place as we do here. Do you know what I mean? When I saw him sitting there looking so lost—well, he just doesn't belong here."

Anna took a deep breath, measuring her words with care. "I can't claim to know any more than you do. I don't have any feelings that seem as strong as yours, but it just makes sense that if Ben sent us to this home, there must be someone here we're meant to help. You haven't had any strong feelings about anyone you've met in this household? Livia maybe? Isidore? That exotic looking slave girl that played the flute at dinner last night?" She couldn't resist pausing to watch him for a reaction.

Brendan's brows furrowed. He shrugged one shoulder. "I don't think so. They all seem completely enmeshed in their lives here. Julia's committed to her dreams and her slaves can only leave with her permission. To run away would be to risk death."

He had a point. She had no clue how they would help anyone here. They seemed blind to their fate and devoted to their visions for the future of Pompeii.

Anna shrugged. "You might as well follow your hunch. I have nothing better. Find out more about Marcus. Oh—and you're invited to Camillus's country estate today for Vinalia and a tour of his property. From the sounds of it, you expressed an interest?" She couldn't stop a smirk from forming at her lips. "— Or Livia did."

"I shouldn't pass on an opportunity to explore Vesuvius. I'll have to find a way to do both." His eyes searched her own. "You focus on Julia for now. Search her out. I'll follow these two leads. I also want to check out an escape route to the east and going with Camillus will give me a better idea of our options. It may be the only chance we'll have with so little warning. We'll still need to leave well in advance of the eruption and give the peak a wide berth to have any chance of surviving the blast. The path of destruction will be vast."

"Sounds like you had time last night to give this some thought."

Brendan gave a snort of frustration and nodded. Poor guy. Sleeping on the floor might be easier on him.

"Also — I'm invited to a country estate with Julia and Basilius."

"Basilius? Anna, you can't —"

"It's not like I want to, but I don't see how I have a choice. I need to see if there is some way I can help Julia, or at least follow this opportunity that has presented itself."

"Anna — somehow he's onto us. We can't be sure why he's here —" Brendan paced in front of her.

"Pompeii is known not only for its decadent lifestyle, but also for its catastrophic end. If Basilius is as evil as you say, then I'm sure he enjoys engaging in both."

"You can't do this. It's too dangerous."

Anna placed a finger to her lips. Brendan stopped pacing and lowered his voice.

"Anna, just promise me — you won't let him get you alone. Stay with Julia at all times."

"Ben sent us here for a purpose, not to set us up for failure. He's not going to let anything happen to me."

"Then I'm going with you. Maybe he sent me here to protect

you."

"Don't be ridiculous." Anna linked her arm through Brendan's and leaned her head against his shoulder. "I appreciate your concern, but you have other important things to deal with. It's obvious you're concerned about Marcus. I won't hold you back from helping someone, even if it's only to make his final days meaningful. And I agree that it's critical for us to know how to evacuate, if necessary. You need to follow what you feel led to do."

"More than anything, I feel the need to protect you."

As pointless as that impulse was, it warmed Anna's heart to hear him express concern for her.

"—to protect you from yourself, when necessary," Brendan added.

Anna rolled her eyes. "Look—for some reason, he seems to want this scrap of fabric that you have. It can't be in our best interest for him to get his hands on that. So keep it with you—and stay far away from us."

"What if he threatens you over it?"

"He's already deceived Julia into believing that he's some fascinating and attractive man of the world. She would never believe me if I told her the truth about him. Who would? But he's not going to want to risk her good opinion of him. Last night, he wouldn't threaten us in her presence. I think as long as you have that piece fabric and you're not with us, he's not going to try anything. I'm sure he's assuming that you'll join us. He would have no way of knowing that you have other plans."

The muscles in Brendan's jaw rippled. She could tell he was searching for an objection he wouldn't find. He shook his head and sighed.

"I can't argue with that," he said, rubbing his forehead. "But I'm not comfortable with it either." His eyes locked onto hers. "Stay by Julia's side. Don't let him get you alone, even for a moment."

Anna pasted a confident smile on her face and gave him an affirmative nod. In her experience, nothing was ever that simple.

10

Whitewashed tombs flanked the narrow street leading to Herculaneum. Pompeii's forefathers had managed to slow urban sprawl outside the city gates, claiming prime real estate for their eternal rest. Time and growth still appeared to have won though. Luxurious homes speckled the coastline along Vesuvius's southwestern slope just beyond Pompeii's northern walls. The mountainside rambled downhill toward the sparkling bay and rose in a steamy peak to their east.

Anna had envisioned a sprawling countryside vineyard like her uncle's. It surprised her to find the doors to the winery right at the roadside. Servants awaited their arrival in a large arched vestibule, ready to take their street shoes. The owner appeared soon after to greet them.

Julia rushed into the elderly man's arms. "Annthea, may I present a dear family friend, Lucius Istacidius Zosimus, master of this fine establishment."

The Isacidii family's elaborate monument tomb on the outskirts of the city had not escaped Anna's attention during their walk to the estate. It was obvious they had significant wealth and influence in the area. Anna dipped her head. "I appreciate your hospitality. Julia is determined to convince me that Pompeii is a city of opportunities."

The weathered winemaker enclosed her in a paternal embrace. "It is a fine city indeed, but it still pales in comparison to our enthusiastic Julia."

"Oh, Zosi!" Julia threw her arms around his neck as they exchanged cheek kisses. "It has been too long." She turned to Anna. "Zosi was one of my father's closest friends. I have wonderful childhood memories of this place. He was the one who convinced us that investing in Pompeii was wise, so I must credit him with much of my success."

The white haired man's pinkish cheeks glowed even rosier under Julia's lavish praise. "I couldn't be any prouder of Julia if she were my own daughter," Zosimus said, patting her hand as she clutched the crook of his arm.

With a awkward lurch, Julia pitched forward into Zosimus' arms. "Oh, not again," she groaned.

Anna stumbled, light-headed as the ground rocked beneath her feet. Dust filtered down from the rafters as the earth rumbled.

Zosimus threw an arm around each of their shoulders and ushered them back into the street. A chorus of screams followed a thunderous crash from the inner rooms.

"Oh, dear. I hope my surprise isn't ruined." Zosimus released them from his tight grasp once the ground trembled to a standstill and stalked off toward his home. Julia trailed close behind, so Anna followed in their wake.

"Jupiter must be angry. I told the magistrates we have not rebuilt his temple soon enough," Zosimus grumbled under his breath as he disappeared through a large doorway. He turned as Julia and Anna began to follow him. "Wait here where it is safer until we are sure the tremors have passed. I will send someone to attend your needs."

Julia shaded her eyes, peering down the road leading to Pompeii. "I do believe our friend Basilius has arrived."

Anna muffled a laugh with her hand as the pompous display

drew closer. She and Julia had chosen to walk, bringing only a page with a sunshade to serve their needs for the day. It was little more than a ten minute walk from the Salt Gate to the Istacidii estate, yet Basilius lounged on a luxurious lectica carried by four men. Dark, muscle-bound and swarthy, the servants were likely from the far eastern outpost of the empire.

Once the men rested the gilded litter on the ground, Basilius parted the curtains and rose from his cushions. A servant assisted him with his sandals, which would soon be removed once again for dining. Two gladiators served as escort, following the procession on foot. One carried a dwarf jester on his shoulder. Had Basilius brought him along as entertainment?

Julia didn't seem repulsed in the least. She greeted Basilius with a kiss to both cheeks. "That was quite the entrance. Did you encounter tremors on your way here?"

"Encounter them? These useless creatures nearly dropped me in the streets. It's not like the occurrence is unusual to Campania. I can only assume they are fresh off the slave ships."

In compensation for his little tirade, he scooped Julia up in a playful embrace. Anna's eyes betrayed her, lingering on his sun-kissed biceps and tousled blond hair. Unbelievable. He managed to turn both her head and her stomach at the same time. He winked at her over Julia's shoulder.

He sidled up to her once he released Julia. "And you, my beauty, do you have anything for me?" His lip curled in a sadistic smile as he leaned in to kiss her cheek.

Anna shrunk back as a wave of sulfurous fumes washed over her. How had that detail escaped her before? "I brought nothing but a spirit of adventure today." She clenched her teeth and turned her head to quell the nausea gripping her throat.

"May I escort you ladies inside?" Basilius offered each of them an arm.

Anna took an involuntary step backward as Julia dove for his arm. Anna mustered a polite smile. "But Zosimus asked us to wait—"

"Nonsense," Basilius said, with a dismissive flick of his wrist. "It's a crime to leave two beautiful women wilting under the August sun when you can invite them into the shade of your home. The crisis has passed." He marched into the vestibule with Julia on his arm. His retinue followed. Anna rolled her eyes, but tagged along after the jester who was now trotting along behind them on his own.

"Ah—Zosimus," Basilius bellowed as their host met them in the atrium. "I rescued two beautiful women I found stranded outside your home."

Zosimus had the harried face of a distracted man. "We've sustained some damage, I'm afraid—and suffered some setbacks with the preparation of our Vinalia feast." He managed a weary, but genuine smile. "The tremors appear to have stopped, and gods willing—we will have that feast."

"What was damaged this time, Zosi?" Julia abandoned Basilius's arm to comfort her old friend.

"I had the salon prepared for our feast, but I'm afraid our beautiful mural has been ruined."

Julia's eyebrows bunched. "No—" She dashed into the peristyle garden and disappeared through a doorway on the far side.

Zosimus shrugged at the rest of them. "You might was well follow me."

Basilius and Anna followed their host through a small, inner garden that paled in comparison to Julia's. Shoulder-high walls between the columns prevented entry to the garden within from all but one side. What Julia had invested in dramatic garden features, this property seemed to have instead received in interior luxuries. They followed her route through a cavernous atrium without a sign of her. Several tiles had fallen from the opening in the atrium's ceiling into the bone-dry impluvium below.

Zosimus turned to them as he hustled through the spacious room. He shrugged and shook his head, despair dimming his eyes as he beckoned for them to follow. "This has always been Julia's favorite room. The murals fascinated her as a child."

They followed Zosimus through a doorway and into a cramped and windowless room. Racing across mosaic tile floors, their footsteps echoed against shadowy ceilings high above. A painted satyr eyed them from a red paneled wall as they passed. Anna paused to touch the lifelike creature. What an unusual place. Zosimus disappeared through a doorway beyond, but Basilius stopped and turned. A smirk curled at his lips over her impulsive appreciation of the wall art. Anna's heart stuttered as she pushed past him, into a sunlit room.

She found herself on a airy portico. Terraced pleasure gardens and trellised grapevines framed a panorama of the shimmering bay far below. The view stopped her in her tracks. She might have ventured on to enjoy the view, but Julia's moans of frustration drew her into an adjoining room instead.

Zosimus gripped Julia's shoulders in a comforting embrace. She gave a mirthless laugh as she wiped tears from her eyes. "You'd think it was my own house, wouldn't you?"

Anna gasped as she entered the room. "I have never seen its equal," she whispered in awe. The floor to ceiling mural was breathtaking. She could empathize with Julia's attachment.

Anna's eyes were immediately drawn to the serene faces on life-sized figures lining every wall in the room. Rendered with a talent so exquisite, it was impossible to enter the room without lingering to study them closer. The mural's figures paused from their various activities as if to observe the intrusion on their activities. Their bodies sprang to life amid dramatic red walls. A satyr played panpipes, gods reclined in the midst of a ritual, a woman danced with cymbals. The scene was fascinating.

On the central wall, a crack split the fresco and a massive chunk of the mural's plaster had tumbled onto the dining couches beneath it. The faces of a few main figures had disappeared into the pile of rubble below.

"Will the artist be able to repair it?"

Zosimus' shoulders sagged. "I am afraid not. This work was done over a century ago when the property was first renovated."

Julia slumped to one of the dining couches, ignoring the dust and debris around her.

Zosimus seemed to mourn the damaged mural as well. "The fresco was commissioned before my family owned this property. We believe that long ago, this was the home of a Dionysian priestess. I like to believe that the priestess is pictured here." Zosimus pointed to a small panel of wall near the door where a seated woman seemed to oversee the various activities in the room.

Basilius paused to study the image of Aidos — goddess of modesty and humility. With delicate fingers raised, she appeared to be warding him off. Her wings spread wide, the goddess raised a whip above her head, as if ready to strike him. Basilius eyed her with an amused smirk.

"As a girl, I loved to imagine myself the initiate in preparation for the next phase of womanhood, dancing with the satyrs. Now Semele's beautiful face is gone forever."

"Ah — at least Dionysus remains with us for the Vinalia celebration. I must admit, the villa has seen grander days. We purchased it after it was damaged in the great earthquake and I've been adapting it for more agricultural uses. We are making interior repairs as necessary, but we've focused on modifications for the time being. I've updated my tablinum where I conduct most of my business meetings. The rest will happen in time."

Julia gathered herself and put on a brave face. "Zosi has added vineyards, a winepress and cellars — which makes this the perfect place to celebrate Vinalia, don't you think? Our wines here in Pompeii are considered to be the best in the empire and Zosimus' winery is the best of the best."

"Speaking of the celebration, my dear, where should we move our feast to? The rest of my family has been delayed in Rome, and Polybius never responded to my invitation. I can't imagine they've left the city with his daughter so near to giving birth. I'm afraid it will only be the four of us today — a party easily moved."

Sea breezes wafted in from the portico lining the bayside room. Anna found herself drawn again by the view.

Zosimus seemed to follow her gaze. "We could move the couches out to the portico and perhaps find a bit of shade to cool us." His steward hovered just outside the doorway awaiting his master's decision. As Zosimus approached him, his servant leaned in to whisper in his hear. Their host clapped him on the back. "Our fine dinner escaped destruction and we will take it on the southern portico."

Under the steward's direction, the dining couches were moved and tripod tables placed in front of them. Servants poured glasses of mulsum and passed trays of onions, lettuce, anchovies and sliced eggs as appetizers.

"I thought a sampling of Virgil's Aeneid might be in order," Zosimus announced, rubbing his chin in a show of melodramatic contemplation.

Julia caught Anna's eye and raised an impish brow as she

109

snuggled closer into Basilius's side. Charming. Roman dinner theater alongside the Evil One.

"Let me set the stage." Zosimus rose with a theatrical flourish. "Our hero Aeneas, shares the sorrowful tale of Troy's fall. Their Greek attackers, appearing to have sailed for home, leave behind an enormous wooden horse rumored to be an offering to the goddess Minerva. A Greek Captive, Sinon, claims that if the wooden horse is harmed in any way, Troy will be destroyed—but if it is brought within the city walls, then Troy will conquer Greece. What will the Trojans do with the mysterious horse, you ask?"

Zosimus crept toward the portico columns, using the sparkling Bay of Naples as his backdrop and began to recite Virgil's saga.

> *"The Trojans, cooped within their walls so long,*
> *Unbar their gates, and issue in a throng,*
> *Like swarming bees, and with delight survey*
> *The camp deserted, where the Grecians lay:"*

Squeaky wheels chirruped toward them through the maze of rooms. The man definitely enjoyed drama. Zosimus crept toward massive paneled doors behind them before continuing with his recitation.

> *"Thymoetes first ('tis doubtful whether hired,*
> *Or so the Trojan destiny required)*
> *Moved that the ramparts might be broken down,*
> *To lodge the monster fabric in the town."*

On that cue, servants burst through the doorway wheeling a roasted suckling pig on a wooden cart. The servants pushed it to the front of their couches so it stood between the guests and the views of the sea on Zosimus' makeshift stage.

"Oh, Zosi, you didn't—" Julia doubled over in laughter. "You did—a Trojan pig!"

Zosimus chuckled. "I couldn't resist, my dear."

The pig, supported by a clever wooden framework, appeared as if it stood on the cart. Below its feet, a platter and knife waited.

"Oh, Zosi—father would have loved this." Tears appeared at her lashes once more, but Julia blinked them back. Anna had never seen this vulnerable side to the shrewd businesswoman. "You've outdone yourself this year!"

"Our gathering grows smaller every year," Zosimus said, his smile fading. "I dare say I miss him as much as you. He was a fine friend."

"You honor his memory well," Julia said, rising to her feet and joining Zosimus beside the small roasted pig.

"Would you care to do the honors?" Zosimus offered her the knife.

Julia swept back from the cart with a hand to her brow, matching Zosimus' theatrics. "No, please—I do not trust this mysterious beast. I will watch from afar."

Zosimus cleared his throat and launched into another recitation with dramatic flair.

"This hollow fabric either must enclose,
Within its blind recess, our secret foes;
Or 'tis an engine raised above the town,
To overlook the walls, and then to batter down.
Somewhat is sure designed, by fraud or force:
Trust not their presents, nor admit the horse.
Thus having said, against the steed he threw
His forceful spear, which, hissing as it flew,

*Pierced through the yielding planks of jointed wood,
And trembling in the hollow belly stood."*

As he mentioned the forceful spear, he thrust the knife into the pig's belly and slit it open. Sausage and black pudding tumbled from the hollowed out cavity, spilling out like steaming entrails onto the platter below.

Julia returned to her friend's side. "Ah—what do we find? No foes hiding within. It is only a pig after all."

A servant sliced bite-sized portions of sausage and placed two platters full on the tripod tables in front of each couch.

Zosimus chuckled as he patted the roasted pig on the head. "Later in his adventures, our hero Aeneas landed in Latium—and, as you may know, a sow such as this selected Rome's future site."

"I suspect Rome's founding swine was a bit more animated than this one," Julia said, rolling her eyes toward the unfortunate beast on the cart.

"Is the lady requesting something more spirited?" Basilius sidled up to Julia. "I brought the juggler I will use to entertain the crowd before the hunt. Would you care for a preview?"

"What do you think, Zosi?" Julia bit her lip and offered her old friend an eager grin.

Zosimus turned to Basilius without his previous gusto. "If the ladies wish it, make it so. Your attendants are dining in the kitchen courtyard."

Without a further word to either Julia or Anna, Basilius beckoned the steward and ordered the juggler summoned.

Nauseated by both Basilius and the magnitude of her mission, Anna wandered toward the dramatic bay view, her thoughts drifting to Brendan. Hopefully, he was making more progress than she was. With Zosimus and Basilius demanding most of Julia's attention, Anna had many opportunities to observe, but few to interact. Meanwhile, her prospects for luring Julia from Pompeii continued to diminish.

Basilius's eyes jolted to hers across the room, piercing her calm veneer. Before she could return to the safety of the table, Basilius sauntered to her side. Anna cast a hopeful glance toward Julia and Zosimus, but the two friends were lost in conversation.

Basilius cornered Anna against the garden wall, pressing close enough for his stench to invade Anna's nostrils. "Do you feel safe here little one? Feeling confident enough to take me on alone?"

"I'm not alone." Anna held fast to that promise. Whatever Basilius might do to her, he couldn't remove Ben from her life. She hoped that confidence shone in her eyes.

Basilius made a dramatic show of looking on all sides. "Your army's in hiding, is it?" Basilius huffed a humorless laugh. "I will take what is mine."

"Julia is not yours." Anna winced at the uncertainty in her voice. She gritted her teeth and summoned her contempt for him. "And you have no power over me."

Basilius's eyes bored into her. "Some don't believe I exist—and I applaud their lack of faith, for it goes hand in hand with denying Ben as well. Others choose to serve me out of self-serving ambition, but my favorites—and I do believe Julia falls into this category—are the ones who worship me without even realizing it, through their passion for the things of this world—MY kingdom. Ben might wish to steal them from me, but this is my domain by his own admission—and I will not relinquish it."

"What is it you want from us?" Anna whispered, wrestling her gaze away from his feral glare.

"Don't attempt to play games with me. You will only arouse my aggression."—he quirked and eyebrow—"I know you no longer carry it with you. As much as I am flattered you kept a part of me close to you for so long—" Basilius ran a finger over her bare arm and she shuddered. "I always claim what is mine."

It was the scrap of fabric he was after? Anna's heart raced. A wave of nausea washed over her, and for a moment, she wasn't sure her legs would hold her. She grasped a pillar next to her and used it to push herself in the direction of Julia and Zosimus. Brendan had warned her not to allow Basilius to get her alone. She staggered to Julia's side.

Zosimus refilled Julia's glass since his steward was still in search of Basilius's juggler. "My wife, daughter and baby granddaughter have been delayed in Rome—but they should return tonight, gods willing." His nose crinkled in mock distaste. "And my son-in-law too, of course."

"Oh, go easy on the poor man. No one in the empire would ever have been worthy of your daughter," Julia said shaking her head.

"Just as no one will ever be worthy of you, my child." He draped a protective arm around her shoulders. "I must watch after you as your father would have."

"Zosi, you know I value my independence far too much to ever submit myself to marriage." Julia turned to the other guests with a wry smile.

Zosimus cast a fleeting glance at Basilius as if to read his reaction to her claims. Anna detected the slightest hint of a smile playing at the corner of his lips.

The likelihood that Julia might abandon her life at Pompeii had never seemed more dismal. Julia valued her independence here far too much to leave. The most she could hope for would be to distract her with a short trip to Rome, but with so little time to persuade her, Anna knew the odds were against her.

The juggling dwarf shuffled to Basilius's side, stubby fingers beckoning his master close enough to whisper in his ear. Basilius squatted and gave a grim nod as the pint-sized entertainer shared his news. Basilius met Anna's gaze, narrowing his eyes before rising to his full height.

"I am afraid I must beg forgiveness for my rudeness and leave at once. Urgent business in town demands my immediate attention." His eyes shifted toward Pompeii as he offered them a tight-lipped smile. "Each event I arrange brings its own unique challenges."

Basilius's dark gaze slid over Anna with the same chilling effect as a cloud over the sun. She thrust her chin forward and forced her eyes to remain on his, thankful for the ground-sweeping gown to conceal her shaking ankles.

Basilius's lips grazed Julia's cheek as he whispered a private farewell. Her eyes fluttered wide. Julia's pout slipped into a wry smile as she shoved him away with a throaty giggle and returned to her seat next to Zosimus.

Basilius cornered Anna as she backed away from the table. "Nothing you do will change what I have in store for this place." He spun on his heel and strode through the doorway with the juggler trotting in his wake. The only thing worse than Basilius's presence was dreading what he might be up to elsewhere. His sudden departure was not a good sign.

11

Brendan plodded toward the Forum on foot, skirting the clamor and chaos of the streets whenever possible. Somehow, he had to save Marcus. If he could save anyone here, he would, but Marcus couldn't even get across the Forum courtyard on his own. The kid needed him and he wouldn't be able to live with himself if he ignored it. If his own life was at stake here—and it seemed to be no matter where he went in time—then he wanted to serve a purpose. He needed to do something meaningful.

Although Brendan hadn't connected with Julia as much as Anna had, her generosity just might save Marcus. When he'd asked to borrow the cart, she'd been more than gracious, offering unlimited use without question. Anna might not approve of his decision to move Marcus, but he couldn't ignore the nagging impulse to reach out to him. He was one of the few in this town without the ability—or the choice—to leave on his own.

Besides, once he moved Marcus to a safer location, he could better focus on his mission to help Anna. A quick trip to the Forum would only delay his arrival at Camillus's vineyard by an hour at the most. He'd even bet he could make the trip to the Forum and back before Anna could complete the elaborate Roman bathing process. What further justification did he need to act on this nagging hunch?

Hair on the back of Brendan's neck prickled. His eyes roved the narrow street. A blur of movement pulled his gaze upward to a window. The figure slid into the shadows of an upper room. It might be nothing but his imagination fueled by mounting anxiety — or mountain anxieties in this case. With each passing hour, his nerves wound tighter. He crossed to the opposite side of the street on raised stepping stones, unsure why he had bothered since the gutters were bone dry. Refuse littering the streets shriveled under Pompeii's scorching summer sun, competing with the aroma of baking bread.

Brendan rounded a bend in the road and the Forum came into view. On impulse, he shot a quick glance over his shoulder as he turned. Indulging in paranoia wouldn't make his time here any easier, but he couldn't stop himself. Pompeii's streets were safe enough in broad daylight. Still, an inexplicable sense that watchful eyes pursued him raised his hackles.

Basilius would soon join Anna and Julia at a private Vinalia Rustica celebration outside the city walls. It wasn't likely he'd waste time skulking about the streets beforehand. Brendan just hoped he didn't have any followers doing his dirty work here like he had in Mutul. Basilius seemed to be more hands-on here for some reason.

Brendan strode into the Forum courtyard, scanning the perimeter for his new friend. As anticipated, Marcus sat in the shade of a toppled column on the far side. He appeared to be talking to his dog, oblivious to Brendan's arrival. It was good the boy had a companion.

A husky voice growled a demand as he approached them. "Ask for help today or we're doomed."

Marcus shook his head. Had the dog just — the dog? Of course! The demand could only have come from the dog. No one else was close enough to have made it.

"The only people in this town who bother to take notice of me are the ones who want me gone," Marcus said, his lowered brows framing a scowl.

"Perhaps that's the answer then," the dog suggested. "One way or another, we need to get out of here."

Marcus's eyes darted up to meet Brendan's at that moment and he froze, slack-jawed as if caught in a lie. The dog twisted on his hind legs to follow the boy's gaze.

Realization dawned on Brendan. "Ben sent you here, didn't he?"

Marcus folded his arms across his chest. "What is it with this Ben? Does he enjoy torturing people?"

Brendan shook his head. "It's not like that. It's all about perspective. Sometimes a new one can do your life good." It wouldn't be an easy lesson for this kid — it hadn't been for any of them. In fact, Brendan knew firsthand what it was like to choose the most difficult means possible in learning what Ben was capable of. He was still mystified by the fact that Ben had been so quick to forgive him when he hadn't yet forgiven himself. Somehow, helping Marcus seemed like a fitting penance. Maybe he could keep the guy from making the same mistakes he'd made.

"Look — can you hang out here for a while longer?"

"Do I look like I'm going anywhere?" Marcus demanded with a bit more attitude than Brendan would have liked.

"I'm not alone here," Brendan said, and his eyes shifted over the crowd of market shoppers. "In fact — now I wonder how many people in Pompeii might not belong here any more than we do." That thought made his stomach twist into an even tighter knot, but he couldn't let fear distract him from their purpose here. The mission seemed simple enough in theory: help one of Anna's relatives. Then they could leave this unfortunate place. "What I meant to say is that I'm traveling with a companion."

"I suppose I am too," Marcus said, turning to the dog.

"What year are you from?" Brendan asked.

Marcus's brows bunched. "1985. Why—what year are you from?"

"You're from the future," Brendan muttered, before he could stop himself. For the first time, he understood Anna's perspective in Mutul. He'd teased her about being old enough to be his mother even though she had been a couple years younger than him when they'd met. Here they were both young adults. She was a knockout. It was more than distracting. He mentally kicked himself. What a shallow idiot he'd been, getting so wrapped up in age and physical appearance. Anna was so much more than that.

"What do you mean, from the future?" Marcus said, jarring him back to their conversation.

"Nothing—sorry. It's just a matter of perspective—and trust me on this. You will understand it all better by the time you leave. If we step back and look at it all from the larger perspective, our lives here on earth are just a blip on an eternal timeline. Time is a bit of an illusion—unfortunately, not one we can control on our own."

"I'm definitely not in control of much here," Marcus said, his brows bunching. He thrust an arm toward his legs as if to illustrate his point.

Brendan rubbed his forehead. "I'm sorry. I get where you're coming from more than I have time to explain at the moment." He ducked down to look Marcus in the eye. "Back where I come from, I'm the crippled kid."

Marcus rolled his eyes. "Like this?"

"Pretty much—yes. Polio left me with partially paralyzed legs. Of course, I've had the benefit of modern medicine and the help of leg braces that you don't have here—"

"What year are you from anyway?"

THE VEIL OF SMOKE

"1957."

Marcus snorted. "Modern medicine?"

"Well—" Brendan couldn't help blushing a bit. "Modern enough."

"Like you said—" A smug smile spread across Marcus's face. "It's all a matter of perspective."

"Are you from Italy?" Brendan asked.

"I'm from Chicago, but my parents were both born in Italy. Why?"

"I'm trying to figure out your connection to my friend—if there is one. Do you have a grandmother named Anna by any chance?"

"Yeah. How did you know that?"

Brendan tried to do the math. "What is your grandfather's name?"

"I don't know. He died before I was born. What is this all about anyway? Why are you asking me so many questions?"

"I'm just trying to make some connections. It's not that important at the moment. Look, can you hang tight here for a while? I made a commitment to be somewhere and it's the only way I can think of to figure out how we're going to get out of here, unless you know the way out."

"What do you mean? Can't we just leave the way we came in? How did we get here anyway? I just woke up a couple days ago and I was here."

"I'm sure when the time is right, you'll go back where you came from. I think the point is to realize that you can't do it on your own. We can't do much on our own power. We have to trust that Ben is working things out in the best way possible for us. None of this is an accident. We're supposed to learn from it—to grow in some way."

121

Marcus nudged the dog with his elbow. "Max here was just telling me you had to be childish about it."

"I didn't say childish—" Maximus corrected. "I said childlike: vulnerable, open to the possibilities, not set in your own way of doing things."

"Huh. I hadn't thought of it that way before," Brendan said, more and more baffled by the turn of events. "I wonder why I'm older here?"

"You said you're traveling with a companion?" the dog asked.

"Yes, but she's—"

"I'm sure that has something to do with it," Maximus said.

That gave Brendan pause. What was Ben up to? What was the real plan here?

"You can rest assured it is well orchestrated," the dog said as if finishing his thought. Brendan gave him a sideways glance.

"I'm sorry, I've allowed myself to get distracted again. I need to scout out an escape route. At least, I think I do. I'm following my gut on that one. Better safe, than sorry," he said, glancing up at the massive cone of Vesuvius towering in the distance.

"I can't argue with that one." Marcus said, shaking his head. The kid was always trying to play it cool.

"So, here's the plan: I'll scout out an escape route this afternoon. When I return, I'll borrow one of Julia's carts. By then it'll be after dark and I'll be able to take the cart through the streets."

"Why can't you during the day?"

"Some rule here. The streets are too narrow. Most of them, you couldn't even pass an oncoming cart on, so I'm guessing they might be one-way. Everyone here walks and the streets are crowded."

"They couldn't make the streets wider? I thought the Romans were supposed to be so advanced."

"Have you seen how these streets are made? They can't just—"

Brendan gritted his teeth. There was no point in arguing with Marcus.

"Actually, no. I haven't seen how they're made. I arrived in this town somewhere over there." He pointed across the Forum courtyard. "Then someone dumped me over here, and this is pretty much where I've been ever since — groveling in the dirt."

Brendan took an involuntary step back. The dog pawed at Marcus's leg as if to quiet him. "I'm sorry, Marcus. I know this hasn't been easy for you."

"No, it hasn't." Marcus's scowl deepened.

"Hang in there, man. I'll get back as soon as I can. I'm sorry. It's the best I can do under the circumstances." Brendan cringed. The words were all too familiar. His father had said as much to him every time he was hospitalized — and again, the switch in perspective was weird.

Marcus shook his head and stared at his legs as if he still couldn't wrap his mind around his current disability.

"Try to keep a low profile. I'll be back soon," Brendan promised. With that, he strode back toward Julia's estate, eager to put his plans for the afternoon behind him.

In the borrowed carriage, Brendan rambled past olive groves, vineyards and hilly fields of wildflowers on his way to Camillus's country estate. Lulled by the rocking sway of his seat and the lack of traffic on the road, Brendan's mind began to wander. Living with impending destruction was exhausting. No wonder the future was meant to be a mystery.

He should have pressed Marcus and the dog for more details — something that might convince Anna he was the one they were looking for. It was easy for him to believe Anna was Marcus's grandmother, but he'd still need to convince her. She seemed hung up on the idea she would be serving an Italian ancestor. It was understandable. Who would expect to meet one of their American descendants in ancient Pompeii? She also seemed convinced she was doomed to be an old maid and didn't seem to have faith that she might one day be a parent — much less a grandparent.

This experience was as much about Marcus as them — maybe more so. What had Ben sent him here to learn? For both Brendan and Anna, their first adventure had been a time for healing. They had developed a strong bond of friendship with Ben. For Brendan, their time in Mutul had been recent in the context of his own lifetime — but for Anna, it had happened many years ago. Her relationship with Ben seemed to have deepened. She'd mentioned spending time with him. In all those years had she traveled again? He hadn't even thought to ask.

Maybe he'd become a bit too self-absorbed since learning how bad his health situation was. He vowed to show more interest in the lives of those around him instead of focusing so much on his own. His problems were out of his hands now. It made sense to put others first, now more than ever. He'd enjoy the time given him to its fullest and try to put the looming dangers out of his mind.

It was fascinating how this experience would benefit each of them in a unique way. This was so much more than a shared adventure. They would each enter and leave the world on their own, but it was the parts they shared that were most meaningful.

As he mounted a crest in the hill, six distinctive landmarks appeared. Camillus had told him to watch for tall cypress trees — three on each side of the entrance to their family vineyard. Livia and her father huddled together, intent upon the vines farther up the hillside. The exuberant redhead turned at the sound of his approaching carriage and waved. Camillus ushered servants ahead to attend Brendan as he raised his arm in greeting.

Brendan pulled onto the dirt road leading to Camillus's country estate. A few servants took Julia's carriage and mules to the stables and another led him into a cool inner atrium.

A young man brought a bowl to wash his legs and feet. Despite the fact that his sandals hadn't touched the ground during the trip, his feet were still covered in dust. Both Camillus and his daughter welcomed him to their country estate with enthusiastic cheek kisses — a habit that never failed to make him blush. In spite of his cultural ignorance, Brendan felt at home with them. There was an allure to first century hospitality, and if his time on earth was short, he would enjoy every moment of it.

They led him toward a terrace, offering refreshments in the shade of a pergola.

"Vesuvius's sunny hillsides were made for vineyards, as you can see," Camillus said, casting an arm toward his vines.

"Looks like a lot of work."

"It takes five men to tend these vines. Until now, much of their work has been turning a spade, but now the harvest begins." A twinkle lit Camillus's eyes.

Livia slipped her arm through Brendan's as they led him into the neat rows of vines fanning out over the slopes below them.

"Not so long ago, these were grain fields, but there is more money in wine. My grapevines are finally established, so this will be an exciting harvest. Much of what I sold last year went to the cauponae here in Pompeii." He nudged Brendan's ribs with his elbow. "But this year, it looks like I will be able to produce a finer grade for export as well."

Sorrow gnawed at Brendan with the mention of Camillus's future hopes. "It must be well managed while you are in Rome."

Brendan stifled the urge to cringe as the words left his mouth. Had he just complemented the slaves before the master?

If he'd just insulted Camillus, the man didn't let on.

"Oh, yes. My vilicus manages the estate well during the growing season. He cares for my vines as if they were his own and keeps the slaves busy throughout the year as plowmen or vine dressers or reapers as the season requires. By the end of the day, some will be treaders as well—but I think I may also put my guest to work today." He gave Brendan a hearty clap on the back.

The heavy-laden branches bore witness to the skillful nurturing they'd received, but their fruits would soon produce only embers. It would be less painful if he could lose himself in the magic of these moments, appreciating the beauty in them instead of dwelling on Campania's impending doom. As Camillus himself had said the night before—life was uncertain. It was wise to enjoy the day.

"I think I could enjoy the country life," Brendan said, taking in a lungful of mountain air. In all honesty, he could imagine a life in this place in spite of what he knew.

"The wine we produce here in Campania is among the best of the empire. We export some of it to the far eastern outposts. This may be a year of great success for our flourishing vineyard, Brendanus. So many of us have started vineyards, that prices of wine will drop. Not so good for the grower, but good for the drinker—eh? But this year looks to be favorable for us both."

Brendan did his best to summon an encouraging smile. He hoped that Camillus and Livia would evacuate before any harm could come to them. Even if they both escaped unharmed, though, their beautiful crop would be devastated.

"By now the Flamen Dialis has picked the first bunch, and so shall we. Would you care to join the workers for a few rows?" Camillus' rubbed his hands together as if a feast had been set before him. "Just look at them. They are lush and healthy. The soils here on the mountainside are like no other."

Livia tucked her skirts up into her belt and smiled at Brendan through her lashes. "I will show Brendanus how we harvest, Tata."

Camillus was so absorbed by the grapes he held, he didn't respond. He crushed one between his fingers. "Perfect!"

Livia plucked one of the darkest grapes from a cluster and held it to Brendan's lips. He took it in his own fingers and Livia's lips twisted into a pout. Brendan popped the grape into his mouth. The ripened fruit was sweet and almost plum-like.

"Jupiter sent no great storms this year," Camillus cooed to the grapes he cradled in hands. "Our fruit has ripened to perfection. The sacrificial lamb must have appeased the old god of thunder, eh?"

"Take only the ripe ones," Livia instructed, holding a dark cluster in her hand and showing him how to cut it from the vine. "Leave behind anything moldy. Here, you try." She watched him select and cut the next cluster himself. "As little stem as possible. It only makes the wine bitter."

The sun crept higher in the sky, beating down on their backs as they moved down the row. It was the most purposeful he had seen Livia. He took advantage of the pause in her flirtations to steal a few sidelong glances. She could be quite charming when she wasn't overdoing it.

"It might be hot enough to turn these grapes into raisins right here in our baskets," Livia said, swiping the back of her hand across her brow. "The cart should be full soon, then we can head back."

Brendan smiled at the idea. Sweat was trickling down his back. As they crested a hillock on the mountainside, a panorama of the valley below tore Brendan's attention from the vines. He shaded his eyes from the morning sun and peered into the distance. "What cities lie east of here?

"Aeclanum and Aquilonia lie on the Appian Way—and that takes you all the way to Brundisium on the Hadriaeticum." Livia fixed her eyes on his. "I have never been to Brundisium. Father only seems to head north to Roma."

Livia plucked another grape and held it at her lips. "If I was free to travel as I wished, I would just keep going—through Illyricum and Macedonia, to Thracia." She raised her eyebrows. The finest gladiators come from Thracia."

"Thracian gladiators are not necessarily from Thracia, dear," Camillus called from the next row. So he was paying attention after all. "That is just the style of their armor."

"Spartacus was," Livia insisted with a pout.

Camillus shook his head at Brendan and shrugged. "Spartacus! This is what happens when a girl is raised only by her father. As long as she is not thinking of Celadus, the gladiator so popular with the girls." He peered at his daughter through the row of vines that divided them. "Your mother would have done a much better job of raising you to be a lady, my sweet. For that I apologize."

"Tata allowed me to watch the gladiators train once." Livia's eyes lit with a mischievous twinkle. "I think he really does enjoy the games, though he's reluctant to admit it."

"Who among us is innocent of morbid fascination when it comes to the events of the arena?" Camillus confessed aloud. "Whether we approve or not, it seizes our attention. I, too, am held captive by a remorseless curiosity."

"Can we go to the hunt while we're here then?" Livia was quite shrewd when it suited her. "I hear they are going to use the awning."

"Livia, dear, we have come for the harvest and to celebrate Vinalia. Jupiter has blessed us with abundance this year. We have much work to do. You would do well to learn the business. I encourage you to look to Julia in matters of independence. As much as I respect Roman tradition, you are my only heir — and one day, you may wish to make the most of it — as she has."

A cart laden with grapes trundled toward them, creaking and straining under the heavy load. Camillus clapped his hands and raised them to the heavens. "Look at the size of this harvest, my child. This is only the first of many cartfuls. Come, let's follow it to the vats. You two will be the first to tread."

Camillus's workers began to return from their hours of work in the rows beyond them. Brendan cast a longing glance at hillside beyond. "Excuse me one moment. I just want to take a quick peek at the view." Brendan dashed between the rows of vines and scampered over a ridge before Livia could follow. From this vantage point, he'd be able to see where the road led. If it swerved northeast, away from the coming lava flow, it could be their evacuation route.

The road did meander toward the eastern valley as hoped, but instead of the relief he'd expected, panic exploded in his chest. Beyond the crest of the ridge, a man stood, arms outstretched and straining with effort. His bold shock of blond hair and red robes billowed in rippling waves of heat. He thrust splayed hands higher. A gust of blistering sulfur fumes assaulted Brendan, as if a lid had been lifted from a hellish stew pot. Brendan's lifted hand did little to shield his face.

In the blink of an eye, Basilius was at his side — another blink, in his face. Tears stung the corners of Brendan's eyes as a wave of heat rushed over him. He clenched his jaw to prevent himself from crying out.

"You can't stop it, but you're welcome to witness the grand event. Be — my — guest." Basilius wasn't just here to passively enjoy the chaos. He was the source of it. Where better to catch thousands of wayward souls unprepared and take them out before they had a chance to find their way? This city was lost. He was claiming them for his own.

A hand thumped his back. Nearly jumping out of his skin, Brendan spun on his heel. Camillus.

"Didn't intend a sneak attack, my friend." His playful host chuckled.

"Look—" Brendan swung back to face the valley, arm extended, ready to accuse. A peaceful and scenic panorama spread beyond his pointed finger.

Camillus nodded, his hand squeezing Brendan's shoulder. "I come to this very spot myself quite often. Humbles a man, doesn't it? Reminds us of how very small we are in the eternal scheme of things."

Not a whiff of sulfur. Innocent blue skies framed the rolling hills leading to the promising valley beyond. Condemnation evaporated from his gaping lips. There was no proof. Nothing these people would recognize as danger.

At the farthest reaches of his vision lay freedom, in a direction that would seem illogical to most. They would need to head toward the foothills and the east side of the mountain to escape. If only he could gather up the local population and usher them away from this doomed place.

"You asked about cities to the east, Brendanus." Camillus must have caught his longing gaze. "I hope this does not mean you have given up on Pompeii."

Brendan fumbled for a truthful answer. "Pompeii is a fine city, with many opportunities, but I need to know what lies beyond these fertile hills as well." He tried to paste a pleasant smile on his face, but inside he was screaming. Get out of this place—get far, far away! All their work, all their plans would amount to nothing.

"I like to know the lay of the land — to understand my surroundings. I have not yet explored the eastern provinces, but I would like to before I consider settling anywhere."

"Pompeii is not quite the city that Brundisium is, but it is a thriving port city all the same. However — in answer to your question, you must first take the Via Popilia north to Nola and Capua to cross the mountains by the Via Appia. It will take you through the mountains and all the way to the port of Brundisium — the gateway to all the ports of the Mediterraneum. From there, one may cross the sea to Apollonia, and beyond to Thrace, Asia, Galatia and beyond." He clapped Brendan on the back. "Explore the provinces, my friend, but come back to us."

Livia ducked under a trellised vine to join them. "Oh, Tata, can we take Brendanus on a tour of Campania?"

"My daughter, our roots are here — quite literally." Camillus thrust his arm in a wide arc toward the vines that surrounded them.

"You could always put your vilicus to the test and travel the empire. You have an adventurous girl on your hands here. Why not satisfy her daring spirit and come explore with us?"

Camillus snorted. "That I do, but it would benefit her to begin to think like a woman. Were she a son, I might encourage the military life, but women do not have the luxury of wandering the empire in such a manner."

"Tata, if you mean for me to be ruled by a husband, I would like to see a bit of the world first. Lady Julia does not let the ways of the world hold her back."

"That is one of the many reasons I encourage your visits to Lady Julia. She was raised as you are, child, the sole heiress of a household with freedoms most women can only dream of. My wish for you, Livia, is to see what a woman of intelligence and resource may accomplish in a world dominated by men."

"I admire Lady Julia," Livia said, as dreaminess glazed her eyes. "But—"

Camillus patted his daughter's hand. "But—even Lady Julia has put down roots. She chose Pompeii for its progressiveness. She made wise investments of both her time and money—and in doing so, secured her future. If you do not wish to rely on a man to protect you after I am gone, then you must do the same. This vineyard could serve you well, if you chose to learn the art of the vine."

Brendan flinched. Camillus's prophetic statement was more than disturbing—Julia most likely had secured her future. There was little hope she would ever leave the little empire she had created. If she left Pompeii, she would leave her fortune and freedoms behind. Brendan braced himself as a wave of despair washed over him. Why had Ben sent them here to witness a horrible event they could not change?

The cart creaked to a stop at the side of the sprawling villa. Servants gathered to carry baskets full of grapes to a large earthenware vat.

Livia hiked her skirts up even higher. "I hope you're not wearing your finest tunic," she said with a wicked grin.

"Brendanus, Livia—step into the cupa!" Camillus grasped the side a large earthenware vat now loaded with grapes. "You shall begin the creation of my personal stock of wine for next year."

Livia bounded toward the enormous clay vessel and climbed into it. Camillus waved Brendan over, urging him to join her. A servant removed Brendan's sandals and washed his feet.

"Get in with me, Brendanus—you will enjoy this," Livia urged, waving him toward her.

"Shouldn't you consider getting a wine press?" Brendan asked, wondering at the moment he spoke if they had invented presses yet.

"Oh, I do have a wine press. I use it for the wine I sell, but only the juice from treading will make my own wine for the year," Camillus said with a wide smile. "It is better for the wine to be stomped. In the wine press, the seeds and stems get crushed as well and make the wine bitter."

Brendan shrugged and stepped in beside Livia. He might as well get the full experience. Grapes popped under his feet. Juice gushed from the crushed fruit and the more he stomped, the slimier it got. Grapes skins wedged between his toes as juice began to swirl around his ankles.

"My feet are making you a finer wine?" Brendan had his doubts, but rather enjoyed the sensation of grapes bursting beneath his feet.

"Faster! Faster!" Camillus bellowed. He gestured to a slave who pulled a flute from a pouch at his waist and played a lively tune. Livia laughed as she began to dance on the grapes in time to the music. Camillus clapped, urging the musician into a faster tempo.

"Dance, Brendanus!" Livia grabbed his forearms in both of her hands to keep them both from falling over. Even the slaves gave in to genuine laughter.

Brendan kicked his knees up higher and did his best to coordinate his movements to the beat of the music. His years in leg braces had done little to develop coordination much less dancing skills. He closed his eyes and couldn't help visualizing running down the mountainside with each step — away from the brewing Vesuvius. He'd just have to trust that Ben had a plan in bringing them here.

After a few minutes Livia wilted into Brendan's arms. "Oh, I feel dizzy," she said, falling against him. At first, he attributed it to exhaustion — or another flirtatious ploy — but a wooden rack of amphorae beside the cupa began to quiver. Camillus and the flute-playing slave clung to each other, eyes wide. The rack of amphorae tumbled to the ground, shattering most of the clay vessels.

The ground seemed to bubble in places. Livia and Brendan instinctively squatted lower, grabbing the sides of the massive vat. A gigantic popping sound exploded beneath their feet and grape juice seeped from a large crack in the clay cupa. Camillus dashed to Livia's side and lifted her from the vat.

Brendan clutched the side and hurled himself over. Solid ground offered little improvement. They rocked on their feet as if standing in rowboats instead of solid ground. The ground shuddered to a rest, but they all stood braced until they were confident the tremors had stopped.

"Oh, Tata," Livia wailed. "That was the biggest one yet. Are they getting worse?"

"Now, now, dear—tremors are common to the region. Don't upset yourself." Camillus's shoulders sagged as he eyed the remains of his cupa.

"Can we salvage any of it?" Brendan kneeled to get a closer look at the damage.

Camillus rubbed his chin with a frown and shook his head. "I fear this may be a bad omen."

Understatement of the century. The question was—were there days left, or mere hours?

12

"Wake up, you urchin."

Marcus grunted as he suffered a kick to the ribs. Operating on pure instinct, he curled into a fetal position. He barely had time to open his eyes before rough hands seized him and threw him sideways across the back of a horse. A large rider jumped on behind him and the man's cloak enveloped both their bodies. Without so much as a glimpse of the man's face, Marcus remained baffled by his circumstances.

Max barked and nipped at the horse's hind leg. The horse lashed out, its hooves clattering against the stones. Marcus winced as a dull thud was followed a whimper, and no more barking from Max.

The rider urged the horse to a trot. As Marcus floundered under the cloak, he could see little other than his captor's muscular leg, the horse's hooves and the stone road.

"Hey, where are you taking me?" He tried to squirm loose, earning himself a punch in the kidneys.

"Somewhere no one will bother to look — not that many would trouble themselves on your behalf," the rider hissed.

"You can't do that. A friend is coming to get me. Put me down."

The rider didn't respond other than to nudge the horse to a quicker pace.

"Max? Max, are you there?" No sign of his companion. No

answering bark. Only the sounds of evening traffic—the clatter of hoof against stone, the creaking of carts and the laughter of evening patrons at the inns and taverns open after dark. Foot traffic in the streets dwindled as dusk descended on Pompeii. Most families returned home for their evening meals. Only the poor, who had no kitchen at home, took to the streets to buy their dinner.

Marcus's knowledge of the town had been limited to the Forum. Now in his first opportunity to leave the area, his view was limited to the street below the horse he'd been thrown across. He was completely at the mercy of his captor. His only defense would be the use of his wits. He racked his brain for an escape plan, but he didn't know who his captor was, much less where he was being taken.

Marcus tried to get a sense of which direction they were heading. He had already established by the harsh rays of the sun each morning, and brief period of shade in the evening, that he'd been dumped on the west side of the Forum. The horse was heading east on the main road just south of the Forum courtyard. They didn't travel long. Within a couple minutes, the rider dismounted. Marcus was able to sneak a quick glimpse at his surroundings before the horse ducked through a doorway.

The horse clomped into a dim room lit by two small windows with iron bars. White plaster walls and a mortar floor suggested the room was not a formal part of the house, yet it didn't appear to have been designed as a stable either. They hadn't attracted any attention on the street with their entrance and the home, although lit with a few lamps, was silent. If he yelled for help, it was doubtful anyone would come to his aid. The effort would probably only earn him another beating from the brute who'd abducted him.

Marcus stole a glimpse of his captor as the man led his horse through the doorway. This guy had the Dolph Lundgren look down — tall, blond and ripped. He had the confident sort of swagger that attracted women, but kept men at a distance. He'd carried out the kidnapping with shameless ease, as if this sort of brazen act was a common occurrence for him. The man hadn't even broken a sweat.

In Marcus's tight knit Chicago neighborhood, a crime of this sort would have been noticed by at least a dozen busybodies — and immediately reported to the police. He might not be able to ride a skateboard on the sidewalk without being hassled, but he could walk Little Italy's streets at any hour without concern. He suspected his abduction in Pompeii had attracted little, if any, interest. It was unlikely anyone would take on this oversized tough guy to save a crippled beggar.

The man rounded his horse, tossed Marcus over his shoulder without a word and ducked into an adjoining room through a narrow wooden door. They had entered a private home, passing into some sort of entry hall. Parts of the wall had been painted to look like marble. The room was fancy, but unkempt and covered in a thin sheen of dust that implied some sort of home improvement project. What few furnishings remained in the room had been covered by drop cloths.

The man jogged up two steps without a hint of strain under Marcus's weight, lugged him through a wide hallway and into an unpainted room beyond. Stacks of room tiles lay in neat rows on the floor, awaiting installation. Marcus's heart sunk. If this house was a construction site, the guy was right. This had to be the last place anyone would bother to look for him — not that anyone here would care. Even Brendanus was a long shot.

The man carried him past a shallow pool in the floor, not only bone dry but laced with the dust of repair work going on in the next room. Up another step and through a doorway, they entered a covered porch area lined with columns surrounding a large garden open to the moonlit sky.

His captor tossed him on the ground and peered into the night sky, meaty fists pressed against his hips. Marcus scooted backward until his back rested against a fig tree. He searched the area for anything that might be used as a weapon. Wooden cupboards lined one courtyard wall. On the opposite side of the garden, an iron brazier served as a makeshift cooking area. Perhaps someone was staying here during the repairs after all.

A small tortoise trudged across the small garden toward Marcus, straining at the effort of moving a cumbersome body with such disproportionate legs. The man flipped it over with his toe, snorting as its legs pedaled the air. "Such stupid pets they have here in Pompeii." He shook his head, his lip curled in disgust, before his eyes darted to Marcus. He cocked his head. "But then your pet hasn't exactly been man's best friend, has he? I thought dogs were a bit more loyal than that. He abandoned you the first chance he got."

"Who are you? What do you want with me?"

The man raised an eyebrow and crossed his arms over his chest. He seemed to have little interest in answering questions. Given the look of annoyance plastered on the man's face and his silent appraisal of him, he wasn't sure the man had a plan for him yet. If the kidnapping wasn't premeditated, then it was the random act of a madman, a thought that twisted his stomach into a knot.

If he could find something to use as a weapon, he might have a slim chance at escape. Of course, a botched attempt was more likely to result in a premature death — but at this point, he had no idea what the man's intentions were. A marble mortar stood near the brazier. There was something he could wield at an unsuspecting captor's head. He'd need to crawl over to get it, and the man didn't seem likely to be caught off-guard. It was something though — the only shred of hope he could grasp onto at the moment.

A slave in a short tunic dashed into the garden. "Help —" he cried, panic etched on his haggard face. "My master and his family — I can't wake them up. They —"

The moment their presence registered in the slave's frazzled mind, his eyes narrowed. He froze in a half-crouch, assessing the strangers lurking within his household walls. An unfamiliar crippled boy in beggar's clothes accompanied by a muscle-bound Adonis seemed to leave him speechless.

Marcus's captor thrust an open palm in the stunned man's direction. As if his arm possessed an invisible extension, the frightened slave hurtled in the opposite direction with the force a cannon. His body slammed against a wooden door and tumbled into a dark room beyond.

"Looks like I missed one," Marcus's kidnapper hissed. His face puckered in disgust. "Let me show you what happens to people who serve no foreseeable purpose."

He grasped Marcus by an arm and launched him several feet off the ground. Marcus floated next to him, weightless as a balloon, as the man tugged him through a doorway into a windowless room beyond. Two squat oil lamps cast dim pools of light on the far wall between two narrow beds. The man yanked him toward the beds. Marcus's body bobbed at shoulder height without any means of stopping or changing direction.

Marcus hovered mid-air, floundering over the bodies of six people. At first, it appeared they might be dead, but a girl on one of the beds rolled over with a soft moan and settled on her side facing him. A cloth satchel she clutched to her chest clinked and slid as she turned. Two bronze coins spilled out and clattered onto the floor.

"A lot of good that money will do her now, right?" The man elbowed him in the ribs as if sharing a joke. "Priorities are a funny thing."

Lamplight flickered on the girl's face. She couldn't be any older than him—sixteen or seventeen at the most. The young woman's other arm cradled a sizable pregnant belly. A man crumpled on the floor next to her held her hand and looked the right age to be her husband. The family looked peaceful enough, but he had no desire to join them in their unnatural slumber.

Marcus acknowledged the implied threat. He couldn't fathom why the man had chosen to harass him in his helpless, homeless predicament. "What do you want from me?" he asked, loathing the whine creeping into his voice.

The man tugged Marcus back toward him. "What is your game, boy? What are you doing here?" The man hissed in his face, leaving specks of spittle on his cheek.

Marcus wasn't sure how to respond. "I was just minding my own business. I wasn't in the way."

"And what was that business exactly?" The man uttered each "s" with snakelike enunciation. Marcus tried to shrink away from his captor's tightening grasp, but his back was against a wall.

Marcus thrust a hand toward his legs. "I'm crippled. There's not a lot I can do."

The man's face drew into hard lines. He raised one well-groomed brow. "You fail to grasp the serious nature of this matter."

"What are you talking about? I haven't done anything wrong."

"You have drawn the attention of a certain adversary of mine. That makes you a person of interest to me." Despite his proclaimed interest, the man released his hold on Marcus's tunic. Gravity again took hold of his body and he dropped to the floor in a heap.

"I haven't—you mean Brendanus?"

"Brendanus, is it? Very well, what does Brendanus want with you? What is your connection with him?"

"I just met him. Don't know much about him at all — I swear. He just offered to help me if he could, but I don't think—"

"You don't think, you don't think." The man mocked him in a whining voice. "That's a problem — DON'T YOU THINK?"

"I — I — I — " Marcus stammered before his voice failed him completely.

"Listen to me carefully. I am sponsoring a wild animal hunt in the amphitheater tomorrow. If you serve no other purpose, you will make yourself useful as my opening act. You could warm the crowd up a bit — get them hungry for a kill."

"I — I — I can't hunt. I can't even walk."

"Finally — you're beginning to understand." The man thumped Marcus's forehead with his finger. His lips curled into what might be called a smile. "I'd be willing to put you in a chariot to draw it out a bit. It'd give you a fighting chance. There wouldn't be much entertainment value in killing you immediately now, would there? The crowds love bestiarii and exotic animals. You might add an unusual new twist to the show."

"What do you want with Brendanus?"

The man's eyes narrowed. "He took something from me."

"But, I—"

The man grabbed him roughly by the neck, choking his words. "But nothing. I will give you a little time to think this through. The key word here is little. The hunt is tomorrow — and you will either give me information I desire, or die in the arena. It's your choice." He gave Marcus a parting kick, spun on his heel and strode out of the room.

13

Hefting a torch to light their way, Brendan nudged Lady Julia's mule toward the Forum. The cart jostled over stones eroded by rain, sewage and the constant grind of traffic. Originally constructed with Roman precision, Pompeii's roads succumbed to countless decades of wear. As the street-seasoned mule negotiated a stepping stone crosswalk, she aligned the cart behind her with practiced ease, guiding their wheels through deep grooves carved into high-traffic areas. The journey required little supervision on Brendan's part, but despite their uneventful trip, a growing sense of dread blossomed in the pit of his stomach.

He urged the mule to a faster pace. Most of Pompeii's respectable citizens retreated indoors at dusk. Shops were buttoned up tight with their paneled wood doors barred and locked. Only a few businesses catering to the evening crowd remained open. Thermopolia continued to serve heated drinks and snacks to those without kitchen facilities. Sailors enjoyed their nights ashore, carousing the western harbor front side of town. After sundown, it became increasingly obvious Brendan did not belong.

So far, he'd accomplished little more than pinpointing a good escape route from the city—an act displaying little faith. More cumbersome than the toga he'd managed to shed, the threat of failure weighed on him. His time, both here and at home, would end if he couldn't overcome the challenges he faced.

Had Ben simply allowed him this time with Anna, in a body

free of pain and disability, as a brief escape at the end of a short life? He had to be grateful for whatever he received, savoring each moment, without getting hung up on whatever might happen next. In the brief time he'd spent with Anna, she'd become his closest companion — and a partner in the greatest adventure of his life. He'd just need to trust Ben to orchestrate events for the greater good of all involved.

Ahead, the road ended at the Forum courtyard, where stone roadblocks limited accessibility to those on foot. If he couldn't find a way to squeeze Julia's small cart past them, he would be forced to leave it unattended while he located Marcus. Other carts hovered at the perimeter. A couple antsy delivery drivers regarded his indecisive pause. Brendan bit his lip and vaulted over the barrier stones on foot. They'd draw less attention if he left the mule and cart behind. He dashed toward the toppled column Marcus favored.

Brendan's sandals slapped the marble tiles of the Forum courtyard as he ran. His frantic footsteps echoed among the tiers of columns like invisible pursuers. Jogging past the Temple of Apollo to the far corner, Brendan was again thankful for the strength in his legs. He vowed to help this disabled boy whether he turned out to be Anna's relative or not.

Brendan rounded the toppled column near the Forum warehouses, skidding to a stop. There was no sign of either the boy or his dog. As much as the Forum bustled during the day, an eerie stillness fell over it at night. Brendan felt doubly guilty now at having left the boy to fend for himself in the dark heart of this doomed city. Had he found a more sheltered place to go at night?

"Marcus?" The echo of Brendan's urgent whisper mocked him in reply. He peered into shadows surrounding the warehouse and even crept into the public latrine. He circled the crumbling temple of Jupiter, calling the boy's name.

He dragged restless fingers across his clammy brow and swore under his breath. There didn't appear to be any signs of foul play, but he doubted the boy would have gotten far on his own either.

No, no, no, no. NO. Not again. How many times would he let his friends down? Here, he had no excuses. He was strong and healthy. He knew better. Was Ben testing him? If so, he'd failed in every way.

He'd widen his search by a block, but if he couldn't find Marcus, he'd need to return to the Forum at daybreak and hope he'd returned to his usual spot. As if in response to his fears, the earth shuddered another warning. Time was slipping away not only for their mission, but also for Pompeii.

LAUREN LYNCH

14

A low, guttural roar resonated across the surface of the pool. Reacting on pure reflex, Anna raced to the edge, scanning the garden for any sign of danger. Pompeii's summer heat grew increasingly unbearable, inspiring their retreat to the swimming pool after the bath suite closed for the day.

"Don't worry. They're in cages." Julia lounged on the poolside ledge, pressing the cool drink in her hand to her cheek.

Anna's heart pounded against her rib cage. "Cages? What is growling?"

"Lions—for tomorrow's hunt," Julia said, laughing. "They probably haven't fed them in a while, so they should be good and restless by now."

"It sounds like they're here in your garden."

"Gives a bit of a thrill, doesn't it?"

At least as much as lingering in the foothills of a restless volcano—but this threat was more immediate. "I would put it more in the category of sheer terror," Anna said, attempting a light laugh that ended up sounding more like a strangled yelp.

"Have you never been to a hunt, Annthea?" Julia asked, leaning forward. "Perhaps we should go. There isn't much going on until Volcanalia."

Anna had heard of gladiator games, but hadn't been aware of spectator hunts until Basilius announced his upcoming event at

Julia's dinner party. "Is it bloody?"

Julia leaned back and gazed up at the stars — a picture of serenity in glaring contrast to Anna's growing agitation. "Oh, a bit I suppose, but it's actually quite fascinating. I don't think Basilius's hunt will be as garish as some of the slaughters they've had at the Circus Maximus in Rome — and he will pay to have the awning set up, so we'd have shade at the top. Would you like to go? Basilius would be thrilled. He might even be able to get us into the seats below."

Anna tried to imagine what the finest seats at a hunt might be. In her opinion, it could only be the safest — perhaps the furthest from the arena. "I'll talk to Brendanus about it. I'm actually a bit concerned about him at the moment. I'd expected an earlier return. I wonder what might have delayed him?"

Julia slid closer to Anna and lowered her voice. "Are you and Brendanus involved in any way?"

Anna's heart skipped a beat. She'd spent half a lifetime pursuing him in time in one way or another. Words could not begin to describe her deep connection to him — her hopes and dreams — if he had a future, if she could save him ... if. "Brendanus is my closest friend, my trusted ally—"

"And rather handsome, don't you think?" Julia gave her a wicked smile and watched for a reaction out of the corner of her eye.

Anna put a hand to her burning cheeks as Julia giggled into her cup.

"Of course, Basilius takes the prize in that department. Have you ever seen such a finely chiseled jaw line? Eyes as blue as the shallows of the bay, flaxen hair, rippling muscles and skin like golden honey — oh, so delicious."

Anna had to remind herself to close her mouth. She wanted

to retch. Basilius certainly had worked his evil charms. "I actually find him rather boorish at times—" How could she get Julia to see him for what he truly was?

Perseus chose that moment to drop from a nearby tree and scamper to Julia's shoulder. He screeched at Anna, as if to put her in her place.

"Hello, my pet," Julia cooed. Perseus wrapped his tail around his new mistress's neck. She offered him a piece of fig from a dish the servants had placed nearby and the tiny creature devoured it.

"Have you known Basilius long?" Anna ventured. The way he had weaseled his way into Julia's life, you'd think he'd been a family friend for years. Of course, she had opened her home and been a gracious hostess to them as well—but surely there was a heavy dose of business savvy in that choice.

"No, no—I only recently met him. I am patroness to a gladiator. When I went to meet with his trainer, I was introduced to Basilius. His troupe was using the barracks for practices."

"You don't find him rather presumptuous?" Anna's heart skipped a beat. Perseus' head turned sharply at her comment, his beady eyes riveted on her. He was listening to their conversation—and not just listening, but understanding. How foolish of her to have not considered that possibility sooner. Of course, he would eavesdrop. He was Basilius's little minion. That explained why Basilius had been willing to part with his companion so easily.

Anna clamped her mouth shut and glared at the monkey. She had hoped to take advantage of these private moments to convince Julia to leave, to open her eyes to the dangers of Basilius—and now the monkey would add an additional challenge to the task.

Faint strains of eerie music carried over the wall from the direction of the amphitheater. The haunting chords brought goose bumps to Anna's arms in spite of the oppressive heat.

Julia sighed aloud. "Ah — this is one of the many advantages of living near the amphitheater. I do love the hydraulis. The musicians often practice at night, when they have the arena to themselves."

The music reminded Anna of an old steam calliope from the circus. It seemed a rather frivolous accompaniment for a show concluding in death. "It's beautiful, but it makes me rather sad."

"With trumpets, it creates a more dramatic atmosphere for the games."

"Tell me about the hunt. How does that work in an arena?" Anna waded to Julia's side and perched on an underwater ledge beside her.

"Here in the city, during these civilized times, we are so far removed from the excitement of an actual hunt. Staged events like this give a vicarious thrill. They feature brawny barbarian hunters and animals imported from exotic locations, far beyond the Mediterraneum." Julia's lips curled into a suggestive smile. "Some hunters ride on horseback and some are actually on foot."

"On foot — against lions? Do any survive?"

Julia gave a flippant shrug. "Most are highly trained, and they have spears. If they are cowards, they only face their lanista's whips. Given the choice of killing or being killed, you can imagine they are quite motivated."

"I'm not sure I could watch that," Anna said, her stomach flip-flopping at the thought of it.

"There is always a chance the hunter will die, but death can happen at any time — to any of us. A man might as well go down fighting. There is honor in it."

"Honor — in a staged hunt?"

Julia cast an open palm toward the heavens and shook her head. "More honor than the average slave receives in death."

Anna had her doubts, but the Roman spectacle of the hunt

wasn't so far removed from hunting practices in her Australian homeland. It would be hypocritical of her to object. Her own father had made a profit from the slaughter of sheep. Still—to make it a spectator sport in the arena…

"Brendanus," Julia called out, rising abruptly to her feet. "We're over here." She waved her arm to attract his attention as he passed through the portico beyond the garden. "Come join us."

Isidore followed in Brendan's wake as he made his way to the pool. The man seemed to have a sixth sense for anticipating need.

"Isidore, my love, please bring Brendan some refreshments." Julia stood and slipped into a robe. "Will you two be joining us for the hunt tomorrow?"

Brendan's eyes locked onto Anna's with a knowing glance. "I am terribly sorry," Brendan replied. "Anna and I have some business we need to see to first and we probably will not be able to attend."

Julia's smile faded. "Oh—I am sorry to hear that. I hope you don't mind if I accept."

"Not at all," Anna said. "Please don't miss out on our account."

Julia excused herself to change into dry clothing, with Isidore hovering predictably at her heels. "My servants will see to your every need in my absence—both tonight and tomorrow."

"That was a chilly response, for Julia. I hope we haven't insulted her." Anna stepped out of the pool, slipped into a thin robe, and sat next to Brendan at the pool's edge. "How did your day go?"

"I did figure out an escape route, in case we're here long enough to need it." Brendan's eyes shone in the moonlight. "And, Anna—this is important. I'm pretty sure I both found and lost your family member in need."

Anna gripped his forearm with both hands, as if it could secure that possibility. "Are you sure? What made you think that?"

"I stopped by to visit Marcus—the crippled boy—before I

left for Camillus' vineyards. I wanted to let him know I'd be back tonight to get him. I overheard him talking to his dog."

"Oh, Brendan, we've all talked to a dog before," Anna said, still not wanting to concede on that point.

"But how many dogs actually hold up their end of the conversation?"

Anna leaned forward with newfound interest. "Okay, you got my attention with that one. You actually heard the dog speak?"

Brendan folded his arms across his chest. To his credit, he did manage to suppress a self-righteous smile. "I did." His head dipped, hiding his face in shadow. "But I lost him Anna — he's gone. When I went back tonight to pick him up in Julia's cart, he was nowhere to be found."

Anna exhaled with force, struggling to process all the new information without giving into frustration. "I'm so sorry I doubted you, Brendan. I should have listened to you sooner instead of giving you a hard time. I just thought — "

Brendan raised a palm to stop her. "I know — and I don't blame you. I just had a really strong gut feeling on this one. I should have listened to that feeling sooner. We can head back to the Forum first thing in the morning."

"So my ancient Pompeian ancestor is a crippled boy? No, wait — if he had an animal companion, he isn't from here either, is he?"

"No — I almost forgot — that's the most amazing part about this. He was from the future. I mean — even more than we are. He was from Chicago in 1985."

"What? How could he be a descendent? I — " That couldn't be right. She wasn't involved with anyone. She'd devoted her life and her free time to her nursing career, committed to helping Brendan in any way she could. Over the years, her prospects for marriage had dwindled along with any hopes of starting a family.

Brendan turned to her, studying her face. "There's no one in your life?"

Anna examined her hands, unable to face him as she admitted the consequences of her hyper-focused life. "No. I don't see how we could possibly be related."

"He said his grandmother's name was Anna. Look—we just need to focus on finding him for now. We'll worry about the details later."

"Maybe someone else took him in for the night," Anna suggested.

Brendan squeezed her shoulders, pulling her closer. "This town isn't exactly welcoming to loners—especially crippled beggars. Marcus apparently didn't have Theophilus to arrange the same kind of luxury accommodations we got."

"If Marcus was called here, there's a reason. And he'll need to find the purpose in his particular situation. He would need to gain a new perspective—humility perhaps, since he's forced to depend on others here." Anna's mind drifted to the adventure she'd shared with Brendan in Mutul. They had both needed to grieve and heal to move past challenges in their lives. Could Marcus have completed his personal mission and left? "Is it possible he was called home?"

Brendan shook his head. "I seriously doubt it. He seemed more at a loss than we are here."

Nausea bloomed in Anna's stomach. "I'm still having trouble grasping the idea of a generation coming after me, much less two—or more. Are you sure he said 'Anna?' The modern Italian word for grandma is 'Nonna.' Perhaps you heard wrong?" Grandmother? Mercy. Her mind rebelled against any hope for that possibility. She'd already prepared herself for a solitary existence.

Brendan continued to shake his head. "No. I don't think so.

Besides — he was obviously sent by Ben. Marcus seemed to be working on a bit of an attitude problem — and there isn't much he'll be able to do for himself in his present condition. He doesn't even have proper crutches. He needs our help."

Anna's heart sank. "Everyone here needs help. I just don't know if there is anything we can do for them."

Brendan jumped to his feet and began to pace as he often did when he was processing an idea. "Something just occurred to me." He rubbed his chin, chafing at a day's growth of stubble.

Anna rose to his side, nurturing a spark of hope. "What is it?"

"Basilius — Fire is Born — whoever our adversary is trying to sell himself as at the moment — he doesn't seem to know any more about our mission than we do."

Anna's spark of hope grew into a small flame. "And this little scrap of fabric he's after seems to make him feel vulnerable. He seems desperate to get it back for some reason."

Brendan gripped her shoulders, eyebrows raised. "True."

"When we were focused on Julia, so was he. So, maybe he's not as powerful as we had feared?" Anna said, clinging to that possibility for everything she was worth. Maybe they actually had a chance to accomplish something here after all.

"He only seems to be able to guess our mission based on our actions. He can only target those around us we seem to make a connection with. Ben defeated him at Mutul. He's still furious about that. He's lashing out — blindly." Brendan's jaw dropped. "He must have seen me with Marcus," he croaked, eyes wide.

Branches rustled in the olive tree above them. Basilius's monkey skittered down the trunk and bolted toward the courtyard garden.

"I'm acting on a hunch, here — I've got to follow that monkey." Brendan darted after the blur of fur scampering toward the shadows.

"Wait, Brendan—" Anna reached for him, but he was already rounding the corner of the pool. "It's not safe on the streets at night—"

"I'll be okay," Brendan shouted over his shoulder as he disappeared around the garden wall.

Anna dashed to the side of the pool, leaning forward until she could see her moonlit reflection wavering on the surface of the water. "Ben?" she whispered. "Ben—are you there?"

LAUREN LYNCH

15

Marcus lay sprawled on the floor where his captor had flung him. The front door slammed shut and a bolt slid into place. Silence — the man was gone. Marcus lifted his head and pushed himself up on shaky arms. Oily light flickered on the room's black walls casting an eerie glow on the unconscious people scattered throughout the room. He dragged himself to a boy slumped against the far wall. The poor kid looked as if he'd also been dropped from above.

"Hello?" Marcus called out to them. He shook the boy's arm. His comatose companions remained unresponsive. Only their shallow breathing hinted at life.

Marcus pulled himself across the floor toward the doorway. The rough mortar of the floors scraped his elbows, but he couldn't have cared less. He wanted out. He would give anything to be back home with his mother — and he didn't care who knew it.

Once he was back in the open courtyard, he collapsed onto his back and let out a wail of frustration. "I swear if I get out of this alive — if I somehow make it home again — I will do whatever my mother wants. I'll sweep floors, or flip burgers. I'll give trade school a try — maybe even college. I'll even make her pancakes. Do you hear me Ben?"

What did Max say he'd need to do? Ask for help? Admit he couldn't do it on his own? Could it really be that simple? Max had said to humble himself. "Are you really there, Ben? If you are,

I admit it — okay? I need help. I know I'm not in control here."

He took a deep breath and decided to make a very literal effort. "Help!" He yelled at the top of his lungs. "Heeeeeeelp — " Who was he kidding? The house was beyond earshot of any businesses remaining open. Anyone still on the streets at this hour probably wasn't the kind of help he wanted anyway. The last hints of sunlight had disappeared from the opening in the roof over the garden.

Marcus closed his eyes and visualized home. He brought Taylor Street to life in his mind — with its mom and pop grocery stores and Italian social clubs on every other corner. If wishing could make it so, he'd already be back in Chicago willingly surrendering to his mother's ambitious dreams for him — at least, he'd try to compromise somehow.

His mother had lived in Little Italy since before the university was built. An only child with a widowed mother, she'd watched her friends' homes torn down and replaced by campus buildings, but never attended herself. Yet she and Pop had scrimped and saved for him to go. He should be grateful, he supposed. Why wasn't he grateful?

Now he was stuck here in a nightmare he couldn't seem to wake from. The man had warned him he'd only have a little time before he returned. What could he do? If he had any clue what that creepy dude really wanted, he'd have given it up by now. Somehow, Brendanus played a role in this. He should have known his help was suspicious. He'd probably only been trying to trick him into the arena himself.

A faint sound — footsteps maybe — threw him into alert. Marcus strained to identify its source. He barely breathed, senses alert.

"Is anyone here?" a feminine voice called.

"Hello?" Marcus's heart pounded as he dragged himself into

a sitting position. Reflected lamplight bobbed on the far wall as a petite silhouette approached from the front of the house. A young woman peered into the garden from the hallway across the courtyard. She took a tentative step into the room.

"Over here." Marcus did his best to appear casual, not wanting to scare her off.

"Oh—" The startled girl nearly fumbled the lamp she was carrying. Her free hand fluttered to her waist. "Where is everyone?"

"They appear to be sleeping. I couldn't wake them."

"You're bleeding," she said, holding the lamp close to his elbow. "What happened? Were you injured in the tremors? Wait—let me light more lamps and I'll get some water. I'll be right back." She passed through a doorway and returned moments later with a pitcher under one arm and a lamp in each hand.

She set them on the ground and kneeled at his side. She gathered her red tunic around her ankles and examined his arm in the lamplight.

"My name is Marcus."

If the girl noticed his withered legs, she hadn't reacted. She simply leaned over him, intent upon cleaning his wounds. Long auburn hair hung loose at her back and swept across his arm as she tended to it. She glanced up at him briefly and smiled. "You can call me Fortunata."

"Do you live here?"

"I'm visiting." She leaned closer, intent upon her work.

"I am too."

"Tell me what happened." Her eyes drew him in, although it was difficult to concentrate on an intelligible answer under her penetrating gaze.

"I was kidnapped from the Forum and brought here." It sounded ridiculous, but again, she didn't show much of a reaction other than a deepening frown as she dabbed at his raw elbows.

"This is all the water I could draw from the fountain. There was barely a trickle coming out. Something strange is going on. Let me check on the others." Fortunata crossed back to the room Marcus had crawled from. When she returned she merely shrugged. "They seem to be sleeping peacefully. I'm not sure what I can do for them. I should go find help. Can I tell someone you're here?"

"I have a friend who was supposed to pick me up in the Forum tonight."

Fortunata returned to his side. "Does your friend live in Pompeii?"

"I—I'm not sure really. I haven't known him long. Why do you ask?"

She leaned toward him and stroked his cheek with silky soft fingertips. "What is your friend doing in Pompeii? What business does he have here?"

Her touch sent a jolt of warmth through his body. His thoughts swirled as his eyelids drooped in ecstasy. "I'm not… really certain."

"And what about you? Is there something you're supposed to do?" Her eyes were so close to his, it seemed her pupils were all he could see. Their immeasurable depths like the vacuum of a black hole he might spiral into if he got any closer. What was it he was supposed to do?

"I need to ask for help." Marcus mumbled, wondering if he should close his eyes and rest for a bit.

Fortunata let out a huff of breath, snatching her warm fingertips back. "I will get help—"

"Wait," Marcus reached for her as she stood. "I really need to find my friend. Can you help me?"

"Where might I find him?" Fortunata's voice had an edge to it now. Perhaps she didn't trust him—or wondered what a stranger was doing crawling away from her comatose household members.

His hand grazed her heel as she stepped away. "Your dress is torn." He pointed to a rip in the hem of her tunic.

"Yes, that was careless of me." Her frown deepened. "I'll be sure not to let that happen again." Her movements appeared wooden — almost crooked — as she disappeared back into the hallway leading to the front of the house.

The front door slammed shut. Strange. Why would a pretty young girl wander the streets of Pompeii alone after dark? The moment she was gone, a rapid pattering of feet skittered his way. Dog nails on tiles — Max!

"He left the door ajar when he came in the second time and I was able to get in." Max sniffed his face. "I can smell him on you. Repulsive."

Marcus latched onto the dog and buried his face in Max's fur. He didn't care how childish it appeared. He had never been so happy to see another living creature.

"We've got to get out of here quickly." Max's eyes were wild as he gave him an urgent nudge. "He could be back again at any moment."

"Wait—" Marcus was still processing Max's first comment. "You said when he came in the second time. The man has only been here once, but he said he'd be back soon. We need to get out of here, but wait — Fortunata was going for help. A girl came home after he left, a guest here—"

"No, that was him again. Crawl — fast —" Max pushed him from behind. "We must leave at once."

Marcus turned backwards, used his hands to move this time, scooting along on his bottom and dragging his legs behind. His arms were nearly as useless as his legs now, refusing to cooperate. His body seemed to move in slow motion, his brain stuttered with every thought. "So you're trying to tell me that the woman who came in and helped me—"

"—was the evil one, again, in another form. He does that. Masquerades as an angel of light, secures your trust—manipulates you."

Marcus stopped moving, his mind lost in thought. "No. You can't be right about that. She was kind. She cleaned my elbows up after I scraped them on the floor. He would never do that."

Max nudged his arm. "Keep moving! Don't stop."

"She said she was going to get help. Why would she—" Come to think of it, it had been odd that she hadn't gone for help sooner. Why would she be more concerned with the minor injuries of a stranger than her friends? He dragged his uncooperative legs past the neat piles of roof tiles stacked on the floor. Amphorae of lime rested nearby. This unfortunate family had been renovating their home. Now they were unconscious in the back rooms.

"I don't understand." Marcus struggled to keep up with Max. "How could you possibly know that was him both times?"

"You really can't smell him?" Max snorted, as if to rid himself of a lingering odor. "It is the most horrible stench—worse than rotten eggs. It's as if he can disguise everything but his scent."

"No, not at all. It must be something only an animal can sense."

Max cast him an odd glance.

"I'm sorry. You are actually a dog, aren't you?"

"That is a long story, but for the time being I am. Yes."

"Max, we have to send someone back to help these people." Marcus tried to pick up his pace.

"Help who?" Max's eyes shifted over the dusty rooms prepped for renovation.

"A whole family—unconscious, in the back of the house.

Poisoned, knocked out, under a spell or something. I think he did it so he could use their home."

Max groaned. "Let's focus on one thing at a time. If we don't keep moving, none of us will make it out of here — and you are my priority. Will you be able to get the door open?"

"I don't know. We didn't come in a main entrance. We came in on a horse."

"On a horse? That might help."

Max scurried ahead while Marcus continued to drag himself around the shallow impluvium and toward another hall. Numerous doorways opened onto other rooms on either side of the large hall. For a moment, Marcus worried there might be more people in the other rooms. He peeked through a doorway as he dragged himself past. Only haphazard piles of amphorae and more dust.

Marcus struggled down two steps and he was back in the main atrium. He leaned against a wall to catch his breath. His elbows throbbed and he wanted nothing more than to rest at the moment, but the man had said he would return soon. He didn't want to end up unconscious like the others — or worse. He had to get out of this place.

The lock on the door in the front room rattled. He couldn't be sure if it was Max or if the creepy dude had returned, but he couldn't take any chances. He rolled through a doorway on his left and shuffled into the shadows in a corner. He had just managed to drag his legs in behind him when an outer door burst open. The horse whinnied in the next room. Resolute footsteps hammered through the front room. A door opened and closed. He hadn't heard the locks slide back into place. At least there was that. His pulse pounded in his ears. How was he going to manage getting through the front door without being discovered?

The man's footsteps faded as he strode down the hallway and

into the garden beyond. Marcus had to make a move quickly, before his absence was discovered. He pulled himself back through the doorway as quietly as he could. He rolled across the large atrium, cringing with every noise he made, biting back the pain of each movement. Tears welled at the corner of his eyes and he suppressed a moan of pain, but he managed to make it across the room in mere seconds. Adrenaline must have kicked in because he was able to scoot through the doorway into the room with the horse.

Max was at his side once again. "Go, go, GO!" The dog's whispered orders urged him on.

"I know you're here Marcus. I can smell fear," the man yelled from the garden. "I will find you in the same way the lion will find you in the hunts tomorrow." Harsh laughter echoed down the corridor to the garden. Was the man closer already? He'd been concealing his footsteps if not his voice.

"Get out into the streets and hide yourself. I'll distract him. I'll bite him if I have to," Max whispered.

"No, Max, you don't know what he's capable of."

"Oh, but I do. Now, go — quickly."

Marcus didn't argue. It would only get them both killed. He scooted toward the door. The man hadn't bothered to close it all the way. Perhaps he'd meant to carry him back out. Marcus nudged the door open and rolled into the street, pulling the door partially closed behind him. The horse nickered.

A caupona further down the street remained open for business, its lamps casting a yellow glow onto the sidewalk in front. Two smarmy men slouched on stools at the roadside counter, sloshing their drinks and bickering over a game of dice. The street was otherwise dark. Marcus pressed himself into the shadows, scanning the area for a hiding place. He dragged himself around the nearest corner to a narrow side street. A small cart rested against the building he'd just escaped from. Too close for his comfort, but it would have to do. With the last of his strength, Marcus heaved himself toward it, scurrying into the darkness below.

Still in the house next door, Max growled, a low rumble. Marcus clenched his fists, resisting the urge to cry out. The dog yelped. What had the man done to him?

"Where is he?" The man snarled.

No sound. Was Max alive? Marcus swore under his breath at his lifeless legs. What could he do? There must be some way he could help. Offer himself up? Create a diversion?

Before he could act, the front door slammed. Footsteps echoed across the stones in the direction of the Forum. He didn't have long. Max would have his hide for it later, but he couldn't abandon him. Marcus dragged himself back across the sidewalk, straining for the door handle.

A husky whimper led him toward the shadows at the back of the stable. The horse reared and pulled at his ropes. Maximus limped from the far corner on three legs.

"Leave at once," Max ordered. "I will follow as fast as I'm able."

Marcus groped his way back over the dusty sidewalk and rolled back into the shadows beneath the cart.

"No, Marcus—you must get farther away. He'll find you here." Max limped toward him, obviously exhausted. Ignoring his own advice, he ducked under the cart with a groan.

"There's not much I can do without crutches or a horse for this cart," Marcus gasped. "—and look at you. You're barely able to move yourself. You shouldn't have taken him on, Max. I'm not worth it. I let only people down."

Max let out a soft whimper as he lowered himself to the ground. "Have mercy," he wheezed. "I was going to run to the Forum and try to find Brendanus, but I'm not able to do that now.

Somehow, we are going to need to get help. We can't do this on our own — but we can't trust just anyone."

"So what am I supposed to do? Crawl into the street?"

"No, no — we need to lay low until we're sure the evil one has moved on. I also need to talk to you about Ben."

"Who is this Ben? What does he have to do with me being here?"

"You have been chosen — and it is time for you to take your part in his plan."

"I can't imagine why anyone would want me to be a part of their plan. I'm a total screw up. My mom had big plans for me. It used to get under my skin, but now I'd give anything to be back there with her."

"I am very pleased to hear it, but it's my job to protect you while you're here and right now I'm not doing such a good job of that. We need to get you out of here. Your friend will help you get out of the city if we can find him, but he won't know where to look if you're not at the Forum."

"Max, I've got to get out of here, get back to my mother and make things right. I've been so caught up in what I wanted to do — in having a good time. I never stopped to appreciate all the sacrifices she's made for me. She always seemed so critical of my choices, but I know she just wants what she thinks is best for me. If I don't get back to her, I won't be able to fix what's happened between us. We used to be so close. Now, we might as well be strangers."

"Pride can make us believe we operate on our own power. When the very thing you exalt to an extreme is taken from you, it humbles you. It might not seem like it at the time — but it's an act of mercy in the long run."

"You're telling me being dumped here in Pompeii with crippled legs was an act of mercy? I'm not feeling it." Marcus gritted his teeth against the pain gripping his body. He couldn't imagine how he'd be able to crawl his way to escape, but if he ended up in the hunt tomorrow, he stood even less of a chance.

"Embrace your powerlessness. Allow yourself to become as vulnerable as a baby—believe as freely as a small child. Growing older causes many to insist on seeing before believing, but you must believe in order to see. Be grateful you're learning this lesson as early as you are."

"What good will learning do me if I can't go back and fix my mistakes?"

"Nothing keeps your heart more vulnerable than love. Accept love any time it is offered and give it every chance you get. Following a path that involves real, sacrificial love will never lead you astray."

Marcus pushed deeper into the shadows of the cart and nursed his regrets. He had rejected so much of his mother's love recently. Instead of talking things over with her, he had resented every act of kindness and lashed out in anger. Surely they could have come to some sort of an understanding instead. Groveling in the dust of Pompeii's filthy streets, it was hard to imagine how he'd live to see the light of day, much less find his way back home, but if he ever found a way out of this mess—he'd jump at the chance.

Footsteps interrupted his thoughts. Someone was headed their way—and the closer they came, the more their pace quickened.

16

Brendan sprinted after the monkey. Scrambling up a date palm, it leaped onto the portico roof, scurrying to its peak before jumping over the edge. Brendan dashed into the atrium, unbolted the door and entered the street in time to see the monkey scamper up the main road toward the Forum. He followed at a distance, hugging the shadows at the edge of the street and trying to keep his sandals from slapping the pavement.

The monkey had been left behind to spy on them. Brendan didn't know if he should be relieved or concerned by it, but he meant to figure out what Basilius was up to. What could he possibly want here? Had Ben sent them to thwart some sort of evil plot?

Basilius seemed as surprised as Brendan when they crossed paths at the Temple of Isis — and curious enough to follow him. He wouldn't leave his monkey at Julia's unless they posed a threat to his plans. Their activities must be as much of a mystery to Basilius as his were to them. If that was true, they had a chance.

Brendan's heart pounded as he chased the monkey through the dark streets. Without a torch to light his way, he strained to keep the shifty little creature in sight.

Half way to the Forum, the monkey paused. Brendan ducked into a doorway and flattened himself against the wooden door, peeking out seconds later. Perseus headed north on a side street. Brendan rounded the corner just as the monkey bounded over a cart then onto a second story porch. He scaled the plaster wall, climbed onto the roof and disappeared into an open courtyard within the residence.

Brendan raced to the corner. Two doors and a shuttered shop faced the street in the building the monkey had just entered. Brendan tried the first door—locked. The storefront was also closed up tight. The third door burst open as he leaned against it. Brendan crept into the dark room beyond, heart hammering in his chest, and pulled the door shut behind him. He tiptoed through a doorway on the opposite wall and into a dim corridor. Light drifted in from the rooms beyond.

"I know you're here somewhere," Basilius growled.

Brendan froze in his tracks, scanning the dark rooms for a hiding place. Construction debris and tiles littered the floor. He managed to sidestep a pile of rubble without disturbing it and did his best not to leave a visible trail in the dust as he leaped through a narrow doorway into an empty and windowless room. Cornered. All he could do now is wait and hope he wasn't discovered.

"I smell your fear—the fetid stench of your miserable existence." A stack of clay tiles tumbled to the ground, shattering under Basilius's feet as he stomped through the cluttered corridor. "You have only forced the hunt to begin sooner, but I am all too happy to oblige. I may merely toy with my prey for the moment—but the lion will feast on your flesh in the arena tomorrow. You will never know Ben. Not as I do."

Brendan backed into the darkest corner of the room, his only camouflage a lanky scaffolding, as Basilius's voice drew nearer. Grit crunched under his pursuer's feet as he inched closer in the hallway. Brendan held his breath as Basilius paused outside the doorway.

"Come out. Come out," Basilius taunted in a singsong voice. "I know you're still here."

Brendan summoned his courage. If this was the end, he

wouldn't go in a cowardly way. Ben had sent him here for a purpose. If it was to die in battle, instead of wasting away in a bed, then so be it. He would face his death with honor instead of cowering in a corner. He lifted a metal bar from the scaffolding as soundlessly as possible, gripping it in his hands like a sword and braced himself.

A low growl resonated from the front room. Basilius bolted toward it. Tile shards crunched beneath his feet as he dashed toward the front door.

The monkey scampered behind him, chattering as he caught up to his master. Basilius made a clucking noise with his tongue. "Why, Perseus, my pet, what are you doing here? You are supposed to be keeping an eye on my latest conquest—and her two annoying guests."

The monkey chirped and screeched. "They are both at her home now? I have another important task to handle first. I'm sure we'll see them all tomorrow. Perhaps I will invite them into the arena for a pre-hunt tour. Accidents do happen. Don't they, my pet?"

The monkey offered an enthusiastic screech in reply.

"The boy will finally make himself useful by serving as the Praegenarii. Not the most exciting opening act perhaps, but he should get the crowd in the mood for a kill. We could give him a wooden sword and send him out to battle one of my lesser beasts. Which one shall we save for him, Perseus? Well, we still have a little while to mull that, don't we?"

Brendan crept from the room. He hugged the wall to stay out of view, still brandishing the metal scaffolding pole.

Basilius opened a side door, disappearing into the room beyond. A horse whinnied as he led it out onto the street. The outer door slammed shut and the latch fell into place. The first door he'd tried to enter from the street served as a stable.

Brendan allowed a lungful of air to gust free. He crept toward the main door and lifted the latch, trying to make as little noise as possible. No sign of anyone—man or beast. He slipped through the doorway and crept toward the closest side street. Back pressed against the wall, Brendan peered around the corner. As Basilius hitched his horse to a small cart, he burst into a raucous howl.

"What have we here?" Basilius guided the horse a few yards ahead, revealing a body huddled where the cart had once stood.

A dog growled, rearing up, bared teeth flashing in the moonlight. Marcus and his dog.

"Well, well. Would you look at this," Basilius hissed. "Isn't it convenient, Perseus? This couldn't have gone better if I'd planned it. Here is my opening act, waiting under the cart for transport. Do you think there is a place in our opening show for the dog as well? He appears to be limping. It would hardly be sporting, but then we'll have to put the lad in a chariot anyway, won't we?"

"Very well, let's toss him in too. If nothing else, he'll be a first course for the lions. Then everyone will be happy, won't they?" The dog gave a weak yelp as Basilius heaved him into the cart.

"No—leave the dog," Marcus pleaded, grunting as he was tossed next to his bedraggled companion. Relief flooded Brendan. The boy was safe for the moment. The old wooden cart groaned as it lurched to a start and made an awkward u-turn on the narrow road.

Brendan slipped behind a folded awning as the cart turned onto the main street, guided by his hulking blond nemesis. Anna's grandson must be saved, whatever the cost. Brendan grasped at hope as the horse plodded toward the Forum instead of heading for the amphitheater. Once they passed his hiding place, he trailed them at a distance.

While Brendan's life teetered in an uncertain balance, Marcus hopefully had a full life ahead of him back at home. Brendan resisted the urge to charge after Basilius in a fit of rage. Any rescue attempt would require a cunning approach. Brendan knew better than most what horrors Basilius could unleash. He bolted to the nearest public fountain and leaned over the edge. His reflection, ashen in the moonlight, gaped back at him.

"Ben? Ben—I need your help. I can't do this without you."

17

"You'll serve me one way or another." Marcus's captor sneered, whipping the horse to a faster pace. The rickety cart tottered over the worn stones of the main road for a few blocks, then turned onto a side street and headed south.

Max sunk to the bed of the cart and rested his head against Marcus's leg. He pushed his fingers into the dog's dusty fur, comforted by the companionship, if nothing else.

Mere days ago, he'd aimlessly wandered the streets of Chicago without a care in the world. The closest he'd come to being tortured was to endure his mother's endless job propositions and college pitches. She'd slip applications into his backpack or leaving school catalogs on his bed. He'd dug in his heels, focusing all the more on booking band gigs and sneaking off to late-night jam sessions. It all seemed so petty now. He wasn't sure anymore why he'd resisted the idea of college. His mom would probably be fine with him studying music as long as he got a degree. He'd probably just overreacted to her pressure.

"I could put you in with a couple gazelles," his kidnapper babbled aloud. "The lions might find them more exciting at first. It would draw out your time in the arena—a blessing or curse, depending on how you look at it. I also have a bear and some ostriches. Perhaps you could ride an ostrich." The man laughed aloud at that thought. "If your dog perks up a bit, he could join the others in a stag hunt."

Max twitched. He pushed his muzzle close to Marcus's ear. "I think my leg is rested enough for me to run. If this idea works, I will jump from the cart, follow at a distance until I know where he's taken you, then bring help as soon as I can."

Marcus sighed. If the dog could escape, why shouldn't he? It wouldn't improve his own situation any if Max stayed. Marcus nodded, certain he was seeing the dog for the last time. Max's plan was probably his only chance at being rescued. He certainly had few hopes on his own.

As Marcus's kidnapper strode ahead to lead the cart around a turn, Max managed to roll off the back and keep the noise of his movements in sync with the horse's clomping hooves. Marcus wrestled with envy as the dog scampered into the gloom of Pompeii's deserted streets.

The cart made several turns before arriving at a windowless building. There was no sign of Max behind them. Hopefully, he'd managed to trail the maze of turns they'd taken. Marcus hadn't showered in several days, so the dog should have no difficulty in tracking his scent, although very little in this town appeared to be any fresher than he was.

The man rounded the cart, fists on his hips. He shook his head and gave a low whistle. "All your friends abandoned you, eh? Adversity is a true test of friendship, I suppose. Looks like man's best friend came up lacking." He snickered at his own joke and tossed Marcus onto his shoulder.

The man jogged effortlessly down a flight of stairs with Marcus's upper body flopping at his back. He heaved Marcus through a doorway into a small, windowless room. Two other guys about his age lay on the ground. A set of iron shackles lay unused on the floor next to them. "Mind yourself and you may remain unrestrained."

One propped himself up on an elbow as Marcus landed next to him.

"Paetas here will show you the ropes—or the chains, as the case may be. He has served for years in the arenas." The man chucked to himself. "Not that I expect you to be around for long."

He turned to Paetas. "Your new friend here will be the opening act for the hunts in the morning. Explain how it all works. If you prepare him well, there will be a reward—if not, you know I'll find a way to make you regret it." He spun on his heel and returned to the portico, locking the door behind him.

"How did you get mixed up with Basilius?" Paetas asked.

"Basilius? Is that what he's called? He kidnapped me from the Forum."

Paetas eyed him from head to toe. "Can you walk?"

"Not without crutches—and they're long gone."

Paetas rubbed his chin. "Basilius is even more cold-blooded than I'd thought."

"Do you fight?" Marcus asked, pushing himself toward the back wall.

Paetas snorted. "Basilius has me dress up as Mercury. Once a gladiator falls, It's my job to find out if he's dead or faking it. I give him a jab with a red-hot iron—to see if he moves or not. Vassus here is dressed as Pluto, our own god of the underworld. He drags the bodies into the underbelly of the amphitheater."

Vassus glared at the ceiling, jaw clamped shut.

"As you can see, he is not very happy about that. Maybe now he'll understand we could just as easily end up hunted in the arena and he'll appreciate his assignment a little more."

Blood rushed from Marcus's head. The room seemed to tilt. At first, Marcus thought it might be another tremor, but the other two didn't react.

"You look a bit pale, my friend. What did you say your name was?" There seemed to be genuine concern in the boy's voice, but Marcus couldn't meet his eyes. Receiving compassion now would only leave him vulnerable at a time when being so could only hasten his death.

"Marcus," he replied, with as little enthusiasm as he had hope for surviving the day ahead. "Please—continue. The least I can do is make sure you're not suffering any consequences for not training me well."

"For the games, we march to the arena. Crowds turn out for the procession. The gladiators wear their ceremonial armor—but this event is just a hunt. I doubt Basilius will bother with much of a parade. I haven't seen any animals here at the barracks. They must already be at the arena."

Marcus tried to stretch his stiff legs. "How much time do I have?"

"We'll leave at dawn. Hunts are always scheduled for early morning in the summer—when the animals are most active. Once the sun is overhead, both the animals and the spectators are only ready for a nap. If the beasts get lazy in the heat of the day, they pretty much lose their entertainment value. Basilius has ordered the awnings to be set up, so that will draw a larger crowd and keep the animals lively a little longer."

"We might as well try to get some sleep. A night of training will hardly increase his odds," Vassus said, throwing an arm across his eyes as if trying to block out the sight of him.

"The whole event is inhuman." Paetas ignored Vassus. "I heard that once, when Caligula was emperor, there weren't enough prisoner participants to keep him entertained, so he had a whole section of the crowd thrown to the wild beasts. Basilius is a bit too much like Caligula for my comfort. Not a one of us is safe."

"If I must die in the arena, I will at least try to find a way to die with honor."

"There is no honor in this. Even the most glorified gladiator is degraded—" Paetas stopped himself. "I'm sorry—I didn't mean—"

"I know what you meant. It really doesn't matter." Marcus's stomach churned.

"Sure it does. You were right—there are ways to die with dignity."

Marcus nodded. Already, he was adopting Vassus's blank stare.

"You're very brave." Paetas gripped his shoulder. "You're handling this far better than I would."

Marcus took a deep breath. "What is the arena like?"

"You'll go through a big arched tunnel at the side leading directly into the arena. The seating starts right above the arena wall. It's only slightly above the top of your head, but for the hunts, they add iron bars on top of the wall to protect the spectators."

"There are just the two ways in—one on each side of the arena. There is only one other passage, but you don't want to take that one. Vassus drags the bodies through a small door on the side."

Marcus had to remind himself to breathe. Panic was creeping in.

"You could actually win this, you know." Paetas's voice feigned confidence, but his eyes betrayed a grim empathy. "You really don't need strong legs unless your plan is to run. You need strong arms. I'd bet yours are stronger than most."

Marcus seized this glimmer of hope. "Are the lions defeated often?"

"Often enough that they keep several around."

"How would I do that exactly?"

"I'll do my best to get you a spear."

"Basilius won't object?"

Paetas shrugged. "I wouldn't think so. His biggest concern is entertaining the crowd. They won't be entertained for long if—well, you just hang in there and give it all you've got."

Marcus didn't have much to give here. He'd just have to hope for a miracle.

"Brace the end in the sand and hold tight—like this." Paetas pantomimed tucking a spear under his left arm, aiming the tip with his right. "If the lion leaps at you, point the spear at his chest and roll with it as he falls."

"What was your crime?" Vassus rolled toward him, meeting his eyes for the first time.

"What do you mean?" Marcus didn't appreciate his insinuation.

"I mean—bestiarii are usually either criminals or prisoners of war. You speak fluent Latin, so I'm guessing you're a condemned man. You don't have any training. They must be making an example out of you."

Speaking fluent Latin. He hadn't thought of it from the listener's perspective. Strange how this universal communication thing worked. It made him wonder what would happen if he died here in the first century. Did he die in his own time too? Or worse—did he not exist at all in his time? His mother might be better off without him. Maybe she would end up giving birth to another child with greater aspirations than his own.

"I'm not a criminal. I was minding my own business when Basilius kidnapped me from the Forum. Some guy promised to help me get out of Pompeii. Basilius thought he was up to something and I was part of it. He called Brendanus his adversary. I just got caught in the middle somehow."

Vassus snorted. "Well he's making an example of you for some reason. You're probably the sacrifice to Jupiter Latiaris."

"Keep it to yourself, Vassus," Paetas growled.

Vassus huffed in indignation and went back to staring at the ceiling.

"Basilius does seem to be making a big deal out of this hunt. He has more ostriches than I could count—a lot of stags too. He has the arena made up to look like a wooded area on one half. We had to set up dozens of trees. They're just mounted on beams buried in the dirt, but I think they'd be sturdy enough to climb if you had to." Paetas's voice carried a lilt of hope.

Vassus snorted again, but didn't bother to look their way.

As the first rays of dawn warmed the horizon, Paetas stood and wiped his arms and legs down with a rag dipped in a bowl of water. "Did you sleep at all?"

Marcus shook his head. "Would you?"

Paetas gave him a sympathetic half-smile. "I'll help you dress for the hunt."

"What will I be wearing?" Marcus eyed an open cupboard containing only leather straps and fittings.

"Not much more than your loin cloth, but you'll get leather leg and arm wraps. I'll make sure you get a Galea and a shield. I might even be able to get you a real spear."

"There is a chance I won't get a real spear?" Marcus hadn't even considered that possibility.

Paetas grimaced at his ignorance, then offered him an apologetic smile. "The praegenarii usually only carry wooden weapons, and sometimes a net or a lasso—it's all just for show, you understand—but Basilius is putting you in as a bestiarii with Brutus and the lions, so I think I'll be able to procure a real spear for you.

Let's get your wraps on first." He bound Marcus's limbs in the leather fittings, taking special care with his withered legs.

"How do you manage to stay positive in a world like this?" Marcus cringed at the hopelessness creeping into his voice.

Paetas paused to look him in the eye. "I worship a powerful God and have faith that I will live forever if I persevere in my beliefs."

Vassus groaned. "It was your faith that landed you here to begin with, Paetas." He turned to Marcus. "Paetas was a small child when the Romans crushed Jerusalem. He was only taken prisoner because he was young enough to be trainable, but old enough to be useful."

"Anything is possible for those who believe, Marcus. You go out there and believe—persevere—maybe you'll even renew Vassus's lost faith." Paetas gripped Marcus's wrapped forearms firmly and ducked lower to keep eye contact. "Believe."

"You were in Jerusalem?"

Paetas gave him a quick solemn nod. "I was called Uzziel then, which means 'God is my strength.' Another name, another life—I am not that person any more, but I still draw my strength from my memories of that life." The sadness in Paetas's eyes was conquered by a genuine smile. "And so you see, sometimes—against all odds—we survive another day, if only to assist a brother in need."

When Paetas finished binding Marcus's leg, he rose and pounded twice on the door. A guard let him out, grunting at Paetas's cheerful greeting.

When Paetas returned he wore a winged helmet and brought a visored helmet for Marcus to wear. True to his word, he had also found him a small, round shield. "Stay away from Brutus. He was trained at the Ludus matutinus in Rome and takes his role as a bestiarii a bit too seriously. He's not any happier about your part in this than you are. He thinks pretty highly of himself, and he fights for money. He won't even use the cage when it's offered."

Marcus could barely swallow. "How soon do we leave?"

"Within moments—it's already hot out, so that will work in your favor. The beasts may get a bit lazy."

Paetas offered him a bowl of lumpy porridge, but Marcus's stomach turned at the sight of it. "What about my spear?"

"They may let you have it for the procession. If not, it will be given to you as you enter the arena." Paetas offered him a stiff smile.

Marcus took a deep breath and put on his helmet, which appeared to have been designed for a man twice his size. If he could keep it on, it might offer protection for his face.

"And here is Pluto, god of the underworld," Paetas offered a mock bow to Vassus and nearly lost his own helmet. Vassus wore a black tunic and a sneering black mask. His skin had been smeared with a greasy gray substance that made his flesh appear corpse-like.

"Your chariot awaits." Vassus announced in a deadpan voice. Marcus wondered if he had finally managed a smile behind his mask.

Vassus and Paetas lifted him, each grabbing an arm and leg, and carried Marcus through the door. He tried not to blush at the undignified process.

"Basilius had a chariot fitted with a seat last night," Paetas explained as they helped him into a crudely fashioned sling.

They led the horse pulling his chariot into the streets and joined the waiting procession.

A burly man sneered at Marcus. "Stay out of my way, breakfast."

Marcus cast a questioning glance at Paetas who mouthed a single word: Brutus.

Brutus's words were meant to sting and hadn't missed their

mark.

Paetas leaned close. "One last bit of advice: ride straight into the tree props at the arena, get your bearings, buy yourself some time and maybe you can think your way out of this. Good luck, my friend."

Marcus had never believed in luck. It also hadn't escaped his attention that his chariot didn't contain a spear.

Paetas led the horse near the head of the procession. He nodded as onlookers, nursing their morning mugs of watered wine lifted them in a friendly salute. A boy in ragged clothing ran alongside the chariot, jabbing the air with a stick in pretend swordplay. His exuberant shouts startled the horse, forcing Marcus to grip the sides of his bucking chariot. He made a shooing gesture at the boy, who stuck out his tongue — evidently a childish response that had survived the centuries.

Basilius joined the parade at the next intersection. A caged cart rumbled behind him, carrying a pacing leopard. All part of the show, he supposed.

In a few short blocks, they reached the amphitheater. Bile rose in Marcus's throat as they approached the arched tunnel into the arena. It turned a corner, hiding the entryway beyond in prophetic darkness. Whimsical music drifted from the depths of the amphitheater, as if to mock his dismal thoughts.

Basilius waved Brutus and Marcus forward with a smirk. The bestiarii hurtled toward the tunnel as fast as his beefy limbs would carry him. Marcus searched the small crowd huddled outside the amphitheater and found Paetas standing near the tunnel entryway. He thrust a fist into the air and nodded his encouragement. "Believe," he yelled. The rest of the group jeered at his cheery demeanor, but Paetas remained unruffled, holding Marcus's gaze.

Believe, Marcus repeated to himself. Believe. He had nothing to lose but his life. Marcus steeled his thoughts and focused on the task ahead. Grim as his outlook was, he was determined to go out with dignity and put on as brave a face as he could muster. He nodded to Paetas as his chariot rumbled into the cobblestone tunnel leading to the arena.

The horse pulling Marcus's chariot nickered, bucking at crowd's frenzied reaction to their arrival. Guards slapped his flanks, prodding him onward. As they charged back into the sunlight, iron gates clanked shut behind them. No turning back.

Trumpets sounded as Brutus strutted to the center of the arena, jabbing his spear into the sky as he acknowledged the spectators on all sides with a guttural snarl. The crowd roared. Doors under the podium flew open and deer darted in, scattering in every direction. Marcus's entrance went largely unnoticed. He took advantage of the opportunity to steer the horse for the trees. A lion leaped into the arena, close on the heels of the deer. The audience, apparently anticipating its arrival, broke into applause.

Brutus assumed an offensive stance, spear raised high. The lion circled, answering each of Brutus' growls with one of his own. A stag bounded between the adversaries and the lion launched after it, pouncing after a chase of mere seconds and ripping into the animal's delicate hide with its powerful jaws.

Marcus slapped his horse with the reigns, determined to flee toward shelter while he still had a chance. His anxious horse was happy to oblige. Marcus steered the chariot toward the simulated forest on the far side of the arena. He paused alongside an umbrella pine at the center and tested its stability with his arm. Typical of the lanky species, its branches loomed high above the ground. In fact, it rather resembled the mushroom cloud that would soon erupt from Vesuvius. If he attempted to climb it, he would become little more than the comedy routine Basilius presumably hoped he'd be. He'd probably send Brutus to shake him down. Both would be thrilled to humiliate him in death.

The trees seemed to have been selected for their uselessness as a potential hideaway. The motley selection had likely been nothing more than unwanted plants removed from some landowner's property—as undesirable as a crippled boy rounded up from the streets of Pompeii.

There was even an olive tree in the cluster—one that had probably never produced. He ripped a willowy branch from its misshapen trunk. Olive branches had long been a symbol of peace. They might not have given him a spear, but he'd go down making a statement.

"Ben?" Marcus thrust the olive branch over his head. "I admit it. I am nothing. I can't do this on my own. I get that now—I get it! Help me, please…"

Hooves pounded the turf behind him. Marcus spun around, shield at the ready. His jaw dropped. Paetas had mentioned stags would be released into the arena, but this exceeded his wildest imaginings. An elk towered over him, crowned by a massive rack of antlers. Marcus removed his helmet to get a better look.

He shaded his eyes from the glaring morning sunlight now streaming over the amphitheater walls. A man sat astride the elk's back—something familiar in his silhouette. "Brendan?" In the sunlight's intense glare he couldn't be certain, and the man didn't answer.

"Come with me," the great elk commanded. The man riding the elk thrust his arm toward Marcus.

With a strength fueled by desperation, Marcus lunged for the man's outstretched arm and was pulled up behind him. The elk braced for a leap. Marcus seized the man's waist as the elk thundered toward the center of the arena, circling the bewildered bestiarii. Marcus waved the olive branch above his head and the crowd cheered.

Basilius gestured and yelled at Brutus from the front row, behind the safety of the bars. Brutus glared, drew back his spear arm and gave a battle cry as he stomped toward them. The elk wheeled on his hind legs and galloped toward the arched arena tunnel. Guards blocked their path to the iron gates. The elk turned and reared. Marcus clung to the man in front of him as the elk's front legs stomped the arena floor, his rear legs hammering the gates. The sentries rolled clear as they were ripped from their hinges. They clattered up the stone ramp before the stunned men could find their feet.

Marcus let out a whoop. As narrowly as he'd just escaped death, he had never felt more alive. They sailed over the city walls outside the amphitheater in a gravity-defying leap, pounding the grassy slope on the other side without slowing. The elk's hooves pummeled the ground as he rounded the wall, kicking up divots of earth in his wake as they galloped toward the Salt Gate.

Max appeared at their side, barking an enthusiastic greeting. When the elk slowed his pace at last, the dog trotted to his side. Brendan jumped to the ground, reaching up to help Marcus slide down beside him.

Marcus gripped his friend's arm and slapped his back. "Brendan, you kept your word. I never expected to survive this. I hoped, even when it didn't seem wise to—"

"Don't thank me. I did what I could on my own, but realized in time that it wasn't possible to help you on my own power. Ben was the only one who could save you." Brendan helped him limp toward a cart waiting nearby. He slid into the back. Max jumped up beside him and sniffed his leather arm wraps.

"Ben—" He nearly choked over the mysterious name,

following Brendan's gaze. "You are Ben?"

The elk towered over the cart. Great dark eyes lowered to meet his. "I am."

Marcus steadied himself against the side of the open cart. "I have so many questions."

The elk dipped his head. "In time, they will be answered. You asked for help and it was given to you. If you continue to seek with all your heart, you will find me — but for now, you must rest." Sweet, warm breath tumbled over him.

Marcus yawned. "It's true. I haven't slept in days." Adrenaline waned and he allowed his body to relax against the smooth floorboards.

∽

Warm fur tickled his nose. Max. Marcus stretched, his aching joints resisting the action. "How long have I been asleep?"

"Long enough to revive you, I hope. We have a rough journey ahead."

"After the last few days, I would expect nothing less."

Max tilted his head. "Eat while you have a chance." He pushed a cloth bundle toward Marcus with a dusty paw.

Marcus unwrapped a round of bread and broke off a wedge, hungry enough to ignore its crumbling density. He chewed a parched mouthful and swallowed hard. "Do they normally put something on this?"

"I'm not certain how long that has been here." Max paced toward the doorway, sniffing the air.

Marcus drummed on a wooden crate with his palms. Dum-dum-dum — da-da — dum-dum. Dum-dum-dum — da-da — dum-dum. Marcus tipped his head back and sang, grateful for the distraction. "Pressure—pushing down on me, pressing down on—"

"Shhh!" Max hissed. "We are in hiding."

"Sorry." Marcus brought his shoulders up to his ears and offered an apologetic grin. "After being saved from the arena, nothing seems quite as dire. Where are we anyway?"

"Not far enough from the arena for my comfort. We are in the stable storage room of the estate where your friend Brendanus has been staying. This alley leads directly to the arena on the next block."

"Why are we back this close?" Marcus couldn't help cringing as he peeked out of a crack in the rickety wooden door. "I thought you'd be getting me out of Pompeii."

"We must wait for Brendanus and his friend to return. I haven't seen them yet."

"What's taking so long?"

Max crept into the main stable room and poked his head through the bars of the gate, craning to check the alleyway. "I expect they'll be back any time now. There are clothes in the satchel next to you. Make sure you're ready when they arrive."

Marcus pulled on a soft tunic, grateful to no longer be half naked. "How did these fancy clothes get in the stable?"

He removed the leather wraps from his arms. Before he could untie the straps on his legs, footsteps in the alley drew his eyes. He pressed his face to the crack, hoping to see the familiar loping of his new friend. Instead, the bulky shape of Basilius's trained bestiarii crouched to peer through a gate across from them. Growling, he spun on his heel, heading toward them. Marcus pivoted, his back pressed against the outer wall. He held his breath as Brutus stomped their way. The door next to him rattled. Another growl.

18

Julia's household staff assembled in her personal atrium as requested, hovering on the outskirts of the room with the same care they might exert when approaching the orchard beehive. If their tentative glances were any indication, her desperation might be beginning to show. "There are very few bath patrons today," she announced. "We must illustrate to our guests how successful these businesses are—or they may move on."

"That—or we must distract them from noticing." Isidore suggested, raising a brow.

"Isidore," Julia said, unable to suppress a giggle despite the mounting tensions. "You do have a gift for lightening my mood. You make a good point though. Let's play up Volcanalia today. Things are slow on this side of town. I will take them on a tour of the docks—show them what a key port city we are. We are halfway between Neapolis and Stabiae on the trade route, we are one of Rome's favorite vacation destinations—let's sell this."

Isidore stepped to her side. "Sarah and Methe, we need to plan a memorable meal tonight. I will search for something extravagant at the market this morning—and Sarah, your raisin cakes would be a treat they won't soon forget."

Julia tucked her stylus into her hair and fanned herself with the wax tablet instead of marking off her list. "After the disaster at the hunt yesterday, I'm afraid our guests won't take us seriously. It was rather more of a comedy than I had anticipated with a crazy stunt involving an elk and a masked rider. Basilius seemed furious at first. I'm not certain the antics were planned. Either way, the crowd loved it. So all is well, I suppose. But our guest, Annthea, left the show early and Brendan was elsewhere attending to business. They are spending more time touring the city than exploring our grounds, so please do whatever you can to make their time here enjoyable. A signed lease will benefit us all."

"Will Basilius be joining us for the cena, my lady?"

"He's been completely preoccupied since the hunt. I'm not sure what his plans are. If he comes calling, please find me immediately."

Rumbling from deep within the ground sent the group crowding into doorways for shelter. A loosened roof tile slid through the opening in the ceiling and shattered in the bone-dry impluvium pool, reverberating in the nearly empty cistern below. They braced themselves for continued tremors, but no more came.

"Well, they seem to be easing somewhat." Julia tried to summon a casual tone. "We must also each do our part in appeasing Volcanus. Tonight, the gardeners will build a bonfire from the brush pile and we'll make an offering of fish. Isidore has already stocked the garden pond with some carp he caught in the river."

"Isidore, be sure to offer our guests some bread, honey and figs this morning, and make sure they are dressed to explore the ports in a couple hours. We won't need a lectica today. The streets will be crowded and it would only slow us down, so make sure they wear comfortable walking shoes."

Julia strode through the bath suite once more. With more restless energy than she had tasks this morning, she actually envied her servants their busywork. Only one slave waited in the bathhouse portico with her mistress's clothing. Wilting on a bench in the far corner of the room, her shoulders drooped. Julia offered her a sympathetic smile. Slaves were the greatest source of gossip—and therefore, advertising—in the empire. It was wise to give them a positive impression to share. Julia strode to the service window at the thermopolium and requested a drink for the waiting servant girl. It was a small extravagance that would likely pay off in recommendations.

As she passed the food service counters, the furnace room attendant—a small fretful man continually bathed in a glossy sheen of perspiration—waved her into his adjoining work area. The furnaces were housed in an open-air space between the main atrium and the thermopolium. The unfortunate man had little shade and his leathery skin had made him look wizened beyond his years. He stood, slightly stooped, as if a lifetime of hefting wood and tending fires had left him incapable of pulling himself fully upright.

"My lady, something is wrong. The water level is very low. Even the public fountain is reduced to a trickle. Perhaps you can check into it when you head to the Forum this morning."

Julia clenched her jaw and inhaled deeply. It would not do to let her frustrations show. Leasing the bathhouse and thermopolium would not come soon enough. She had lost her peaceful mornings entirely in her efforts to make a successful display of the complex.

"I will do that. If necessary, bail some water from the pool. Our visitors may soon become the proprietors. We must appear at our best."

"Yes, my lady." The eager attendant grabbed an empty amphora and immediately headed for the pool.

She must remember to check the public fountains as they passed them. If they were running dry, the situation was indeed dire. The water system had been designed to divert water to the public fountains before the private residences if the flow dwindled for any reason. In the aftermath of the previous decade's major earthquake, the city's underground pipes had required many repairs. Perhaps after the recent bout of tremors, they needed additional maintenance.

Julia backtracked, returning to the thermopolium, where steaming crocks built into the countertop bubbled unattended. Now the servers had disappeared? The street was virtually empty. Pompeii's citizens must be as eager as she was to make their offerings to Volcanus. The ports would be crowded this morning. Nonetheless, she would somehow find a way to put a positive spin on this turn of events for her guests. Perhaps they could find time to stop at the temple for a sacrifice to Isis as well. Surely the goddess would see all her hard work and have mercy on her. Julia couldn't ask for better business associates. She would make every effort to bring that relationship about.

She waved a morning greeting to her next door neighbor as he guided an overloaded cart toward the nearby Salt Gate. As he plodded closer, it became obvious the small cart contained his entire family and as many personal belongings as they could cram in around them.

"Rufus," Julia called. "What is this? You can't abandon our city during the harvest—and in a cart at this hour, no less."

"I fear the gods are angered, Lady Julia." The man wiped a grape-stained hand over his weathered face. "I have a bad feeling. The city is sweltering and the fountains have run dry. Tremors have damaged my home yet again. My children were up all night crying. My wife has begged me to take her to her parents in Stabiae. I will do that today and return as soon as possible. We have only just harvested our grapes. I still have much work to do—but with a family, a man cannot be too careful." He gestured toward his wife, who urged the mule-drawn cart toward the gate without a backwards glance.

"Rufus, you are the paterfamilias," Julia scolded. Perhaps a little shame would set him straight. "You know what is best for your family. Keep them here with you. With so much work to be done, you need their help."

Rufus flapped his large purple-tinged hands like the henpecked cockerel he'd become. "As paterfamilias, I must keep peace in my household."

"Old fool," Julia muttered under her breath. She turned her back on the weak-willed family and headed back inside her garden oasis. Nothing could tear her away from her beloved Pompeii. She'd summon her guests for their jaunt to Volcanus's seaside temple, then sell them on the city and all its opportunities on the way. "Isis will redeem me," she said aloud, although no one was nearby to hear.

Julia marched back through her thermopolium, out the back exit and toward the swimming pool. Evidently, the sole patron of her bath facility had chosen to take advantage of the tepid pool, despite the fact that the water level was now down by several inches. The ample matron's personal attendant knelt on the ground behind her, juggling both a parasol and a fan. Julia waved in greeting and offered a polite smile, but made a beeline for her private gardens. It was simply too hot to make small talk. Her lounging guest seemed to agree.

Julia rounded the brick wall separating her ornamental gardens from the bath suites and sat on the marble ledge of the fishpond. She swung her feet over the edge and dipped the tip of her toes into the cool water. Isidore's carp gathered below her in anticipation of food. A shadow loomed over her shoulder. "You're hovering,

Isidore," Julia said without turning.

"Mistress, you know I served in Rome when it burned. Volcanus nearly destroyed the whole city. Pompeii is parched this season. The fountains have run dry and even our own cistern is nearly so. Please—we must appease him with sacrifice as soon as possible."

Isidore so often seemed to know her mind. It was both a pity and a piece of good fortune he was her slave. "Yes—yes, Isidore. I agree with you completely—and we will sacrifice your carp before the evening meal. Bring me my street shoes. I will also stop by the temple to make a sacrifice to Isis while we're out."

Isidore disappeared into her personal atrium as footsteps padded down the creaky steps leading from the upper guest rooms. Brendanus loped into the garden, blinking in the stark sunlight.

"Brendanus." Julia shaded her eyes with her hand before waving him over. "Come join me."

He offered his arm as she lifted her legs over the ledge of the pond. Soft hands betrayed his life of comfort. Tousled brown hair swept over his forehead as he leaned to help her to her feet. Boyish good looks might be his most charming quality, but a world-weary smile lingered today, stealing the sparkle from his eyes. Although his social awkwardness might not give him an edge in business, she found it both amusing and refreshing. At least clients would find him good-natured.

She'd double her efforts, if that's what it took. She needed the property leased, but beyond that, she wanted it to be them. There was something about the two of them—a quiet confidence and peace she found attractive.

"Annthea should be ready soon. I'll go nudge her along, then we are yours for the morning." Brendan's brow creased. "Are you certain we can't talk you into joining us this afternoon? We'd love to get a better feel for the area—explore the valley—perhaps as far as Nola."

Julia pressed her lips into a flirty pout. Oh, what might have been if she'd grown and bloomed without protective thorns — instead of being cast into a gutter, adopted by an elderly freedman and raised to survive a world that viewed women as little more than chattel.

"The countryside? What do you want with that? The city has all the excitement, beauty, history — and opportunities a young man could ever desire." Julia cast her arms wide.

"You've been quite convincing in that regard, but I still want to make some contacts outside the city walls — get to know this place inside and out."

Julia gave him a playful nudge. "You are planning to visit suppliers for a certain thermopolium, perhaps?" She raised her eyebrows, hoping for some sort of confirmation. "I cannot accompany you this afternoon, but I can provide unlimited use of my carriage, and a letter of introduction for a couple farms and vineyards nearby. They will be eager to do business, I assure you."

His face was unreadable. "Your knowledge of the area would be invaluable."

"I am sorry. The town is in a bit of an uproar this week. It's nothing to worry about — I assure you — but I must remain on hand." Julia's gaze shifted to the dwindling water in the swimming pool. "There will be all the more opportunities here soon. People panic, they make bad business decisions. Those of us who keep a level head profit while others give in to emotion. You'll see."

Isidore returned with a towel and sturdy sandals, kneeling to dry her feet. After she made the appropriate sacrifices to appease the gods, she'd need to deal with their water issues before it affected business at the bathing rooms.

Brendan cleared his throat and shifted on his feet. "Forgive me for being so presumptuous, but could you spare your girl, Sarah, to assist us in our errands?"

Sarah? Julia bit back the impulse to make an excuse and mustered a pleasant smile instead. She'd just committed to doing whatever it took to secure the lease. The girl had already made her raisin cakes and could be released from her afternoon chores. Julia dipped her head. "I suppose we can manage without her for a few hours."

19

"Anna, Marcus is safe! Safe, hidden in Julia's stables and waiting for our return so we can get him out of here." It made it all the more exciting to share the details of the daring rescue with his closest friend.

"You were amazing, Brendan—and it was incredible to see Ben again, if only from a distance. Basilius was horrified, but managed to act as if it had all been part of the show once he realized the crowd was entertained."

"I'm not surprised. He's quite the opportunist." Brendan gathered an armful of her clothing from a wooden cupboard and shoved it into a travel bag.

"I have a feeling he'll manage to put a spin on it that works to his advantage." A hoarse chuckle escaped Anna's throat.

"And you—so discerning and confident. It makes this whole agonizing trip worth it just to see you grow stronger." Anna nudged him with her shoulder. "You were right all along. I should have listened to you sooner. You have a gift, and I hope I've learned not to question it."

"Then why do you look sad?" Anna's untamable curls broke free from the ornate heap of nets, braids and combs the servants had piled on top of her head. It was one of her traits he found most adorable.

"I'm just disappointed in myself." Anna looped her arm

through his and rested her head on his shoulder. "But I'm so happy you were able to come here with me, Brendan — for so many reasons. I could never have done this without you. What am I saying? You did everything."

"Don't be silly. I had an advantage. I saw myself in Marcus. How could I not react to it? If I hadn't been here to distract you, I'm sure you would have sensed it."

Anna let out a shuddering breath and squeezed his arm. "We're better together, you know."

And there it was — the unspoken dread. They'd almost completed their mission. What would happen then? Every moment was a conflict — the constant, overwhelming urge to escape Pompeii, yet the yearning to stick around here by her side.

Brendan pressed his cheek into her hair. The scent of rose petals drifted up from the top of her head. He inhaled deeply and closed his eyes. This was one memory he'd hold close — something time and distance wouldn't be able to steal from him. After an indulgent pause, he shook himself back into the present. There was no time to waste. His future might be grim no matter where he found himself, but he still needed to get Anna and Marcus some place safe.

He pulled himself away and gripped her arms. "Oh — and I also received permission from Julia for Sarah to join us this afternoon."

"You did? That was a gutsy move, Brendan."

He returned her devious grin. "Well, I'm following my gut instincts on this. Ben told me to heed my inner calling. All along, I've felt this need to help Marcus. I had to act on it."

"Why don't you head down to Julia. I'll take your things to the stable. We can slip them into the cart when we leave. If they notice our things are gone and come after us for cart theft, so much the better."

20

Bonfires blazed throughout Pompeii, a twisted testimony in the city's conviction to tame Volcanus's destructive powers of fire. Pompeians took to the streets, reveling in the tradition of appeasing the god of fire at a time when summer heat put crops at the greatest risk of burning. As a sacrifice to Volcanus, Pompeians cast live fish into the flames.

Under other circumstances, the festivities might have held more fascination for Brendan, but as acrid smoke swept over the city, it only served as a disturbing reminder of the volcano poised to wreak havoc on the unsuspecting city.

"For you, my lovely." A flour-dusted baker bowed as he offered Anna a round loaf of bread fresh from the oven's flames. He extended it in a cloth-cloaked hand, and quickly wrapped it to hand to her. "In honor of the mighty fire-wielding Volcanus."

Anna dipped her head and tried to hand him a coin. The baker kissed his fingertips and waved her away with a sly smile.

Vendors continued to hawk their wares in the streets, enjoying the festival atmosphere. In Pompeii, it was business as usual, but Brendan itched to leave it all behind. Over the next couple days, the city would be engulfed by ash and pumice, preserving the lively town in a deathly time capsule. Watching the daily lives of its residents playing out in ignorance was a surreal sort of torture.

The wind had changed direction, blowing inland instead of taking its usual path out to sea. It carried a warning essence of smoke — easily disregarded as originating with the bonfires despite the hint of sulfur. Brendan folded his arms across his chest, anxiety-fueled fingers tap-tapping at his biceps.

"I need to speak with the magistrate before I visit the temple. You two go on ahead. Enjoy your afternoon in the countryside. Why don't you visit the harbor this morning with me first though? You really should make a sacrifice before you leave and it will give me an opportunity to show off our flourishing harbor."

Anna pleaded with her eyes, frantic over the last-minute opportunity to convince Julia. She'd grown attached. Despite his efforts at keeping an emotional distance, his heart was also heavy. Each hoped to entice the other with equal intensity. It was becoming evident neither was in a position to budge. Perhaps their paths were hopelessly, irreversibly set.

Brendan trailed behind Julia and Anna as they passed through a dank pedestrian tunnel in the city walls, blinking at severe morning light as they reemerged. Brendan filled his lungs with pungent salt air, thankful for the bay's open expanses after a morning of negotiating Pompeii's festival frenzied streets. A steep stone ramp led down to the water's edge. Beyond the seawall, a red concrete altar pyre awaited large-scale sacrifices to the god of fire.

Sunlight sparkled on the Bay of Naples, adding to the celebratory atmosphere. Clusters of people gathered at each bonfire, hurling flailing fish into the flames. While a few participants approached the act with a level of reverence, most were raucous, cheering with each unsettling sacrifice.

Anna shuddered visibly, lacing her fingers through his as they followed Julia toward the harbor front. She leaned close to him, her voice lowered so Julia wouldn't overhear. "Do they really believe this sort of sacrifice could save Pompeii from fire? Or is it a twisted tradition they actually take pleasure in?"

Brendan shrugged. "They do seem to be enjoying the day." Even the merchant sailors and foreign slaves appeared to be joining in the revelry. The waterfront exhibited more of a circus atmosphere than any sort of religious demeanor.

Pompeii straddled the banks of the Sarnus River, just north of its mouth into the Bay of Naples. A few industrious fishermen tried their luck along the riverbank, seeking a gift for Volcanus rather than their next meal. Julia selected a live sea bass from elderly vendor selling a variety from the back of his cart. He offered her a toothless grin as he took her coin.

Julia headed toward the crackling bonfire, holding the floundering fish as far from her delicate gowns as her willowy arms would allow. Stopping short, she gaped at their empty hands. "Where is your sacrifice?"

They'd reached an awkward impasse. They would not be making an offering to a lifeless god any more than she would abandon Pompeii and the independent life she loved.

Anna stiffened. "Our God would not permit sacrifice to another."

Julia's lips parted. She seemed to stop herself before protesting. Instead she turned, raising her flailing fish before the flames.

A powerfully built figure rounded the bonfire behind Julia, a confident swagger setting him apart from the milling crowd. Basilius lifted a glistening mackerel, a sneer distorting his lips as he heaved the thrashing creature into the flames. Not a hair out of place, no sweat on his brow as he stood within feet of the raging fire.

He glided to Anna's side, gaze locked onto hers. "So passionate, our Julia," he murmured. Her upturned face followed his, as a flower might track sunlight. "Surely there can be nothing wrong with pursuing the deepest desires of your heart."

"You could leave this place—release it from destruction. You'll never know if they're truly yours if you take them this way." Brendan clenched his fists as he envisioned wrapping them around Basilius's neck, choking the smug smile from his flawless face—but that was surely the reaction Basilius meant to inspire. Ben would not approve. Brendan bit back his anger.

A guttural laugh escaped Basilius's frozen smile. "Is that what you think? That I care? Knowing they are not Ben's is enough. This is a minor diversion—a festivity really. It's not like it's war."

"Isn't it? Then why not keep this between you and me."

"Is that what you wish?" Basilius's eyes cut to his. "Something a bit more intimate? Julia and I already share a certain bond, but I might be persuaded to focus my attentions elsewhere, if—oh, I don't know—perhaps you decided to follow me. We could hang out here and enjoy the festivities. Who knows what might happen?"

Brendan took an involuntary step backward, shaking his head. "This is all a joke to you."

Basilius stepped to his side. "I understand more than you think. Why should you be denied a normal life? Ben isn't offering you much at the moment, is he? The chance to live and love and achieve your dreams isn't so much to ask. I can give that to you."

Was he that transparent? How had he left himself so vulnerable to Basilius's wiles?

"I have wandered the earth for millennia and found that I am rarely surprised by man. It was just a piece of dumb luck that you managed to rip the fabric from my heel—and more ironic than you'll ever know." Basilius feigned half-lidded boredom, but bitterness laced his words. "And you kept it all these years. I'm flattered."

Brendan hoped there might be a chink in his seemingly flawless armor, but held his tongue.

"You might say I'm a scholar of human nature. I can read you all so well. Every last one of you thinks as I do deep inside. No one wants to bow and scrape before a distant god. All we want is our independence, to be masters of our own fate, to be in control of our destinies."

Brendan groped at the belt holding his tunic. He'd hidden the scrap of Basilius's robe within its folds, guarding it carefully once Basilius revealed interest in it.

"Go ahead and run." Basilius threw his arms wide as if to embrace the city. "I'm only claiming what is already mine." His hungry eyes followed Julia as she headed back up the ramp toward the city walls. A satisfied sneer spread across his lips. "Oh, yes. She is mine, most assuredly."

Brendan closed his eyes and turned his head, shutting out Basilius so he could think. When he opened them, his face wavered on the surface of the bay beside him. His eyes shone fierce. Ben's eyes. *Draw power from me. Resist him and he will flee.*

The battle might not be his, but he didn't have to cower either. Brendan forced his eyes to meet his adversary's heated glare.

Brendan clutched the scrap of fabric in his fingertips. Once, he'd held it close out of desperation ... the very fabric snatched from Fire Is Born's heel in Mutul before he'd stepped through the fire portal. It had been a symbol of hope to him — of remembrance — a shred of evidence amid his doubts. Basilius, the prince of lies, leveled his eyes at him over the dancing flames, practically daring him. What would happen if he just ... let go? He'd be forced to nurture his faith instead of grasping at proof. Would his connection to Basilius end? Or would he pursue him all the more?

"Marcus is not yours," Brendan growled. "We are not yours." He thrust his arm closer to the flames, searching Basilius's face for a reaction.

Basilius's eyes darted to Brendan's hand. "Take your broken boy, you fool. He doesn't belong here. I have many years yet to charm him."

"Ben, protect us!" Brendan released the scrap of fabric. For a few protracted seconds, it danced in an updraft, lingering in a current of heat. Basilius dove for it, fingers sifting smoldering fragments. As his body followed the trajectory of his lunge, it burst into fragments of light and disappeared as it had in Mutul.

"Strange. I don't think anyone else could see him." Anna surveyed the crowd. She hugged her forearms as if bracing against a chill instead of a feverish Pompeii afternoon. "We haven't seen the last of him, though, have we?"

Brendan scanned the horizon. "No. I'm sure he'll be back with a vengeance, but he's more vulnerable than he lets on."

"That may be, but he's clever. I won't be letting my guard down." Anna tugged him toward the road leading away from the waterfront.

Brendan quickened his pace to keep up with her. "It's not only Basilius we need to watch for. He has followers to do his dirty work for him. Like Lobo in Mutul."

"I only met Lobo when he appeared to be you. It was horrifying being tricked like that. Do you think Basilius would do that here?" Anna's wary eyes darted over the sea of faces.

"Sure, if it suited his purposes. He appears to be able to do anything he chooses."

"He can't go after Ben anymore. He can only come after us. He'll try to hurt Ben by destroying us."

Vesuvius loomed in the distance. A growing veil of smoke obscured its peak. Brendan took Anna's hand and led her into the prophetic darkness of the city wall. "We need to hurry back to Marcus and get out of this place."

21

Julia perched on the edge of her fishpond. She had been abandoned before. She would get past it. She was a survivor. Fortune had always favored her—from the day Spurious found her in a Roman gutter and took her to his lavish home, she had risen above her circumstances.

"May I bring you anything, my lady?" Isidore, faithful to the end.

A small luxury might soothe her frayed nerves. "A glass of mulsum and one of Sarah's raisin cakes would be delightful, old friend." Isidore headed for the kitchen.

"How do you do it?" she called after him.

Isidore turned, his face a question. "Do what?" It did not escape her that he had not added his ubiquitous "my lady."

"Serve me day in and day out, anticipating every need, without ever showing a trace of resentment?"

Her faithful servant studied his feet. "My greatest hope is to serve to such satisfaction that you one day see fit to reward me with my freedom."

His honesty hit her like a punch to the gut. She fought the urge to double over as his words ripped through any remaining illusions of endless devotion. Isidore had served faithfully. She had no right to any assumptions. "Your freedom is your greatest hope." The words escaped as a whispered acknowledgement. Of course he would desire freedom. A knot formed in the pit of Julia's stomach all the same. His greatest hope was to leave her — and yet, he was not unlike her adoptive father.

Spurious had achieved a freedman's status after many years in service to the imperial family. Had he not been freed, he would not have been able to rescue her. Had he not been generously rewarded, she would not now be living in the luxury she had grown accustomed to. It had been foolish of her to equate Isidore's pleasant and excellent service with happiness, and yet she had done it. She had imagined him content — willing to serve by her side as a lifelong trusted companion. "You have been my most faithful and loyal servant, Isidore. You have truly lived up to your name — you are a gift of Isis."

"I thank you, my lady." Isidore dipped his head and turned once again for the kitchen.

It had always been her plan to free them all eventually. When would that day arrive for a man who made himself indispensable to her? She tried to imagine her life without Isidore and cringed. Perhaps she could look for someone to replace him in the marketplace tomorrow — have Isidore train him to be as fine a steward as he was over time. Then she might one day be able to give him the freedom he desired.

The servants carried a dining couch to the garden and placed it in the shade of the pergola where an occasional breeze might offer relief from the incessant heat. Sarah arrived with a bronze tripod table and set it up in front of the couch. Julia settled onto the cushions and arranged the fabric of her tunic around her ankles. The garden was quiet as a tomb. Even the peacock with its incessant squawking was nowhere to be found.

Julia rubbed the back of her neck. So much time and money invested in her property, and still she did not have it leased. Perhaps her efforts at entertaining Brendan and Anna had fallen short. Now they seemed uncertain, and had taken to wandering the countryside. They would not even return in time for the afternoon meal.

Isidore appeared at her side with a glass of mulsum. The honeyed wine normally lifted her spirits. She gulped at it without thinking and was grateful that no one other than Isidore had been present to witness her unladylike indiscretion. Something in her restless spirit remained unquenched as she lay wilting under the relentless summer sun. Sarah's decadent cake was nothing more than tasteless crumbs on her tongue. A low grumble drifted up from the bowels of the earth as if echoing her complaints.

Julia's clay statues teetered on the ledge of the fishpond. One toppled into the water and sunk from sight. Julia groaned and looked to Isidore, the man who made everything right. His face was pale and drawn—eyes locked on the sky to the north. Julia followed his horrified gaze. A thick column of smoke towered above the mountain. A display of Volcanus, perhaps?

"What is it, Isidore?" She tugged at his arm.

"We must run, my lady—we need to leave at once—escape to the seaport." In an uncharacteristic lapse of decorum, he grabbed her hand and tried pulling her to her feet. "I will pack your jewels. Get your money and a few small valuables."

Julia tugged with equal force in the opposite direction. "No, Isidore! We must stay. Cowards have left Pompeii time and time again. Their loss has been my profit. I have invested all that I own in this place. I could never—will never—leave it."

"This mountain delivers destruction upon us, my lady." Isidore's eyes seem to dart over the potential escape routes. "We must leave while there is still time."

She shook him loose. "I—will—NEVER—leave!" Her attempt to scream the words over the growing roar of the mountain left her throat raw.

Isidore's face was a mask of terror. Her stoic steward had become disturbingly ruffled. It was all too much to endure. Julia wrestled with overwhelming disappointment. Knowing she would likely regret the impulsive decision once the crisis passed, she barreled ahead anyway.

"We don't have time to go before the magistrate, so this is the best I can do." Julia grabbed him by the forearms. "Hunc hominem liberum volo—I wish to free this man," she recited the simple declaration of manumission. She turned him in the opposite direction and nudged him toward the atrium. "Go." If he truly cared for her, he would stay. If not, she had misjudged him and would do well to be rid of him.

He turned back to her, shaking his head, disbelief etched on his face.

"Go—I said, GO. Go to the sea. Escape this place if that is what you truly wish," she screamed. She gave him a shove before she could humiliate herself by pleading with him to stay.

He backed away from her, eyes brimming. "Thank you, my lady."

"Go," she said, her voice hoarse with disappointment. She turned to the fishpond. The beautiful bearded red mullet Isidore had given her floated on its side. The mountain's violent wrath reflected on the pond's surface. Flakes of ash fluttered around her, forming a film on the pond, hiding the horrid fish from view. Julia stumbled to her feet as the ground lurched again.

One of her personal attendants rushed to her side. "Lady Julia—I have gathered your jewels. What else would you like to take with you?"

"We are not leaving!" Julia screeched, her throat burning with the acrid stench creeping into her garden oasis. The girl sunk to her knees, wide eyed, as the color drained from her face.

Julia took the chest of jewelry and headed toward the summer triclinium. "Only cowards abandon what they have worked so hard to achieve." From cover of the dining area, she could watch the ashes drift to the ground without getting any filthier. Perhaps she would have the staff prepare a private bathing session for her. That would soothe her frayed nerves.

The sky grew dark as she curled up on a dining couch beneath her magnificent wall fountain. Not a trickle remained of its lovely cascade. Not only had the water supply run dry for private residences—every drop had evaporated from the stones in the scorching heat. She clutched the jewelry box to her chest. Her father would be so proud of what she had accomplished here. It had always been his dream for her to be a successful landlord. He had purchased the initial property with the domus she now lived in, but she had been the one to buy the property across the street. She had been the one to convince the magistrates to give up the street that divided them—one that led to the amphitheater itself—and to build the fine estate she now possessed. She had achieved everything he had dreamed for her and more.

"Methe," she called to kitchen servant cowering in the corner of the room. "We must make a sacrifice to Isis. Make the preparations." The sobbing girl stumbled toward the kitchen. Julia stepped back into the garden. She would clear ashes from the brazier in the garden sacrarium. It was the best she could do at the moment. Strange foamy rocks hailed down around her, floating as they hit the fishpond. Despite their light and powdery composition, they still stung when they pelted her skin. She pulled her palla over her head and dashed to the sacrarium where thick vines sheltered her from much of the debris accumulating in her garden.

"Mother Isis, you offer shelter to the weak and the

orphan—deliver us from this torment!" A hard black rock burst through vines draping the pergola and hit the ground next to her with enough force to embed it halfway into the ground. Had she been standing a step to her left, it might have crushed her skull. Julia covered her head with her arms and dashed to the closest reception room, passing into the darkened hallway. None of the lamps had been lit—but then it was still day.

"Isid—" Out of habit, Julia had meant to call on her favorite, but now it was mere foolishness. Had he been there, the lamps would have already been lit. He would have met her needs before she'd had an awareness of them—but he was gone. Until that moment, it hadn't occurred to her she might never see him again. She staggered as a wave of nausea washed over her.

Drifts of ash spilled into the rooms opening onto the portico. Julia groped her way through the darkened hall and up the steps to the servants' quarters. Small windows overlooked her herb gardens. The lush grounds she had happily wandered mere hours ago crumpled under the ash and stone blanketing everything in sight.

It would take months to clean up this mess. The city would be paralyzed for much longer than it had after the great earthquake. Nearly two decades later, they were still burdened by reconstruction and repairs from that event—and now this. Perhaps she should have left with the others. She clutched the chest of jewelry, uncertain what to do with it. No—long ago she had committed herself and the whole of her wealth to Pompeii. For all its freedoms, it was now her prison, she could no more separate herself from it than she could from her own heart. It had become a vital part of her being.

Darkness descended over the city, entombing them under a thick mantle of soot no sunlight could penetrate. The sky was blacker than night with no moon or stars to illuminate it. The only source of light was the pillar of flame blasting from the top of the mountain.

"Mother Isis, Queen of Heaven, protect us!" Julia wailed. "Lady of Green Crops, you gave birth to heaven and earth — restore us!" Isis was deaf to her pleas. The only response was the rumbling wrath of the mountain.

22

For hours they'd cast wary glances over their shoulders as they walked. Now, an abysmal rumble stopped them in their tracks. A gray cloud of ash mushroomed on the horizon, barreling south until it enveloped the bay. They'd managed to get miles from Pompeii before Vesuvius erupted. Even at this distance—upwind from the blast—grit filled the air, sifting down around them like sand in a doomsday hourglass. A smothering darkness crept toward them, lit only by flashes of lightening or bursts of flame shooting from mountain's widening peak.

"We should have been able to do more." Anna rested her head on Brendan's shoulder, unable to look away. "We've taken Julia's carriage. What if she changed her mind and decided to leave?" Each passing mile should have brought an increasing sense of relief, but instead, sorrow overwhelmed her.

"Julia made her decision, Anna," Brendan said, putting his arm around her. "You did everything you could to encourage her to leave. If she stayed, it was her choice. Her heart, her life and her wealth are in Pompeii. It's everything to her. Don't forget, the choices we've witnessed played out centuries before we were born."

"She thought Isis would save her." Tears welled in Anna's eyes. "Couldn't Ben reveal himself to her? Convince her like he did with us?"

"Many people never see him, Anna. They're too confident in their own abilities—too set in their ways and reliant on themselves to ever notice him. The older you get, the harder it is to just let go and trust. We were both going through difficult times when Ben took us on that first adventure. We were both still impressionable kids."

"So what are you saying—that Julia never had a chance?"

"With Ben, anything is possible, but the outcome is not for us to know right now. You did what you could. She had another small carriage and two carts if she chose to leave."

"You rescued Sarah and me," Marcus piped in from behind them. "And two of Julia's mules." An endearing smile shone stark white against his ash-smudged cheeks.

Sarah remained conspicuously silent. Anna cast her a guilt-ridden glance. The girl was a stone wall, strong and unyielding. Spine rigid, arms crossed over her chest, she turned her back on the city. Anna vowed, if given the time here, she'd reach out to her.

"You're right, Marcus, thank you. I need to focus on the positive aspects of this journey or the rest will crush me." Like so much volcanic residue. They'd been sent to help Marcus. Wallowing in the misery of this place would achieve nothing. "It was never our mission to save Pompeii—although I do think it was meant to be a wake-up call for all of us. I should be rejoicing that we were able to help you and Sarah—and to escape with our lives."

Sarah shook dust from her feet. "In Bereishith, it is written: 'Then Adonai caused sulfur and fire to rain down upon S'dom and 'Amora from Adonai out of the sky. He overthrew those cities, the entire plain, all the inhabitants of the cities and everything growing in the ground ... the smoke was rising from the land like smoke from a furnace!' History repeats itself."

When the girl found her voice, she didn't hold back.

Anna held in a sigh. The girl needed her compassion. "Was Lady Julia such a bad mistress?"

THE VEIL OF SMOKE

Sarah's posture softened. "No. Lady Julia was kind enough. I believe she bought me out of compassion. I was safe with her. In the end, she was more of a prisoner than I. Lady Julia was bound to her earthly riches. She put her faith in herself and her lifeless Egyptian goddess. She could not bring herself to leave that cursed city."

Anna tried to exhale her sadness. "Were you in Pompeii long?"

"Since the Romans destroyed Jerusalem nine years ago, slaughtering my people and taking the few children left as slaves." Sarah looked as if she'd just swallowed a mouthful of bitter herbs. In her dark eyes, untold horrors brewed.

"I'm so sorry, Sarah." The poor girl couldn't have been any more than six or seven when she'd first arrived in Pompeii as a prisoner of war.

Marcus's gaze was locked on the tower of ash mushrooming behind them in ever increasing height. "Um ... shouldn't we be trying to get out of here—fast?"

As if on cue, another thundering boom echoed toward them, the aftershock palpable. A broadening cloud of debris launched into the sky before the wind pulled it southward. Although they'd put distance between themselves and Vesuvius, heading north into the wind, the murky cloud drew closer this time.

"We need to push on and get to Capua and the Via Appia before the sun drops behind that cloud of ash and we no longer have the light to travel." Brendan threw a mantle over each mule's head, hovering at their heels to urge the skittish animals on.

Julia's solid carpentum, covered by a carved wooden arch, was an ornamental and luxurious carriage, if not entirely practical for outrunning a volcanic cloud. It tottered along the worn stone road on two large wheels. Marcus hunched on the front seat under a cloak. Anna urged Sarah to rest in the back for a while. Although the carriage would have held the four of them, Anna chose to walk beside Brendan as he led the mules, calming them throughout Vesuvius's violent display.

Darkness crept toward them, masking the late afternoon sun. Ashes fluttered around them like snow. A dead quiet pressed in, breached only by an occasional rumble of thunder. Before long, the road began to disappear in drifts of ash and pumice. Brendan prodded the mules on, tapping the road with a stick to navigate the hidden stones.

For hours, they plodded in silence, barely able to see beyond their outstretched arms. The stench of sulfur permeated the thick veil Anna had wrapped around her nose and mouth. Unshed tears and fumes burned her eyelids. "How long?" Anna coughed with the effort to speak. "How long have we been walking? Is it night?"

Brendan checked his wrist and snorted. "Old habits—I keep trying to check my watch. He pointed to a yellowish glow in the distance. "The sun is getting closer to the horizon. We need to move faster. Once the sun sinks below the ash column, it will be even more difficult to tell where we are." He was right. Very few landmarks were visible now and it would only get worse.

Anna continued to cast wary glances over her shoulder. Dread hammered away at her confidence. It was more than Vesuvius. At moments, she was sure someone followed on their heels. She tried to shrug off the suspicion as a nagging paranoia. Despite constant vigilance, no one appeared behind them.

The wind shifted and a wave of sulfurous fumes engulfed them. Anna pressed her veil over her nose and mouth, unable to block images of what Pompeii's stragglers must be experiencing from her mind. She glanced at Brendan through stinging tears. Above the sleeve he'd clamped over half his face, his eyes mirrored her alarm. With each assault the mountain rendered, their small group retreated further into the seclusion of their unspoken thoughts.

Slow progress kept them on the road. Brendan and Anna each shouldered a mule, coaxing them onward. To the northeast, the sky hinted at its presence, offering a bleak orange glow. Angular shapes appeared in the haze ahead. Buildings. Nola. As their motley group skirted the city walls, a woman in a humble farmhouse near the road hauled her skirts above her ankles and trundled out to meet them. She waved them toward her home.

"Gods be praised. You've survived the destruction raining down upon us. How did you escape with your life?"

"We left before the mountain erupted. In Pompeii, the sky is black as night and heavy with ash. I can't imagine many will follow behind us. The few who showed an interest in leaving all seemed to be heading south."

The woman wrung her hands, eyes fixed on the looming darkness. "My husband and son went to market today to sell our harvest of spelt. I must wait for their return, but it looks as if the end of the world is upon us."

Brendan placed a comforting hand on her shoulder. "As long as the wind continues to push the ash and debris to the south, you will be safe here in Nola."

"I pray you are right." Tears streaked her ash-stained face.

"Is there public water nearby?" Brendan tugged the miserable mules from the road, brushing as much ash as he could from their backs. "We must push on if we're to make it to Capua today."

"I have some water inside I can spare. Follow me." The woman emerged from her home with a basin of water, ladling cupfuls for the human travelers before offering the basin to the mules. "I made some cheese today and there is plenty to spare—and some bread that is still warm from the hearth. Please take some with you." The woman lumbered back into her home and returned quickly with a cloth bundle.

Anna hugged the woman, thanking her for her generous hospitality. "I'm sure your family will return soon. We made it from Pompeii unscathed." She climbed onto the seat next to Marcus, and placed the bundle of food in her lap. Offering up a prayer for this kind woman and her family, she held up her hand in a silent farewell. The woman paused to wave back, before returning to the futile busywork of her broom.

∽

Surges continued to tumble down the ever-shrinking Vesuvius, covering the foothills with layer after layer of ash. Each surge was followed by a lingering stench of sulfur, as if the bowels of Hades had been unleashed on an unsuspecting world. They plodded onward throughout the evening, determined to escape the widening reach of the mountain's fallout.

Blundering in thick darkness, they somehow managed to stay on the road. Bleak milestones measured their slow progress. Few discernable objects remained in the ash-shrouded landscape. Inscrutable forms skulked in the intermittent flash of lightening, offering little reassurance. Anna's feet slogged onward even as her mind and spirit rebelled, her will to survive prodding her past exhaustion.

As day broke, hazy forms took shape on the horizon. Capua. At last. Beyond it, the Appian Way—their path to escape. By a simple deviation of the wind, cities to the north of Vesuvius had been spared. Other than a dusting of ash, the luxurious city appeared unharmed.

Soldiers from the fort in Capua stood in tight formation, at the ready to march into Pompeii and Herculaneum. Brendan led the cart into a grassy field, deferring to the ranks dominating the road.

Brendan pulled Anna aside. "Wait here. Try to get some rest. Emperor Titus's army is marching south. I'll see if I can get any information. Maybe I should even join them in a search for survivors."

Anna's fingers dug into his arm before she could stop them. "Don't leave us."

His eyes pleaded from their mask of soot. "I may be able to help."

Panic laced her voice, but she was beyond caring. "This isn't the twentieth century, Brendan. Women aren't safe alone on the streets." How could he even consider it after walking throughout the night?

Brendan's eyes shifted over her shoulder to the carriage. Sarah slumped on the front seat. Marcus slept in the back, the faithful Max curled beside him. His lips pressed into a grim line. "You're right. We need to stick together. Wait here while I speak with the soldiers. I won't leave your sight. I'll be back as soon as I have a better idea what's going on."

Anna nodded, releasing her white-knuckled grip on his arm. She closed her eyes, forcing back tears of desperation.

A strong hand cupped her chin. When she opened her eyes, Brendan's unyielding gaze penetrated the panic gripping her. "We're all overtired. Don't worry. I won't be long."

An ashen figure staggered from the thick veil of smoke.

Brendan's head tilted. "Anna, look—"

Someone had been following them.

23

The man staggered into view as Titus's army faded into the murk, marching for Pompeii. Obscured by his cloak as much as the haze, he hunched over the gutter and retched as the ranks filed past stirring up what ash had settled. A rope held slack in his hand disappeared into the dust cloud behind him. He lurched ahead once more and the lead rope pulled taut. An old woman riding a mule soon emerged behind him. The final rows of troops sidestepped them, fading into the miasma. Any refugees straggling in on their own would be left to the mercy of the Capuans.

Hair loose and wild, the mule rider sat doubled over, blanketed in gray ash, eyes closed. She seemed to be mumbling or praying aloud. He couldn't differentiate at such a distance whether she was driven by madness or faith.

As the pitiable couple drew closer, another man followed in their wake.

Brendan rushed forward, grasping the foremost man by the shoulders. "Have you come from Pompeii?"

The woman nodded instead, coughing too hard to speak. From a distance, her stooped posture and ash-covered hair had made her appear old. Now, Brendan could see her youthful skin was merely encrusted in soot. Brendan took the mule's lead rope, guiding the three exhausted travelers toward the public fountain where Anna sat huddled.

He lifted the girl from the mule's back and helped her to the fountain where Anna offered her water and their remaining bread. The two men collapsed to the ground at her side.

Brendan studied the girl as Anna wiped layers of grime from her face with a damp cloth. He leaned closer. "Wait — do I know you?"

The girl's eyes flashed terror before she ducked her head, grasping her cloak around her. "Please—"

Anna lowered her head to meet the girl's gaze. "Yes, you're from Lady Julia's estate. Methe, isn't it? Do you have any news of Julia? Did she also leave?" Anna's head snapped back up, her eyes searching the gloomy horizon as if her friend might materialize from the haze of ash as well.

The girl buried her face her hands, shoulders heaving. "No — please—"

Brendan squatted in the ashes beside the girl. "Lady Julia did not leave, did she?"

"Please — I beg you. Tell no one you have seen me," the girl pleaded. Her eyes were fierce as she lowered her voice to a whisper. "I did not plan to run. The punishment for runaway slaves is severe."

"No one else came with you? They all stayed behind?" Anna gripped her shoulder.

"Lady Julia would never leave. I was making preparations for a sacrifice to Isis when Sarah's brother came to the servant's entrance looking for her. The city was in chaos. The festival for Volcanus should have appeased him, but instead—" Methe shook her head and lifted one shoulder.

"How did you end up here? No one else seems to have come this direction." Brendan's gaze returned to the dusty murk southeast of Capua. It defied logic to head north past the mountain, yet that was the only quick path to safety. Most would head south where the wind would carry the bulk of the fallout.

"Many were fleeing for the seaport, but Lady Julia refused to leave. When Sarah's brother and his friend showed up, I took them to the stables to see if she had returned. A young mule was pounding at the gates wanting to get to his mother — one of the mules pulling the carpentium. You had not returned." Methe shook her head, her eyes distant. "When we opened the gate, the mule broke free. We chased him, but he was quick to escape the city gate and head for the Nola road. All we could do was follow. By the time we caught him, we had to keep going to escape the rocks raining down—"

"Uzziel?" Sarah sprang from the carriage seat. Creeping closer to one of the men on the ground, she pressed shaking fingers to her lips. She tilted her head and studied his face. "Is it really you?"

"Sarah?" The young man bolted to his feet. "My sister — only the hand of God could make this so."

"How — How are you here? After all these years ..." Sarah's fingers traced his face. "Even with the soot, and the short hair — I could never forget. How did you find me?"

"I was with you when you were sold to Julia Felix of Pompeii. I was so relieved it was a woman — one who appeared compassionate. I could only pray she'd keep you. When Basilius took the show to Pompeii, I began my search. Julia Felix was well known and close to the arena, so it was not difficult to find her. Then chaos erupted, as if from the pit of Sheol — and I knew it was time. I had to find you and take you away from that place ... but you were gone." Uzziel embraced his sister. "In the end, it was a mule — not me — that found you!"

"Paetas?" Marcus, roused from his nap, now perched on the cart's narrow seat next to his faithful protector, Max.

Sarah's brother released her and reeled to Marcus's side.

"Marcus, the miraculous survivor! What a strange day of improbable reunions. Basilius was furious when you made your grand exit, but the crowd was so awed by the show, he ended up claiming the opening act as his own device. The audacity of that man knows no bounds."

"Paetas." Marcus gripped him in an uncharacteristic display of affection, no longer trying to play it cool. "I am so relieved to see you. We've both survived against the odds. I owe you a major debt of gratitude. Without you, I would have given up. I can't imagine how hopeless I would have been without your help."

Paetas waved away the thought and offered him a lopsided grin. "It was nothing. I wish I'd been capable of doing more for you. But now, my show-stopping friend, we are both free of our bonds—and I can be Uzziel once again."

"You know each other? Our meeting is no accident then." Brendan clapped Uzziel on the back before turning to the quiet young man beside him.

Uzziel seemed to notice his unspoken question. "My stoic friend here is Vassus, but I may call him Asher now, since he is more fortunate than he believes."

Vassus snorted. "I suppose we were fortunate to escape with our lives, but what will become of us now that we are fugitives? You may have people to return to, but I have no history of anything but slavery."

Uzziel nudged him with his shoulder. "You will see. We will make a new history for you. If any of my people survive, they are scattered, but we will search for them. My people have a long history of slavery and hardship, so they have learned to create a web of communication. They know how to leave a hidden trail. Do not despair, old friend. You have been one of my people for years."

Vassus shook his head, releasing a cloud of ash. "Spartacus

began his slave revolt at Capua more than a hundred years ago and it didn't end well for him."

"Vassus, my friend, what could be worse than serving Basilius?" Uzziel gripped his friend's arm. "I would rather be crucified than return to that life. Now that I have found my sister, I will run any distance to keep her safe. As prisoners of war, my sister and I would be returned to slavery no matter the circumstance. I cannot let that happen. If you wish to turn yourself in, I understand, but I hope that you will join us."

Vassus gave a despondent nod. "You are right about that. Life as a slave to Basilius is no life at all."

Brendan placed a hand on Uzziel's shoulder. "I no longer believe in coincidence. We each ended up here for a reason. Now we need to figure out what that is. We should travel together. If we appear to be a household, we will draw less attention."

Uzziel rubbed the back of his neck. "Where are you headed?"

"To Brundisium, then we'll take a ship to the east." Brendan liked the idea of a larger group. It would offer safer travel.

Uzziel cast a questioning glance at Vassus and his sister as if to encourage their approval. "We are traveling east as well." They appeared wary, but didn't object.

Sarah finally nodded. "Our homeland is east. Some may remain who might connect us with distant relatives."

"Any among our people who survived the Roman onslaught were likely scattered throughout the Empire. It may involve some time and travel, but we will see where it takes us." Uzziel rubbed his chin.

Brendan leaned against the dust covered well. "The soldiers told me Titus is heading down from Rome to survey the destruction and assist any survivors. We should leave quickly. The soldiers may be distracted by search and recovery, but slave catchers will also be arriving soon."

"Titus led the assault on Jerusalem. He'd only help us right back into slavery." Uzziel pressed his lips into a somber line.

"What did Titus have against Jerusalem? I know Rome is driven by conquest, but why destroy a city they've conquered?" Brendan took a deep breath. Perhaps it might have been best to leave his questions unspoken.

When Sarah and Uzziel remained silent, Vassus leaned toward Brendan, his voice low. "They dared to rebel."

Brendan rummaged in the back of the carriage. Why did surviving feel like a mark of shame? He yanked the carefully rolled toga out of it. While dreadful as a wardrobe item, it might serve well as a makeshift tent.

Max jumped up next to him and pressed his scruffy muzzle close to Brendan's ear. "It will soon be time for Marcus to go home. Head north to the Volturnus River."

Brendan would have pressed the dog for details, but didn't want to reveal Max's supernatural skills to their travel mates. They'd already had a stressful day. Why complicate it more?

Sarah served the small supply of raisin cakes she'd brought with her. They gulped water from a roadside well and washed the dust from their hands and faces. Methe lit an oil lamp Marcus had brought from the stables at a street shrine before they headed off-road.

Brendan took first watch, guarding the small group as they slept. Exhausted by the day's events, they drifted off to sleep in mere moments. He propped himself against a tree trunk, cupping the lamp in his hands. The flame cast a warm glow on his sleeping friends, flickering on their peaceful faces. Let it chase away the darkness all night if it could. There was no point in trying to hide it. He allowed the flame to mesmerize his tired mind.

∽

"Have you slept at all?" Anna set the lamp on the ground at his feet and curled up next to him. Reflecting the glimmer of flickering light, her eyes wandered to Vesuvius's wasted silhouette before drifting back to his.

Brendan tried to rub the pain from his burning neck muscles. "Not yet."

Anna pulled his head onto her lap. "Sleep, then." While Brendan's mind initially resisted rest, his exhausted body finally succumbed as Anna stroked his sooty hair.

When he woke hours later, sunlight crept over the Apenninus Mountains. The dust-cloaked valley retained an otherworldly pallor. Anna had spread her mantle over him and a thin film of ash had covered it even as he slept.

His traveling companions were already up, shaking dust from their clothing as best they could. Uzziel and Vassus harnessed the mules to the carriage, ignoring their braying complaints. The mottled gray landscape to the south was devoid of landmarks, as still and lifeless as an ashen tomb.

24

By mid-morning, the group had traveled high enough into the Apenninus Mountains that the air began to clear. The landscape carried only a fine dusting of ash. Strong winds had scattered the bulk of Vesuvius's debris far down the shoreline to the south.

"I'm sorry we haven't had a chance to talk much yet, Marcus. How did you end up in Pompeii?" Anna sat next to him on the carriage seat, her eyes kind as they searched his.

Marcus tucked his legs under the seat. He had conflicting feelings about Anna. On one hand, there was the bizarre possibility she might actually be his grandmother. She also had a way of speaking to him in soothing motherly tones. While he found that comforting, it also reminded him of his mother and gave him a sick feeling in the pit of his stomach.

There was also the fact that she was young and beautiful, and far from looking like a grandmother yet. He kept his legs out of view so she could focus on who he really was—someone who had changed inside—and so much more than the body he was now confined to. Once they were far enough northeast of Vesuvius that only a stray breeze carried flakes of ash, she let her hair down. She turned her head upside down with a girlish laugh and shook the ashes from her long curls. It was nice to see a playful side to her—like sunshine piercing her veil of sadness, if only for a moment. Without the film of gray dust on her hair, she looked even less like the grandmother she might be—one day—however that worked.

Anna leaned close. A stray lock of hair slid from her shoulder, grazing his arm. "Did you lose a parent — or lose your way somehow? When Brendan and I were on our first adventure together, our circumstances were similar. We had both lost parents and were dealing with some pretty stressful life circumstances."

Marcus shuffled his withered feet. His body was always so uncomfortable here. "I did lose my father a few years back — well, back in my own time," he said with an awkward shrug. "My mom took it really hard. I miss him a lot too — but after Pop was gone, it was like she pinned all her hopes on me. I've never been the greatest student, and we've never had much money, but she really wants me to go to college. That was part of my parent's American dream, I guess. They really put a lot of pressure on me to live that out for them."

"In my time, higher education is a luxury not many get to take advantage of. Would that possibility be so bad?" Anna's eyes twinkled, teasing him with a history he knew nothing about. He'd have to ask if she'd gone.

"Going to college? I guess not, but it's not my dream, you know? She's always nagging me to get a job instead of appreciating my musical talents, or encouraging me to pursue my dreams."

"Can't you do both?"

Marcus groaned. "That's totally something my mom would say."

Anna's eyes grew distant. "Huh." Her forehead scrunched, like she was still thinking about it. The whole grandma thing had to be weird for her too.

"She could do better with the money she's saved than put it towards college for me. She could even go herself if it's so important to her."

"I'm guessing she wants you to have as many options as possible for your future. I would want that for my child too." Anna's eyes narrowed. When she squinted like that, with her brows all crinkled up, she looked just his mother always did when she was lost in thought. "Your mother didn't go to college herself?"

"Nope. Her mom didn't approve of my father and his crazy dreams. She ended up running off to America with Pop when they were only eighteen. They got married at a clerk's office in Chicago, which totally freaked out my—"

Anna chuckled. "Grandmother? I know—weird, right? Could that possibly be me? I went running off to America myself to study nursing and—well," her eyes shifted to Brendan. "To pursue my dreams too, I suppose. I plan to return to Italy eventually, but …" Her voice trailed off and she bit her lip.

Marcus glanced at Brendan, before his gaze drifted back to Anna. "Are you and Brendan—" He hesitated.

"Best mates—at least I've always thought of us that way. I guess his perspective is rather more condensed. In his natural timeline, he's younger than he is here—not much older than you, actually."

"Really. Huh." His eyes shifted back to Brendan as he tried to picture a younger version of his new friend. Best mates. Was that some sort of Freudian slip? She'd said it with a strange accent—one that sounded more Australian or British than Italian. She was definitely a mystery.

"I know how strange it all is—and believe me, having more time to process it doesn't lessen that awkward aspect at all—but I've come to believe that age isn't as restricting in a friendship as you might think. Each year of our lives is a stepping stone on a pathway stretching into eternity. The things that make us what we truly are—our experience, our unique perspectives—are far from limited by mere age. Shared interests and beliefs are more of an important factor when it comes to enriching each other's lives. We view time from a limited human perspective, but we connect on many more important levels."

"You've traveled time together before—you and Brendan."

Anna nodded. "More than once."

"How does this work? How do we get back to—you know—our normal lives?"

"If you're anything like Brendan and I, you're here to learn something important. When you've done that and the time is right, you'll be sent back. Have you gained a valuable perspective being here?"

Tears stung Marcus's eyes, but he blinked them back. "I've been kind of harsh lately … giving my mother a hard time. I should've been talking things over with her instead of blowing her off. I don't know why I've been pushing her away. I know she means well. I just want to get back and make things right."

"We all have a tendency to fight for control, but sometimes we just need to step back and take a broader view of things. Chose our battles wisely, you know? Surrender our path to what's meant to be, not necessarily what we're hoping for in the moment." Her eyes crinkled at the corners. She shrugged. "Try to decide what's important in the long run."

Marcus took a long deep breath and nodded. A weight seemed to lift as he exhaled.

"Has being here changed you?" Anna unwrapped a bundle of cloth and took out a loaf of bread.

"I thought I had it all figured out. I guess I've been trying to barrel ahead with my own plans without much thought about where I was headed down the road. I've taken my abilities for granted—even the ability to walk. I'll never do that again."

Anna broke off a chunk of bread and handed it to him. "You know Ben now. Do you trust him?"

"I do. I get it now. He totally saved my sorry behind. It was the coolest thing — being rescued that way. It made all the difficult parts of being here worth it."

"Good. Grandmother or not, it makes me very happy to hear that."

"Thanks for getting me out of Pompeii." He bit into the hunk of bread. It was dry and a bit smoky smelling, but his empty stomach was grateful.

"I wish I could tell you that I knew to help you ... but I didn't. I don't seem to have developed any motherly instincts. It was Brendan — not me — that was drawn to you." Anna pressed her lips together and seemed to examine her hands. "I should have been able to find you on my own, but I guess that's why I needed Brendan — well, one of many reasons."

Marcus gave her a teasing nudge with his elbow. "He seems to feel the same way about you. And, hey, don't sweat it. You're not a mother ... yet."

Anna's face flushed. "Your grandmother — does she look like me at all?"

Marcus bit back a smile. She'd been flustered enough about Brendan to change the subject. "It's hard to say. She's really old. I think she must have been pretty old when she had my mom. And she lives in Italy, so I've only seen her once."

"Well, in my own timeline, I'm older. I'm not married and don't have any children — so I'm having trouble believing you could be my grandson ... but I suppose it's possible. Anything is possible for those who believe, right?"

"You really believe that?"

"I do." She tucked her hands under her knees and dipped her

head. "I really do."

Anna smiled at something over his shoulder. Marcus followed her gaze. Brendan and Sarah were deep in conversation. Sarah was completely oblivious to the fact that Max was following along beside them and blatantly eavesdropping on their conversation. Marcus snorted, also amused by his canine companion.

"Tell me about your grandfather." Anna bit her lip.

"I never met him and I really don't know anything about him. He died before I was born."

"Your mother never mentions him?"

"No, but I'm starting to realize that I have some family mysteries I should be asking about. I always got the feeling my mother wanted to leave the past and old traditions behind. She and my father really had this American dream — like they could create a better life outside of Italy. America must have seemed glamorous and modern to them. Part of that dream must have been hopes for future generations, but I was their only child. So …"

"I think that's your common ground there — with your mum," Anna said, nodding as if this revelation solved all his problems.

"What do you mean?" Marcus had to laugh. He and his mother hadn't seen eye to eye on much of anything lately.

"Your mother, and your mother's mother, both seemed to have had plans for their children that differed from what they wanted for themselves," Anna said, putting her arm around him. "Ask about her past — what she felt at your age. I'm guessing you'll have more in common there than you might expect. Maybe you'll find an answer that you'll both be at peace with. At the very least, you should be able to understand each other better. She may have gone a bit overboard lately, but I'm sure she has your best interests at heart."

He hadn't thought of it quite that way before. "I guess they were rebels too." He was unable to repress a smile at that thought. His parents had always spoken of Italy as if it had been the kind of place to leave behind. Honestly, he'd wanted to escape it himself since the moment he'd arrived—but his family's roots ran deep here. He couldn't help being curious now. As difficult as his time in Pompeii had been, it had also been an eye-opening glimpse at his ancestral homeland.

"Kind of sounds that way to me—especially if I'm the one they're running from." Her mouth bunched into frown that morphed into a sheepish grin.

"But you live in the United States now, right? How did that happen?"

"Oh—I wanted to help a friend, but I also have an old family home in Italy that's pretty important to me too. I'll get back there—here—eventually."

"How old is it?"

"It's been in my mother's family for centuries."

"Wow—like a castle or something?"

Anna smirked and shook her head. "You know, I might have described it that way when I was first brought there as a child, but it would be referred to as a villa."

"So you miss it."

Anna's shoulders sagged. She grieved for her family home in the way he did his own, but there was more there too—an untold story that caused her pain. Curiosity raged at the back of his mind, but he resisted pressing her on it. She would tell him what she wanted to.

Anna nodded slowly. "I do. So many twists and turns in life are unexpected, don't you think? Well, I guess you haven't had quite as many years to discover that yet ... and now I sound like the fossil I just might be." A girlish giggle erupted, countering the grandmotherly sentiment.

"You know—I've been dying to leave this place since I got here, mostly because I was hungry and dirty and totally uncomfortable. Being here has been pretty awesome though too. Just being in this ancient and crusty place. Was anything in this country ever new?"

Anna groaned. "It is old, even now, isn't it?"

"And just look at it. One day, the dust will clear and it will be a happening place again. But now, it's just eerie. Like another planet or something."

Anna closed her eyes. Her lips trembled. "—and sad too—so very, very sad."

Marcus put his arm around her. How weird would it be if Anna was his grandmother? She was young and gorgeous at the moment. Nothing about her seemed like the old lady he'd once met, but her youthful body did seem to carry a seasoned soul. It was enough to give him pause. He gave her arm an awkward pat.

Anna scooped a handful of ash from the side of the carriage and let it filter through her fingertips. "Ancient legend tells of a phoenix—a bird of great beauty. At the end of its long life, it builds a nest of spice twigs and bursts into fragrant flames. Then, from the ashes, the phoenix is reborn. Just like us, Marcus. I think our whole group may be getting a second chance here."

Brendan appeared at the side of the carriage. "Max wants us to take Marcus to the river now." He turned and caught up with the others as they walked ahead of the mules. "We need to return Marcus to his family. If you continue up the road on foot, we'll catch up with you by nightfall. Make camp out of view, but keep an eye out for us on the road."

Uzziel gripped Marcus's arm before pulling him into a vigorous hug. "May the God of our ancestors direct your steps and lead

THE VEIL OF SMOKE

you to your destination in joy and peace, protecting you from all calamity. I will never forget you, my friend."

"I could never forget you either, Uzziel. You were there for me when I thought all was lost. Big time."

∽

"Come with me, Marcus. It is time." Max nudged him with his nose.

Marcus turned to Anna, memorizing the details of her face for future reference. "Gotta book. Just in case you are my grandma, I'm going to give you a hug."

"You'd better, even if I'm not." Anna gathered him into her arms and squeezed. At least she wasn't pinching his cheeks. "I'm so thankful Brendan was wise enough to find you, Marcus." She pulled back and looked him in the eye. "Try to meet your mom halfway, okay?"

Marcus nodded. "I will. I promise." Being here had given him a whole new outlook on what was most important.

"And go visit your grandmother, will you?" Anna pulled him into another tight hug, her breath hot on his ear. "Even if it's not me. I know it would mean a lot to her—and you, I bet."

Max cleared his throat—an odd sound coming from a dog. "Please carry Marcus to the water," Max commanded. He seemed to be herding Brendan toward the shore.

"Whoa. What do you have in mind?" Marcus locked eyes on Max.

"You can swim, right?"

"Sure." Marcus squinted at the dog. "But I'm not exactly in peak condition at the moment."

"A little trust, please."

239

Brendan lifted Marcus out of the cart and carried him down the bank to the river's edge. Max stepped into the water and Brendan waded in after him. When Max was chest deep, he stopped, but urged Brendan deeper into the river.

"Lower him into the water and back away."

Brendan waded into the lazy current up to his waist, then released his grip on Marcus once he was floating on his own. He reached out to shake hands. "I wish we had more time together."

Marcus snorted and pulled him into a hug. "You've seen Anna more than once, right? It could totally happen."

Brendan nodded. His lips curled into a smile, but his eyes held a shadow of sadness. "I hope we do, Marcus." Brendan turned and waded toward the shore.

"Take care of her," Marcus called after him.

Brendan turned back to him, a smile in his eyes for the first time in days. "I will—with everything I've got." He waded back to the riverbank and sat on a large stone.

Max paddled out to Marcus. He swam up nose to nose with him. "Relax, Marcus," he said, and inhaled deeply. Purple vapor drifted out of Marcus's nose, swirled in front of his eyes briefly and disappeared into Max's nose. "I want you to dive underwater and push hard with your legs."

"But—"

Max shook his head. "Trust."

Marcus nodded. He took a deep breath and pushed himself underwater with his arms. He slid into the cool depths of the lake. He savored the weightless sensation of his body in water, the easing of his aching joints. He spread his legs wide and thrust them back together.

As his body glided through the river, the grime and filth covering him seemed to drift away. Like a healing balm, the water soothed his parched skin. He scissor kicked. His leg muscles snapped into high gear and pushed him yards ahead. His feet uncurled and pointed. He dolphin kicked. His legs had never felt so strong. After a couple minutes of joyful submersion, his lungs burned with the urge to breathe. He used his arms and legs in unison to push his body toward the surface. He broke the water and gulped hungrily at the air.

His body heaved forward, but his legs were unable to move. They were tangled in something. He looked down. Blankets. He had bolted upright in bed, dizzy and disoriented. He slumped back into luxurious softness. How many times over the past few days had he wished for the soft comfort of a mattress and pillow — or had it all been a dream?

No grimy soot coated his arms, although he had been cleansed in the river. Or had he? He wasn't wet. He unraveled his legs from the tangle of sheets and blankets. They were whole and strong and healthy — just as they'd always been. He sprang to his feet and did a couple squats. Never again would he take his healthy limbs for granted. In fact, he had an overwhelming urge to go for a jog to test their limits. He could take the stairs instead of the elevator and head out to Addams Park. He could run all the way to the lake shore, even all the way up to Lincoln Park if he felt like it — anything to shake this feeling of disorientation.

Marcus pulled on a pair of sweat pants, a worn T-shirt and the running shoes he hadn't used since quitting track last year. He bent over and touched his toes, did a couple lunges and jumped in place a few times. He was stronger than ever.

"Marcus, are you up? I'm making pancakes," his mother yelled from the kitchen.

He bounded down the hall and swept his mother up into a playful embrace. She held a spatula in one hand and a measuring cup full of batter in the other. Her open mouth held an unspoken question. She tilted her head and pressed her lips together, reading him like a book. The woman was a human lie detector. "What's gotten into you this morning?"

He planted a kiss on her unsuspecting cheek. "I'm going to take a quick run—can you keep some warm for me?"

His mom shook her head, but her smile told him that she would make a few fresh pancakes for him as soon as he returned. "What's up with you, Marcus?"

He leaned forward and touched his toes. She did not have the hours it would take for him to answer that question. Even if his time in Pompeii had been a dream, it had energized him—motivated him. He gave her his most charming smile and shrugged. "I guess I just woke up with a fresh perspective this morning, Ma."

She planted her spatula fist firmly on her hip. She would never be put off that easily. He would either need to come up with an acceptable explanation, or put his newfound perspective into action quickly.

"Oh—coffee!" he said, with an appreciative groan. "I have really missed coffee."

His mother simply shook her head and chuckled at his foolishness. He stole a couple of gulps of the pungent black brew from her mug and gave her another peck on the cheek. "I'll be back in a few," he promised. He grabbed his left ankle and raised it until his quadriceps muscles burned nicely. Even standing had never felt so good. He jogged through the front door and headed for the stairwell.

"Did you talk to Mr. Salvatore about a summer job?" she yelled after him. "You only have a few weeks of school left."

Marcus jogged into the stairwell and leaped down steps three at a time.

25

"You understand what I'll return to more than I do." Brendan traced the outline of her fingers with his free hand. "Hanging out here for a while might be my only real chance at life."

Anna didn't respond right away, her hand fumbling for tight curls at the nape of her neck, a nervous habit she'd been trying to break since childhood. She stopped short of entangling her restless fingers and took Brendan's hand instead. "I'd love to stay here with you for a while—for as long as Ben allows us to. I have nothing to rush back to—no family, no work that can't wait." She ducked her head. "Nothing, really."

Brendan seemed to search her eyes, probably weighing whether he wanted her medical opinion or not. In his trusting gaze, she read an acceptance of his fate. He nodded, asking no more. Instead, mischief threatened in his lopsided smile.

"Hey—why are you still dry? This was your mission, and here I am doing all the dirty work." He scooped her up in his arms and dashed toward the water. Anna kicked and screamed as he bolted into the river, but it was great to feel water on her grimy soot-encrusted skin.

"You can say it, you know." Brendan removed his tunic sash, using the dampened fabric to wipe ashes from her face.

"What?" Anna splashed him and ducked as he sent an armful back.

"That I was right." Brendan pressed his lips together, suppressing a smirk.

Anna tapped her chin with a finger, pretending to think it over. "You did find Marcus. I don't think I ever would have picked him out from the whole population of Pompeii on my own. How did you do that?"

Brendan groaned. "Oh—once I saw him, I couldn't get him off my mind. Every time I enjoyed the use of the sturdy legs I have here, I remembered him sitting there in the dust, without much hope of helping himself. Without leg braces, I wouldn't have gotten far either. I just really—felt for him, you know?"

Nagging empathy. An overpowering sense of connection, as if they were linked by some invisible force. Anna nodded. She did know. Marcus had weighed on Brendan's heart the same way he tugged at hers. She'd spent her life getting medical training and searching for him for that very reason. "Could Marcus really be my grandson?"

"Seems pretty likely, don't you think? You haven't lost hope have you?"

She shrugged, her cheeks burning. "No, I guess not ... not completely anyway. Here, my body's more youthful and life seems somehow more full of potential, but back at home, my career as a nurse consumes most of my time. Anything is possible though, right?"

"It is easier to believe here, isn't it? We could do anything we wanted to—within first century limitations." Brendan ducked underwater, emerging dripping and fresh-faced next to her, boyish and buoyant with an endearing haze of stubble on his cheeks. Every effort she'd put into tracking him down and helping him was worth the sacrifice.

"So what's next?" Brendan floated onto his back next to her, surrendering to the river's gentle pull.

Anna grasped his arm to keep him from drifting past. "I haven't sorted that bit out yet."

"Now that sounds more like the Aussie girl I know."

"Righto, mate," Anna quipped in her childhood accent. "You knew me when I was fresh off the boat from the Outback. I hadn't accepted Italy as my home yet and I thought my Uncle Enzo didn't want me around. I was so lost then."

"That seems like yesterday to me. From my perspective in time, it nearly was."

"We may never get used to that aspect of our relationship. Here you are, so soon after meeting me. I had many years to process it all, to learn to trust Ben, to search for you—"

"You searched for me." Brendan's hand grazed her arm underwater and lingered.

"Of course I did." Anna's stomach flip-flopped at the confession. "I had a bit of growing up to do first—but when I returned to Italy, you hadn't been born yet. That bit is hard to wrap your mind around, isn't it?"

Brendan shook his head, but it didn't make things any clearer. "It is strange. You're older and wiser, and I've barely progressed at all. You passed me up."

Anna snorted. "You're wiser than you know, then. You could see what I couldn't here."

"Do you think this is what heaven will be like? We'll all be the same age? All equal?"

Anna mulled that for a moment. "I suppose that makes sense. I imagine our bodies would be in ideal condition—at the precise point where they'd stopped growing, but not yet started to decay."

"Decaying—now there's a nice thought." The clinical side of Anna, the one trained in nursing, and maybe even the one matured past its peak had kicked in. The word didn't seem to affect her at all, but it made his skin crawl.

"Think about it like the life of a plant if that makes it easier. We grow, we bud, we bloom — then we wilt and wither and die. But here — in this time — we both arrived here in full bloom, so to speak — at our peaks, together."

"That is a nice gift, Anna. A very nice gift."

"More of a gift than you might know."

"Anna, I have to ask you again — " Brendan struggled for words that wouldn't offend. "Is there no one in your life you want to return to?"

"No. I was so focused on learning nursing — so obsessed with the idea of healing you — that I managed to sidestep that possibility." Anna shook her head. "But I failed. All that effort, and I haven't been able to do much for you.

"But you did. You brought me here. You made this possible. Ben must have other plans for us. I don't feel — well, I'm just not ... finished." Brendan's eyes seemed to plead. There had to be more for him. He was so full of life here.

Anna's fingers entwined with his and squeezed. She'd go ahead and say it. "Maybe there is a chance at more time for us here."

"But ... Marcus has to be your descendent. He had a grandmother from Italy named Anna he didn't know much about. That has to be you. You need to return to Italy for him."

Anna's reflection wavered on the surface of the river. Ben was conspicuous in his silence. Was he leaving this decision to them? Would it somehow alter Marcus's life if she stayed? Selfish or not, every impulse screamed for her to stay. She turned back to meet Brendan's eyes. They glistened, mirroring her despair. "I have no life to return to, Brendan. I never found anyone who could hold a candle to the friendship we've had. Life without you and the adventure we shared wasn't the same. No one else could ever understand."

◆

Water droplets clung to Anna's rampant curls. It was nice to see her hair loose again. Anna had the kind of beauty that was even more spectacular unbridled. Brendan allowed the current to carry him closer to her. "Do you think there is a possibility we could stay longer?"

Anna's eyes widened. In them, the future baited him like an unopened gift, full of possibilities. "Here is a thought. On another adventure Ben sent me on, I needed help from someone who called himself an ambassador. I wonder if Ben would allow us to do that for others?"

Why hadn't that possibility occurred to him before? "Wait. You've traveled time without me?" Brendan choked back a surge of envy, but managed to focus on the upside of that news instead.

"Are you jealous?" Anna's face flushed pink, but an impish grin played at her lips. "You are."

Brendan shook his head. "You don't have to enjoy it so much."

"I think you missed the point of that revelation. The ambassador—the man who helped me much as you did here in Pompeii for Marcus—encouraged me on my journey. I couldn't have done it without him."

Would Ben allow it? He'd jump at the chance. "The others are heading east. We could join them—if Ben is willing. Uzziel mentioned that they'd go as far as Cappadocia if that's what it took to live among their people once again."

"With first century limitations, traveling that far could take a lifetime." Anna held his gaze.

A stifled smile twitched at Brendan's lips. "I'm willing to take that chance if you are."

"It would be a dangerous trip—long, lonely stretches of road with bandits. There are more wild beasts here: lions and bears."

She wanted to play the devil's advocate? He tugged her closer. "I'll protect you."

"Maybe Uzziel will teach me to use a sword and I'll protect you." Anna arched a brow.

Brendan pressed her fingers to his lips before allowing a smile to curl across them. "I was hoping to live a little longer than that, but I'll enjoy whatever time I can get with you."

EPILOGUE

Anna closed her book, stroking the cover with a gnarled hand. Could these possibly be the same nimble fingers Brendan had once entwined in his? Strange how memories of those years still captured her thoughts when so many others escaped. She reached for the balcony's iron railing to steady her as she stood. Best to stretch her legs while they'd still cooperate. While gentle morning rays had warmed her brittle bones, the sun now beat down in earnest. Let it rouse the grapevines. She'd retire to the cool recesses of the library to enjoy an afternoon cup of hibiscus tea.

She lifted an unsteady hand to her brow, squinting to bring the garden gate into focus. A strange young man had invaded her front gate, pausing to chat with the caretaker trimming her rosebushes. Instead of continuing on his way, he followed the pathway leading toward the villa. Odd. An unexpected visitor. On foot, no less. Bother. Hopefully, Sonia would send him on his way. Still, curiosity got the better of her and she drifted toward the front hall instead of heading directly to the library.

Marcus shifted his leather backpack from one shoulder to the other, the weight of it more from sketchbooks and journals than the light weight clothes he'd squeezed between them. Classes at the University of Chicago had kept him even busier than he'd expected. He'd been looking forward to his semester in Rome. Perhaps the change in scenery would inspire a stimulating thesis topic.

He'd had plenty to distract him. The woman who'd inspired this trip, for one. Would she be as he remembered? Would she recognize him?

He stepped into the dim foyer as a frail woman descended the last few steps and made her way to the door. One and the same. Despite the whiteness of the untamed curls escaping her simple braid, he'd have recognized her anywhere.

"Grandma ... Anna?"

Her eyes widened. A smile warmed her pale lips as she opened her arms wide and allowed him to fold her into a long-awaited embrace.

"Marcus. At last. I knew you would find your way."

(NOT) THE END

*Read a sample chapter of
book three in the TimeDrifter Series
at the end of this book!*

**Be sure to join the emailing list on www.laurenlynch.com
to receive updates on the future book releases in this series.**

AUTHOR'S NOTE

THE HOUSE OF JULIA FELIX was located immediately north of Pompeii's amphitheater.

Julia Felix, the wealthy daughter of an imperial freedman, led the privileged life of an independent woman in an era when women had few rights or opportunities. Julia owned one of the largest estates in Pompeii, a large property that combined two city blocks by eliminating the street between them — one that ran directly to the amphitheater. Some of that property was sacrificed to widen the street on the east side of the estate. Much of her large estate was used as vegetable gardens and orchards. The remaining third was used to house her bathing and food service establishments in addition to her luxurious entertainment areas and home. When the site was excavated, several bodies were found in the garden. One was that of a woman carrying a jewelry box containing earrings, rings and a necklace. It is my personal belief that ambitious Julia had way too much at stake to ever leave Pompeii.

For a free downloadable map of the estate, visit www.laurenlynch.com

THE HOUSE OF JULIUS POLYBIUS was located just a few blocks west of the estate of Julia Felix. Thirteen skeletons were found in two rooms at the back of the house. One woman wearing gold jewelry clutched a bag of coins. She is believed to have been the wife of Julius Polybius. A younger woman (an older teen) was in an advanced state of pregnancy and thought to be

Polybius's daughter. A young man was slumped nearby—most likely her husband. The children in the room must have been either siblings or cousins of the pregnant woman. In the peristyle garden, just outside the door to the room where they were found was the body of a turtle—probably a pet. Skeletons found in two adjacent rooms could have been slaves or workmen. The house was being remodeled at the time of the 79 A.D. eruption and showed damage that was most likely from the earlier massive earthquakes in 62 A.D. Election slogans were found painted at the entrance and on nearby walls for C. Iulius Polybius. While many of Pompeii's residents evacuated at the earlier signs of trouble, Polybius's family decided to ride it out. If he was either running for office or in active leadership, he may have wanted to stay as long as possible as a show of support and confidence in the city's future. Add to that his daughter's near full-term pregnancy, and you can understand why they chose to stay instead of running when things became dire. (For dramatic purposes, I chose to portray them as unconscious, under Basilius's evil spell.)

LUCIUS ISTACIDIUS ZOSIMUS is believed to have owned the villa and winery northwest of the city know today as the Villa of Mysteries. The triclinium contains the famous fresco of the Dionysiac Mysteries (the mural that Julia loved), dating from the first century B.C. This well-preserved villa features many elegant wall decorations. It was situated on the southwestern slopes of Vesuvius and would have had a panoramic view of the Bay of Naples. Buried under 30 feet of volcanic ash, it took two decades to fully excavate the site. Nine bodies were found in the villa. It would appear that Zosimus and his family did not survive the eruption.

ACKNOWLEDGMENTS:

Historical portions of this book were based on
the writing, research and observations of:
Mary Beard, Gaius Plinius Caecilius Secundus (Pliny the Younger), Peter Connolly, Carolyn Osiek, Christopher Parslow, Charles Pellegrino, and Loretta Santini

Many thanks to my gifted editor,
and fellow Christian speculative fiction author, Nadine Brandes
www.nadinebrandes.com

My thanks and appreciation also go out to
those who read and critiqued my manuscript:
Amy Austin, Judie Kerstetter, Joanna Muir, Tiffany Provence,
and the ACFW Critique Group

And boatloads of gratitude and love to my
husband, Patrick, and son, Brendan,
who support my writing in many ways

To download printable discussion questions
and view other bonus features, visit:
www.laurenlynch.com

You may also connect with Lauren on:
www.pinterest.com/readlaurenlynch
www.twitter.com/LaurenRLynch
www.facebook.com/laurenrlynch

GLOSSARY OF LATIN TERMS USED IN THE BOOK:

Amphitheater: An oval stadium with stepped seating where gladiatorial contests, games, and other events were held.

Amphora(e): A large, two-handled narrow-necked storage jar.

Atrium: A formal entrance hall and reception area usually at the front of a large house.

Balneum: A public or private bath suite.

Bestiarii: Criminals, prisoners of war, or trained and paid fighters who fought exotic animals in the arena.

Caldarium: The hot and steamy room in a bath complex with an under-floor heating system, used in the sequence of bathing rooms.

Campania: The southwestern region of Italy where Pompeii is located.

Carpentum: A horse or mule-drawn covered carriage with two wheels (seating 2 or 3).

Caupona: An inn or tavern where hot meals were served to patrons at tables.

Cena: The main meal of the day, eaten in the evening.

Compluvium: An opening in the roof, to allow rainwater to fall into a shallow rectangular pool (impluvium) set into the floor of an atrium.

Cubiculum: A bedroom, usually small and often with a built-in bed.

Flabellum: A long-handled fan.

Flamen Dialis: Chief priest of the Roman god, Jupiter.

Frigidarium: The cold room in a bath complex, normally with a plunge bath.

Galea: A bronze helmet with a face mask.

Hydraulis: A water organ. Water adjusted the flow of air in its pipes to produce music.

Impluvium: A shallow rectangular pool in the floor of an atrium to catch rainwater from an opening in the roof (compluvium) above to channel it into a cistern below.

Lanista: The trainer, or manager for a team of gladiators.

Lectica: A litter, or portable couch, carried by four to eight slaves (transportation for the wealthy).

Ludus matutinus: The official training academy for hunters and animal fighters in the arenas of the Roman Empire.

Mulsum: A mixture of wine and honey.

Palla: A traditional outer garment similar to a shawl worn by women and fastened by brooches.

Paterfamilias: A Roman citizen and male head of a household holding legal authority over the family's property and his dependents (including his wife, children, clients, and slaves).

Peristyle: A courtyard or room surrounded by columns (colonnaded garden).

Praegenarii: A mock gladiator used as an opening act, or during intervals between fights.

Sacrarium: A shrine where sacred objects were kept in a temple or household.

Salve: A Latin greeting used in Ancient Rome.

Servi publici: "Public slaves" belonging to the State of Rome.

Sistrum: A bronze rattle, with a sound similar to a tambourine, used in the worship of Isis.

Tepidarium: The warm room in a bath complex, heated under-floor for a pleasant feeling of constant radiant heat.

Thermopolium: Casual restaurants offering hot food and drinks served from a counter (often open to the street).

Triclinium: A dining room, often with three bench seats or couches.

Vilicus: A slave who managed all the operations of the farm villa, including the other slaves.

Volcanus: The god of fire, forging, and smelting—believed to ripen fruit with his warmth.

Volcanalia: The festival of Volcanus (celebrated August 23) when crops were most at risk of burning due to high temperatures and dryness. Live fish were thrown into bonfires as a sacrifice to placate the god.

Read a sample chapter from Book Three of the TimeDrifter Series:
THE TOWER OF REFUGE

1

Progress registered in a blur, measured by the recurring intrusion of Roman milestones. All Brendan's hopes latched onto the journey itself. Despite the determined pace, their destination remained unsettled. Amid overlong days of trudging, one aspect motivated him. Time ... more time to find out who he could be in a healthy body ... more time with Anna.

Was his mission at an end now that Pompeii was annihilated? Would he be forced to return to an uncertain — and likely short — life? What really mattered now anyway? His most meaningful moments revolved around Ben and Anna, and the followers they'd met along the way.

The life he'd return to paled in comparison. It was little more than an existence — a string of events he'd survived, void of deeper purpose. Dread hounded him. He couldn't imagine being separated from Anna again, and yet, he couldn't visualize a normal life either. Even worse — although she doted on him, he could't be sure she felt much more than pity. Even if she did care for him as more than a friend, she didn't deserve getting pulled any deeper into his troubles.

He'd just have to live in the present. Here and now, each second was precious. Each might be his last with Anna — his last moments in an able body, free to wander as he chose.

An outburst of laughter drew Brendan's eyes back to their travel-mates. Paetas, since reclaiming his Uzziel identity, had become even more cheerful and lively. Vassus, his equal opposite in almost every way, provided a twisted sort of balance with his dark moods. The vinegar to Uzziel's honey. Every group had one.

"Denarius for your thoughts." Anna hooked him with an impish grin.

Brendan snickered at her corny attempt at humor, hoping his burning cheeks didn't betray him. How much should he share? Brendan turned away as if he'd found a sudden interest in the sheep pasture on his side of the road. "We sure are an odd group."

"Not that I disagree—but what made you say that?"

"Despite all our differences, we seem to share at least one common purpose. It's like we're each trying to recapture what we've lost—as if we can piece together fragments of our former lives."

"What would you like to reclaim, Brendan?" Sunlight glinted off her brown curls. Since they'd left Pompeii, she'd taken to wearing her hair long and loose like Sarah, covering her head only when strangers crossed their path. With each passing day, he could see more of the girl he'd known in Mutul. Her eyes gripped his, gentle and sincere.

Brendan shook his head and lifted a shoulder. "I've noticed a growing hopefulness in each of you. For myself, I'm almost afraid to hope. I don't want to set myself up for disappointment."

A humble farmer's cart rumbled off the narrow stretch of road they'd traveled since leaving the last mountain village, deferring to Julia's luxurious carriage. Following Sarah's lead, Anna lifted her veil over her head. Dust from the farm cart's wheels tumbled their way. Brendan raised his hand in greeting as the man passed. The farmer acknowledged his wave with a weary nod.

Anna pulled the veil over her nose and mouth, muffling her words. "Have you spoken with Ben about your hopes?"

He took a deep breath as the dust settled. Max poked his head out the back of the carriage, his ears perked their direction. Brendan gave Anna a covert wink and lowered his voice. "It appears you're not the only one who wonders."

He wasn't about to let those sad, soulful dog eyes ruin the moment, but they held way too many secrets for Brendan's comfort. Once Marcus was gone, he'd expected Max to disappear as well, but their canine companion remained. Brendan hadn't wanted to appear rude by broaching the subject, but he couldn't help questioning Max's presence. What purpose did the dog serve now that his charge had returned to his own time? Brendan couldn't help wondering if they could give him the slip somehow. Maybe he was being paranoid, but Max's watchful eyes seemed to follow his every move.

"Ben did tell us we'd never be alone." Anna offered him a wry smile.

"In this case, the scrutiny's not quite as comforting as it could be. And, no—I haven't begged Ben for more time here, although I'm tempted. I'm not sure I'm ready to hear his answer." He wanted to stay, and so far Ben had allowed it. Why push it? Brendan twisted the iron signet ring on his forefinger as he glanced her way. "Have you?"

"I speak with Ben often—and yes, sometimes about you." Anna looped her arm through his, but didn't elaborate.

"Care to share your thoughts?" Brendan stopped to shake a pebble from his sandal.

A chariot rumbled up behind them as another carriage approached from the front. Traffic was getting heavier. The road widened, signaling another city ahead.

Anna stopped and waited beside him at the side of the road. Her brows puckered as she hesitated. "I can't discern what he has planned for you. That is between you and Ben, but regardless of

3

what you decide, I will stay by your side." She glanced at her feet, face flushed. "No matter where we end up."

Brendan pressed his lips together and took her hand. "You don't know what he has planned for us?"

Anna shook her head. "Talk to Ben, Brendan."

When he didn't reply, she tugged him back to a walk. "It's not just about getting the answers you want, Brendan. It's about finding peace and comfort, no matter what happens."

Brendan could still visualize Ben trampling the snake in the jungles of Mutul, but when Lobo had opposed him, he'd taken a meeker stance. Their gentle giant of a friend always remained in control. Although he did display moods, they were used for expression rather than in weaknesses. Every time Brendan tried to grasp Ben's meaning, the truth slipped through his fingers. His fearsome friend never failed to both inspire and baffle him.

The trees to their left thinned as they crested the next slope, revealing the sparkling waters of the Hadriaticum. The road they traveled—the Via Appia—ended in Brundisium, their gateway to the East. At least four times larger than Pompeii, this bustling port city meant business.

"Ben won't lead you wrong." Anna's pleading eyes held such hope. The weight of her expectations hung like a burden lodged between his shoulder blades—dangling in a spot he couldn't quite reach.

It was more than he wanted to deal with at the moment. For now, couldn't he just be a guy on a journey to nowhere—biding his time, enjoying the scenery? He shook his head. "Look at them. They still don't have a clue that he's not your average dog, do they?" Max bounded up to their travel companions, tail wagging.

"He'll reveal himself if and when he choses to. I think it's adorable how he plays with them." Anna's lopsided smile softened his edges. "Vassus, though ..."

Brendan's gaze shifted back to their new friends. Uzziel was scratching behind Max's ears. Vassus crossed his arms over his chest and took a step back as the dog's tail thwacked his legs. "He's still in survival mode. I'm not sure we can trust him."

"Uzziel does." Anna shook dust from her skirts.

"Uzziel is too kind."

"I don't think that's possible."

"I thought you believed all things were possible." Brendan couldn't resist raising a brow.

Anna tilted her head, eyes searching his. "For one who believes."

Brendan nodded. "Then we'd better be careful what we believe."

Sarah dashed their way. "Shall we have lunch here before we head down into town?"

Rolling sheep pastures surrounded their descent back into throngs of humanity. Lingering in the foothills was an obvious temptation. "Good idea. We can plan our next steps."

Uzziel tipped his head back and sniffed the air. "The wind carries its tidings from the east. I can practically smell sweet calamus and cassia on the breeze."

Vassus ignored Uzziel's reverie. "We'll need to sell the carriage and mules. As extravagant as they are, they'll fetch a considerable price—enough to carry us all as far up the coast as we care to go with plenty to spare for supplies."

"No—no." Uzziel shook his head emphatically. "We must only take a ship as far as Dyrrhachium. From there we can walk the Via Egnatia and gather information as we travel. Surely there will be news in Thessaloniki or Philippi, then we will know where to go next."

Vassus clamped his mouth shut and took a deep breath. While he didn't appear pleased, he nodded.

Brendan cared little about their route or mode of travel. Since their escape from Pompeii, he'd focused on little more than survival. But now he was quite certain what he wanted to do next: he wanted to steal time.

*Join the emailing list on www.laurenlynch.com
to receive updates on new releases,
bonus material and book giveaways!*

VEIL OF SMOKE
DISCUSSION QUESTIONS:

1. In *The Veil of Smoke*, Anna and Brendan can see Ben in their reflection. When we are Christians, how does the Holy Spirit interact with us? Read the following Bible passages and make note of what you discover:

   "Don't you know that you yourselves are God's temple and that God's Spirit dwells in your midst?" (1 Corinthians 3:16)

   "Do you not know that your bodies are temples of the Holy Spirit, who is in you, whom you have received from God? You are not your own." (1 Corinthians 6:19)

   "And I will ask the Father, and he will give you another advocate to help you and be with you forever." (John 14:16)

   "And if the Spirit of him who raised Jesus from the dead is living in you, he who raised Christ from the dead will also give life to your mortal bodies because of his Spirit who lives in you." (Romans 8:11)

2. When Anna and Brendan are sent to Pompeii, they are left to discern the details of their mission on their own. It was as if Ben wanted them to learn how to serve without being led—or as if the journey was part of the lesson. Have you begun to develop discernment? How can you become more sensitive to the leading of the Holy Spirit? Read the passages below and make a note of what each verse teaches us about wisdom and discernment:

   "And this is my prayer: that your love may abound more and more in knowledge and depth of insight, so that you may be able to discern what is best and may be pure and blameless for the day of Christ." (Philippians 1:9-10)

> *"My son, if you accept my words and store up my commands within you, turning your ear to wisdom and applying your heart to understanding—indeed, if you call out for insight and cry aloud for understanding, and if you look for it as for silver and search for it as for hidden treasure, then you will understand the fear of the Lord and find the knowledge of God." (Proverbs 2:1-5)*

> *"If any of you lacks wisdom, you should ask God, who gives generously to all without finding fault, and it will be given to you." (James 1:5)*

> *"From infancy you have known the Holy Scriptures, which are able to make you wise for salvation through faith in Christ Jesus." (2 Timothy 3:15)*

How will growing in wisdom and discernment improve your ability to serve God?

3. Basilius displays his deceitful abilities even more in book two as he charms Julia—and even Anna, at first. In what ways is Basilius like Satan? How has Satan deceived you? How have you been drawn in by the things of this world? Read the following passages, making note of what the verses reveal and how they apply to your life.

> *"Satan himself masquerades as an angel of light." (2 Corinthians 11:14)*

> *"See to it that no one takes you captive through hollow and deceptive philosophy, which depends on human tradition and the elemental spiritual forces of this world rather than on Christ." (Colossians 2:8)*

> *"I am sending you out like sheep among wolves. Therefore be as shrewd as snakes and as innocent as doves." (Matthew 10:16)*

> "Don't you know that you yourselves are God's temple and that God's Spirit dwells in your midst?" (1 Corinthians 3:16)

4. When Marcus was stranded in the marketplace, many seemed to turn a blind eye to his situation, but a little girl shares her bread with him and Brendan reaches out to him. What does the Bible tell us about helping others? How can you be obedient to these commands in your everyday life?

   > "If anyone has material possessions and sees a brother or sister in need but has no pity on them, how can the love of God be in that person?" (1 John 3:17)

   > "And do not forget to do good and to share with others, for with such sacrifices God is pleased." (Hebrews 13:16)

   > "Whoever is kind to the poor lends to the Lord, and he will reward them for what they have done." (Proverbs 19:17)

   > "The King will reply, 'Truly I tell you, whatever you did for one of the least of these brothers and sisters of mine, you did for me.'" (Matthew 25:40)

5. In the TimeDrifter series, Ben repeatedly tells his followers that he will never leave them alone. How does this compare to Jesus in our lives? Read the following verses and make a note of how we are never alone when we are believers.

   > "So do not fear, for I am with you; do not be dismayed, for I am your God. I will strengthen you and help you; I will uphold you with my righteous right hand." (Isaiah 41:10)

   > "Be strong and courageous. Do not be afraid; do not be discouraged, for the Lord your God will be with you wherever you go." (Joshua 1:9)

> "Be strong and courageous. Do not be afraid or terrified because of them, for the Lord your God goes with you; he will never leave you nor forsake you." (Deuteronomy 31:6)

> "And surely I am with you always, to the very end of the age." (Matthew 28:20)

6. In The Veil of Smoke, Brendan, Anna and Marcus witness the destruction of Pompeii. Knowing that the people they meet are going to perish is very difficult for them and they long to save them. How does this compare to the unsaved people we know? Read the Bible verses below. How can we share our faith with others?

> "Let your light shine before others, that they may see your good deeds and glorify your Father in heaven." (Matthew 5:16)

> "But in your hearts revere Christ as Lord. Always be prepared to give an answer to everyone who asks you to give the reason for the hope that you have. But do this with gentleness and respect." (1 Peter 3:15)

> "But the Lord said to me, "Do not say, 'I am too young.' You must go to everyone I send you to and say whatever I command you. Do not be afraid of them, for I am with you and will rescue you," declares the Lord." (Jeremiah 1:7-8)

> "He said to them, "Go into all the world and preach the gospel to all creation." (Mark 16:15)

LAUREN LYNCH has lived in nine of the United States, but currently calls a log cabin in North Carolina home, along with her husband, teenage son, two dogs, a cat, five chickens and even the occasional bat.

For more information, visit:
www.laurenlynch.com

Made in the USA
Charleston, SC
15 July 2015